Dare To Love

Cara D. Smith

Warning

This is a work of fiction. Names, characters, businesses, places, events, and incidents are either the products of the author's imagination or used in a fictitious manner. Any resemblance to actual persons, living or dead, or actual events is purely coincidental.

The following story contains mature themes, strong language, and sexual situations. It is intended for mature readers.

Dedication

For Steven and Isaac

One more time, for the people in the back!
The following story contains mature themes, strong language, and
sexual situations. It was written for a mature audience

Contents

Prologue
Austin

February

I can't decide who is more intoxicated, my future sister-in-law
Fern or my buddy, Ryan. He easily has seven inches and a hun-
dred pounds of pure muscle on her, but she uses his size to
her advantage, and hip throws him over her fucking shoulder. He lands on
the lawn with an audible "oof." It's amazing to see and a little scary to
know that someone as small as her can go toe to toe with one of the best
fighters I've ever met and hold her own.

I know he can counter that move, but he obviously didn't expect her to
know how to do it. Unless he's too damn drunk to stop her, which answers
my question. He handles it well, though. Better than I would. I'd probably
come up swinging with something to prove. Then again, he teaches women
to kick his ass twice a week. That requires a particular sort of patience.

"I've always wanted to try that," Fern says, bouncing on the balls of her
feet. Her cheeks are flushed pink, either from excitement or alcohol. Since
she just finished kicking my brother Mason's ass at beer pong, it's probably
the latter. *I'm sensing a theme here* . . . "We weren't allowed to do hip throws."

Ryan sits up and shakes his head hard. "Muay Thai?"

She nods. "Ten years."

"Impressive." He stands and brushes dried grass clippings off his hands and ass. "You ever consider teaching? We have some ladies at the gym who are more comfortable learning from a woman."

Fern shrugs. "I'm not opposed. It's been a long time since I practiced." She grins and shoots my brother a sideways look. "Jabbing aside."

I've watched her and Mason spar. She's vicious. When she gets "into the zone," as Mason calls it, she can do some fucking damage if she's not careful. Or if he's not quick enough. *And the dumbass tells her not to hold back* . . . No one ever said he was smart. After all, we could be at a strip joint right now instead of celebrating the impending end of his bachelorhood in his backyard along with his fiancée and her friends and family.

"Is it over?" I follow the voice to see Tara hiding her face in her ex-husband-slash-boyfriend Gabe's chest.

"Yeah, Princess," Gabe says, grinning down at her like a lovestruck sap. *They're fucking everywhere.* I get enough of that googly-eyed shit from Mason and Fern, and now they're doing it again too! "Fern showed him who's boss."

"Fern has boobs," I say quickly, angling for a laugh to break up the love-fest. That shit makes me twitchy. "Anyone with boobs is the de facto boss."

"And don't you forget it!" Fern says over the laughter, brushing her hands together as if dusting them off after a job well done.

The onlookers disperse, noisily dividing themselves into teams for beer pong, cornhole, or one of the other games strewn about. I take a moment to bask in the success of pulling off this party since my counterpart in the bridal party was all the way in Nebraska for the planning phase.

Fern's new friend, Jamaica, catches my eye where she sits all hunched over on the sidelines. That happens more than I'd like to admit lately. I don't mean to look at her. She's off limits, but damn . . . She's gorgeous. I can't help but stare sometimes. It's not like I want to run my fingers through her hair to find out if it's softer than it seems like it should be to sort of float around her head like it does. And I don't wonder if her flaw-less, warm brown skin is as smooth as it looks . . . Such things never cross my mind. Nope, not at all . . . *Fern would kill me.*

Jamaica catches me watching her, something else that happens far too often. She narrows her eyes at me and cocks her head to the side just a bit, watching me like I'm some sort of creepy-crawly she can't decide if she should run from or squish. That look has me itching to stir some shit. She makes it too fun to resist teasing her because she gives as good as she gets, and she always comes out of her shell a bit more after I do. *It's a win-win.*

I know just what to say to get her to serve up some sass that'll leave my head spinning for days. And I *know* this is something she can laugh about because I heard her and Fern joking about it earlier today. It'll pop into my head at random intervals—likely when I should be working—and my reputation as the crazy Chambers child will be cemented because someone will walk in on me smiling and laughing to myself.

I walk the few steps between us and drop into the chair next to her. "Even you, Jam, with those mosquito bites, are still the boss. They must work out in your favor, though. You probably save a ton of money by buying those little round Band-Aids instead of bras."

Her breath whooshes out as if I just socked her in the gut.

Oh, fuck. I hold my breath, scared to even blink until I know what's going on here. I've clearly misjudged and put my foot in it this time, but I don't know what kind of apology is necessary yet. Will simple suffice, or do I need to make a spectacle of myself to appease her? I didn't want to hurt her feelings, just rile her up and get her to laugh, even if it's at my expense because she puts me in my place.

She crosses her arms over her chest, but I don't think she realizes she's doing it. *She's protecting herself.* That brings me up short. It doesn't matter what kind of reparations she needs from me; I'll start at the bottom and work my way up until she's happy.

She shifts in her seat, angling her whole body away from me. "You're such a jerk," she mutters, her nifty Jamaican accent softens the insult somehow. I still don't understand how she has that accent when she grew up in London with an Irish father, but her mother *is* Jamaican . . .

"Look, I'm sorry—"

"At least *I* don't overcompensate for what I lack by making fun of what I perceive as flaws in other people," she snaps, cutting my apology short.

I clutch my chest over my heart, not that it matters because she's not looking at me. I'm glad she's not because I'm not sure my face won't betray how much that really does hurt. *At least we're even now. Turnabout is fair play.*

"Oh, ouch! I think I'm gonna need you to take me to the burn unit after that one," I say, hoping she doesn't see how true it is. Yes, I apparently had it coming, but *damn*. She's not pulling her punches. "For the record, I *never* said there's anything wrong with a flat chest, just that you have one. It was a joke. I apologized. *I'm* not overcompensating for anything, but I think *you* might be with that attitude."

She whips her head around to glare at me. "Oh, so you're just an asshole by nature?" *Holy shit. She* cussed! Her top lip curls into a sneer instead of the smile I'm aiming for. *What's happening here?* I might not see her often, but this isn't how she usually reacts to my teasing. "I don't know how Fern puts up with you," she says.

Heh. Fern doesn't put up with me. Fern verbally hands me my ass on the regular. It's great. I love it. "She has a sense of humor?" I tease, hoping to steer this conversation any direction but the one it's going.

Jamaica cants her head and looks down her nose at me. The hatred burning in her eyes is so strong I lean back. "You're not funny; you're mean."

Now, wait a minute! I blow a raspberry at her to cover my pain. I don't get the hostility. I've told her I was only teasing, I've apologized; she ignored it. So why is she lashing out at me? *I'm missing something, but damnit, there's no reason for this.* It was a *joke*. It's what I *do*. "I'm not mean! You just don't know how to laugh!"

Her chin lifts a bit more. "I laugh when there's something funny."

Is there any way to win here? I only wanted to make her laugh . . . I didn't come over here to hurt her feelings. Or mine. "You need a better excuse. I'm hilarious."

Fern's voice carries across the yard from the cornhole boards. "Jamaica, you wanna be my partner?"

"Thank God," Jamaica mutters. She stands up and walks away without so much as a "kiss my ass."

What the hell happened? It was just a joke! I apologized! This wasn't supposed to blow up in my face!

Jamaica

I've never played this game, but it seems simple enough. Stand here, aim for the hole in the other board, throw the bag. I can do this. I can do anything that gets me away from Austin. How can he be so . . . horrible? Who says things like that? *People like my ex, that's who.*

Unbidden, memories flood my mind and I relive some of the terrible things he used to say.

"You're lucky. You know that?"

I squirm, pleased with the words. Compliments from Jordan are hard-won. "Why's that?" I ask, shamelessly fishing for more.

"Because no one else would want you. Look at you! No ass. No tits. No hips. Are you sure you're half black? But you found me. I will always want you."

I bite my cheek to keep from crying. I will *not* let Jordan make me cry again.

And I won't let myself cry because of Austin, either. *I can't believe I* liked *him.* That crooked smile of his, the one that made my heart stutter when I first saw it, it's a front. It hides lies, just like his eyes. Yeah, his brother Mason's eyes are dazzling, but Austin's are more interesting than Mason's vivid blue. The gray in them gives them a little extra something. *More room to hide lies!* And the way he laughs with his whole body . . . It starts with a slight crinkle to the corner of his eyes, then he smiles. He always does something with at least one hand, and the sound comes from deep in his belly every time. He laughs without reservation. It's how I imagine he does everything in life.

But his laughter is always at someone else's expense. How did I not see that before?

He's the biggest prick on the planet, and he gets away with it because of his good looks and his last name! He's not even a well-meaning prick, just the attention-seeking variety! I don't understand how anyone can tolerate him, much less find him funny. He's just . . . Infuriating.

Fern waves her hand in front of my face, startling me. As my teammate, she's supposed to be standing across from me, next to the board I'm throwing at. "Jam? Earth to Jam!"

I shake my head to clear the wayward thoughts and look around. Mason and his friend, Chris, are watching me from their places. "Sorry," I say, forcing a smile. "Got lost in thought."

"You okay?" Fern asks. "It didn't look like a happy thought."

"I'm good," I tell her as I heft one of the bags, getting a feel for the way it moves and the weight of it. I don't want to spoil their good time whining about Austin being a twit.

She frowns at me, looking deep into my eyes. I know her well enough to know she doesn't buy it, but she chooses to drop it. "Well, whatever it was, channel that into your throw. We're down by two!"

"Can do."

She runs back to her place and gives me a thumbs up. I imagine the hole I'm aiming at is Austin's face and let the bag fly. It hits the back rim, if that's what they call it, and falls in.

"Oh, my gosh! I did it!" Not only did I make us a point—I think, scoring this is wonky—but I have a nice mental image of myself throwing a bag and smacking Austin square in the nose. I can't *wait* to do it again.

"Way to go!" Fern cheers while Chris golf claps for me.

Mason launches his bag. It arcs gracefully through the air and falls short but still lands on the board with a thud that's felt as much as heard. My next bag lands just shy of the hole, but skids a bit and balances half in, half out, just hanging there, waiting to fall. He launches his second bag and knocks mine in. My third bag lands in the grass on the far side of the board; his hits the base of the board and skids halfway up. I overshoot my fourth bag but leave it teetering on the far edge of the hole. *Come on! Fall!*

This is surprisingly fun. Sports weren't my thing in high school, but my competitive side loves games like this.

It's down to Mason. He releases his final bag. It soars across the space between the boards and hits mine, knocking it in before his falls off the back.

"Yes!" I cry. It was only my first turn, but I did great. I think. At any rate, I didn't let Fern down! She runs over to give me a quick high-five before she and Chris start the next round.

Chris crosses his arms over his chest and fakes a glare, splitting it between Fern and me. "I don't know how, but you're cheating!"

I tense, ready to defend myself—I don't know how to play well enough to intentionally cheat—but notice his smile and relax. He has a nice smile. *Not as nice as Austin's.* I give myself a little shake, hoping I can pass it off as a chill, to get that thought out of my head. I don't want to think about that jerk anymore. He doesn't deserve space in my head. *He's just like my ex.*

I have horrible taste in men.

That's the only explanation for it. Jordan was toxic, and so, apparently, is Austin. And it took me too long to see it in both cases. *At least this time, I caught on before he had a chance to really hurt me.*

"You just don't want to lose to a couple girls!" Fern calls back, smiling at his good-natured teasing.

He shakes his head. "Hey, if we're gonna lose, I'd rather lose to girls. Y'all at least look cute while you're stomping mud puddles in our asses."

"Are you saying I'm not cute?" Ryan asks him, shouting from the beer pong table. It looks like his team is losing. I can't remember the name of the man he's playing with. Derrik? Darren? That's it. He's Mason's assistant. They're playing against Nicole, Mason's sister, and her husband, John.

Chris grins at him. "Gabe's cuter."

Ryan opens his mouth, presumably to argue, but closes it quickly. He frowns and looks around the yard. "Where *is* Gabe?"

Mason clears his throat, drawing our attention. "He and Tara snuck off after the first game of beer pong," he says, referring to the match between Fern and him. He smiles, and it goes a little lopsided, reminding me of his brother's. "I don't think they'll be back."

My breath catches in my lungs. I know what my old friends would say under these circumstances, but I don't know about this lot. This is the first time something like this has happened while I've been around. Will they call Tara horrible names now? *Please, no.*

I like these people. I don't want them to be that way. We're all adults here, and Tara and Gabe are together. If they want to leave for some private time, what's so wrong with that?

Ryan grunts. "Good. 'Bout time that fucker got his priorities in line."

"No shit," Chris adds. He grabs a bag from the stack at his feet and nods to Fern. "Ready when you are, Fern."

Really? That's it? I let out the breath I was holding. That was so . . . anticlimactic. *Thank goodness.* I don't want to find new friends.

"Where's my brother?" Mason asks the crowd in general, interrupting the memories before they really get started.

Like the others, I do a quick sweep of the yard. *Because it's what everyone else is doing, not because I want to see him.* It doesn't matter, though. He's gone. *Good riddance.*

Chapter 1

Jamaica

Thirteen weeks later . . .

*R*onni and I lock eyes across the table where her hands are resting, fingers splayed wide to prevent smudges while I apply her second coat of fingernail polish. She looks like a walking, talking—sassy—porcelain doll today with her hair done up just like Fern's and her full-skirted junior bride dress. I fully supported her brief consideration of a little tuxedo to match her father, though. *"But I'm not joining this family like Fern is. I'm already part of it. So I can't be a junior bride. Does that mean I'm a junior groom?"*

They told her she could wear whatever she wanted, but the dresses swayed her in the end.

"Fern, you've got to eat!" Her sisters, Ivy and Sage, take turns pleading with her. I've lost track of how many times they've tried to shove food in the poor woman's face today.

Ronni's eyes roll so hard at her soon-to-be aunts that her eyelashes flutter. I bite my lip to keep from laughing. It's a good thing we're almost done here. My friend needs someone to rescue her, and her knight in shining armor is locked away on the other side of the castle.

In their defense, she *does* need to eat. She's paler than normal. Skinnier, too. They're going about it all wrong, though. I imagine she's nervous. Who wouldn't be? She's getting married in—I glance at the clock over the door of the guest suite we're all prepping in—a little over two hours. She needs something simple, not alcohol and a taco. *Who feeds tacos to a woman in a wedding dress?*

Bless quick dry polish. I carefully screw the brush back on the bottle and set it well out of reach of tiny hands.

"Let those dry," I murmur to Ronni before I push to my feet, moving upward more than normal in my heels. "I'll be back. I need to move," I call over my shoulder on my way out the door. No one questions me this time. They're used to me popping in and out now. I'm not good at sitting still unless I have a book in my hand. And I hate being stuck in that room, big as it is. Fern is great, but her family is too fussy today. And there are too many bodies packed into that space.

The guys were smarter. *There's an oxymoron . . .* They didn't order a big meal, but a variety of things they can grab on the move. They probably didn't have much to do with it. Miss Lola, Mason's grandmother, is probably the guilty party there. She tried to be the voice of reason when tacos were suggested, but the others insisted it would be amazing. Fern just smiled and let them have their way.

I walk to the other side of the bloody mansion Mason's grandparents call home as fast as I can in heels. *What was I thinking?* They're cute, though. If I have to wear shoes, at least they're cute ones. Fern probably won't complain if I go barefoot if I end up with a blister. She's an anti-bridezilla if I've ever met one.

I stop outside the guys' suite and knock hard enough to hurt my knuckles to be sure they hear me since I can hear them through the door. Then I turn around and cover my eyes to be safe. Last time I was voluntold to come here for something, Ryan answered the door in his underwear and socks. Can't complain about the view—ten out of ten! But it might not be Ryan this time. They should all be dressed by now because they've already had their turn with the photog, but I don't want to risk seeing Austin in his skivvies.

It's hard enough to get him out of my head without *that* snapshot floating around my brain. As it is, I have to remind myself several times a day that he isn't really the nice guy I believed him to be—that he's not worthy of my *anything*, let alone the stupid crush I've harbored since the day we met. *It'll be over soon.* After the wedding, I won't see him as often.

"You rang?" someone deadpans, straining to drop their voice low enough to imitate Lurch from *The Addams Family*. The speaker pauses then chuckles a bit. "You're safe, Jam. Sorry about Ryan earlier. We thought it was Tris."

I turn around and peek between my fingers to make sure he's not lying. Gabe is fully dressed, but he's rocking that tux. I drop my hands to frown at him. "So you sent a mostly naked man to the door?" That's idiotic. That poor girl . . . woman would've had a heart attack! It's easy to forget that Trista is a grown woman. She's the size of a twelve-year-old, and she kind of dresses like one, too.

Gabe shrugs. "He says it's an inside joke and will say nothing more." Somehow, I doubt they let it go that easily. I haven't spent much time around Ryan, but I'm not surprised he's good at keeping secrets. "What did you need?"

"Fern won't eat," I say softly, hoping my voice won't carry to the groom, who is probably as anxious as his bride. We don't need him to go make things worse.

"What?" Mason shouts from elsewhere in the room, obviously eavesdropping and definitely concerned. *Damnit.*

"Down boy," Gabe says, flinging an arm across the door as if he could stop Mason from barreling out of that room and down the hall with that one simple movement. The door opens wider, and every inch of the doorframe over Gabe's shoulders fills with faces. Thankfully, none of them are Austin's.

"They're trying to feed her *tacos,"* I say, hoping they're bright enough to spot the problem here. Yeah, I love tacos as much as the next girl, but come *on*, people!

Mason's loud sigh breaks the stunned silence that follows.

"But she loves tacos," Austin says. I recognize his voice by the thrill it gives me, and that just pisses me right the hell off. I refuse to be attracted to a mean-spirited jerk like him.

"Who doesn't?" I ask, striving for a light tone so he doesn't know that I'd love to choke him with a taco. "But it's not the smartest thing in the world to feed someone who is nervous. And wearing white." They should've dressed her last, so she didn't have to worry about staining her dress, but her mother was too excited to wait.

"Good point," he says.

"I know I saw a charcuterie tray come in here earlier. Did you eat it all?" Crackers are a good start for Fern. Maybe once she has a few of them down, her appetite will wake up and she can try some of the meat or cheese.

"No," Mason says. He turns and bulldozes his way through the guys between him and the food. When he returns, Gabe leans a bit to allow him room to pass it out but otherwise blocks as much of the door as possible. "Text me? Please? If this doesn't work, we'll figure something else out."

Translation, send someone to buy her anything and everything he thinks she might be tempted to eat. "Sure thing," I tell him, taking the mostly-untouched tray. And I will let him know, but only so he doesn't come beat the door down because he's concerned. "Thanks, guys."

Chapter 2
Austin

*J*amaica walks away, carefully clutching that tray of meat and cheese like her life depends upon getting it to Fern safely. *She's good people.*

Despite working side-by-side all day yesterday and the day before to set this circus up, we've barely exchanged a handful of words. It's not that we have nothing to talk about; she's giving me the cold shoulder. She's still pissed at me for the joke at the bachelor party.

Maybe I should try to apologize again? No . . . not a chance. If I was out of line, she was, too. She wouldn't even give me a chance when I tried to tell her sorry. Instead of getting all pissy with me, she could've been reasonable about it and told me that it was a no-fly zone instead of calling me names. As far as I'm concerned, if I owe her an apology, she owes me one. We're even.

"You keep staring, people are gonna think you like her."

The whisper in my ear makes me jump. "Motherfucker!" I was so intent on figuring out Jamaica's problem, I didn't notice Chris standing behind me. Just like Ryan taught me, I pivot on the ball of my foot and punch Chris in the arm for being a dick.

"I *don't* like her. She's too . . . sensitive. And she don't like me," I tell him, though I know it won't make a bit of difference. Mason might be my big brother biologically, but Ryan, Chris, and Gabe claim me too. And they view it as their God-given right to harass the shit out of me, just like big brothers would. It doesn't help that I'm lying through my teeth.

I *do* like her. Or I did. Now, I'm not so sure.

It doesn't matter. She's Fern's best friend. I don't do relationships. There was absolutely no chance of anything happening between us *before* I pissed her off. That doesn't make this situation better, though. Her friendship was better than nothing. I want that back.

"Yeah, I hear the words coming out of your mouth, but the way your eyes were glued to her ass just now . . . That tells a different story," Chris says.

He's got me there. Grinning, I shrug at him. "She can be sensitive and still be fine."

Chris blinks at me. "I think you just described like . . . seventy-nine percent of the female population, bro."

Bitter, much? "Where do the other twenty-one percent hang out?" He's sort of seeing someone new, and it's serious enough she's met his kid. Surely, he can answer that question.

He shrugs. "Fuck if I know. If you ever figure that out, though . . . What did you do to piss her off?" he asks, nodding the direction Jamaica disappeared.

"Something I said at the bachelor party," I tell him, sighing. Her words to me that night still sting all these weeks later. I am *not* mean. So I might be a bit of an ass, but I'm an equal-opportunity ass, and I don't *try* to hurt people. She's got me all wrong.

Chris grunts. He pulls me back into the room by my elbow and closes the door. "And that was . . . ?"

In retrospect, it wasn't the smartest thing I've ever done, but I wasn't trying to hurt her feelings! It was a joke—obviously not a very funny one, but a joke either way. I glace over to where Granddad is deep in conversation with Fern's father and grandfather. *Please don't let them hear me.* This will be bad enough without Granddad's disappointment.

The collar of my shirt suddenly feels two sizes too small, but no amount of tugging provides me with relief. "I uh, told her that she was still the boss even if her boobs are the size of mosquito bites."

"Mère de Dieu," Ryan mutters. It must be bad for him to cuss in French. He only brings that out when he's trying to impress a woman or when things are well and truly FUBARed.

"Reasons Austin is single for fifteen-hundred, Alex," my brother says, falling back on his old Jeopardy standby. *I hate that fucking joke.*

I force my shoulders down, away from my ears, hoping none of the other assholes in the room noticed my defensive reaction, before I turn to face them. "No one invited either of you fuckers to listen!"

"Are you seriously dense enough to think we can't hear you?" Ryan asks, arching one eyebrow at me. The pierced one. Though he took his bar out for the occasion—unasked by the bride or the groom. I'll laugh for days to come at the memory of Fern confronting him last night, hands on her hips, telling him to put it back while he rolled his eyes and did what he wanted to anyway. "Don't answer that. If you really said that to her, I already know."

I roll my eyes. "No, I figured you were too busy being idiots to pay attention."

Mason scrubs his face with one hand. "Did you seriously *not* hear Jam telling Fern how she was teased about her flat chest in high school? I know you were there that day!"

Oh, shit. My face, even the back of my neck, gets hot. "I must've missed the finer points," I mutter. I came in to them laughing about how lucky Jamaica is because she doesn't have to buy sports bras. Jamaica started it even! "It's obviously not something I'd say to just anyone, but that conversation made me think I was in the clear!"

Every other man in the room, and there are a lot of us packed in here, groans. Even Fern's father is shaking his head at me, and the man barely interacts with us. I've watched him all morning, worried that he secretly hates Mason and is waiting to make his move to ensure the wedding never happens. I've worked too damn hard to let anything sabotage this wedding. Well, the wedding was my idea, anyway. Mason and Fern did all the work, but I don't think either of them minded.

"It doesn't matter if you think she won't mind, there are some things you should never joke about, Austin. You apologized when you realized you crossed a line, right?" Mason asks. I can't decide what would be worse, this lecture from him or from Granddad. I hate seeing that cold disappointment on either of their faces. *It should be Dad.* They've done their best to fill in where he left off, and that's why I hate letting either of them down. I wasn't easy to raise, and neither of them should've had to do it. That's easier to admit now than it was as a kid, though.

"I know, I know," I mutter, hanging my head. I heave a sigh and look up, straight into Mason's eyes, which are so much like Dad's, it's like he's glaring at me from the other side. "I apologized, but she ignored it and called me an asshole! And a jerk! And mean! And she said I'm overcompensating for something!"

"So?" Mason demands. "You *insulted* her."

"But—"

Mason shakes his head without breaking eye contact, giving me the full force of his glare. "Flowers. Lots of flowers. And not leftovers from the wedding."

"And chocolate. And wine," Gabe adds. He knows a thing or two about ending up on the top of a woman's shit list, so I should probably listen. But . . . Groveling isn't my thing, and it really doesn't sit right with me in this situation.

"She should apologize to *me* too." I'm not the only one who crossed a line here. She hurt me too. Not that I'll say that out loud.

If sighing in sync was an Olympic event, every member of the gold medal team could be found in this room. "Sit down like a couple of mature adults, explain yourself, apologize, and I'm sure she will too," Chris says.

That doesn't sound too unreasonable. I think I can do that. I've pissed off my fair share of women, but it's normally over something like forgetting to call or kicking them out when the deed is done. Not a joke.

The guys are right. I started this. I need to be the one to make the first move toward fixing it.

Chapter 3

Jamaica

*T*he walk back takes longer. My luck, I'll catch a heel on something, fall on my face, and scatter food all over the floor. Then,
I will have risked running into Austin for nothing, Mason will
freak the flip out, and Fern still won't have any food in her belly.

When I reach the door, I balance the tray on one arm with all the care
I show holding my sister's baby so I can open it one-handed.

"Oh, Jamaica, you're a genius!" Fern's little sister says, rushing to close
the door behind me. They all act like Mason is constantly roaming the halls
when he's the one who laid down the law and said he and Fern wouldn't
see each other before the ceremony, not even for pictures. This is his first
wedding, and he's determined to do it "right."

I shrug while they shove things out of the way on the table closest to
Fern. "Just figured we have a better chance at getting her to nibble on
crackers if her stomach is bothering her."

"Is there enough for two?" Tara asks wryly, dropping her hand to her
baby bump. The poor thing can't keep anything down. She arrived with a
supply of crackers and gingersnaps to get her through the day because the
baby seems to find them the least offensive. *Have kids, they said . . .* She

offered to share, but Fern refused, insisting that Tara needs them more. Turns out, she was right. Tara's rations didn't last through lunch because she shared them with all of the kids. *She'll be a good mum.*

"The guys barely touched it," I tell her. Hopefully, she can get some nourishment from it too. I heard Gabe talking to Ryan last night on the walk from the rehearsal to the tent where we had dinner. He's concerned because she's losing weight. That's one of the coolest things about being included in this group of friends, even if it is only because of Fern. They treat me like I've always been here. They don't try to hide things from me because I'm new. Fern smiled at them, said, 'hey, this is my new friend,' and I was in.

How'd that work out last time?

These people don't have the same vibe, though. There's no undercurrent of tension here. I was stupid enough to ignore the warning signs before. It won't happen again. As long as I keep my guard up around Austin, I'll be fine.

Fern catches my hand and squeezes, pulling me away from the brink of memories I'd rather forget for the day. "Thank you, Jam."

I've never met a person as appreciative as Fern. Doesn't matter what you do for her; she thanks you like you did backflips over the ocean on her behalf. Sometimes, I wonder if she was always that way or if it's something she acquired after tragedy and a bitter mother-in-law left her drowning in debt. "That's what friends are for. Don't thank me, just eat. Before Mason comes and beats down the door."

She winces and quickly selects a cracker. "He heard you, huh?"

I nod, watching her closely to ensure some of that cracker makes it into her stomach. "I don't know how, but yes."

Grinning, she rolls her eyes. "The man can hear a mouse fart, I swear." She salutes me with the cracker and bites it in half.

My mission accomplished, I search for my phone amid the chaos on every available horizontal surface so I can send Mason the text he's waiting for. No matter what, I know the guys won't let him come down here. There *might* be enough of them to stop him, but I'm not sure I'd bet against him when Fern or his daughter, Ronni, are involved.

"Jamaica," Marilyn, Mason's mother, drawls, "you're just in time."

I tap 'send' and look at her across the room. I could be wrong, but I *think* she's eyeing my curls, and the crow's feet at the corners of her eyes are more pronounced than usual, a sure sign she's displeased with something. She's been unhappy about something often enough this week for me to know the signs. My stomach sinks. "The hairdresser is ready for you."

Behind her, Fern's mother, Lily, purses her lips. Their family must have a thing for plants, because every woman in this room who is a blood relation to Fern is named for one. Lily's eyes dart from Marilyn's back to her daughter to my hair. I get the distinct impression that she doesn't care for how Marilyn is trying to run the show and is poised to step in on Fern's behalf if she feels her daughter is being railroaded.

"Oh!" Fern cries before I can come up with something polite to respond with. "Jam, I thought you were wearing your hair natural?"

I could kiss her. It's not something we've talked about, but I don't like letting someone I don't know style my hair. Had I said something before, I'm sure she would've brought someone in just for me, someone who knows their way around ethnic hair. Someone I've vetted. But I didn't. I didn't want to inconvenience her. I'm honored she included me, and I don't want to be a pest and make her regret it.

"If you don't mind," I tell her, ignoring her future mother-in-law's scowl and her mother's smile.

Marilyn is one of those women who like things to be just so—very Type A. I bet it's making her crazy that Fern isn't dictating our every move today. The tension between the two of them is killing me, but I know it has nothing to do with the wedding and everything to do with Marilyn putting her foot in her mouth a few months before Fern and I met.

"Not at all," Fern says with a smile for me. "I love your hair."

I automatically reach up to "fix" the curls I'm learning to embrace after years of relaxers, flat irons, and braids. I knew she wouldn't care. She's left everything about our look up to us so far—dresses, shoes, makeup, and hair. Instead of trying to force us to fit into the little box of what she wants, she encouraged us to be ourselves. There are seven bridesmaids, and none of us match aside from the pretty eggplant purple she chose for our dresses—and she chose that because it would complement every skin tone.

A tap on the door sets them all in motion. The other bridesmaids lunge to put themselves between Fern and the door in case it's Mason out there. It's silly when we all know that we're next with the photog, who is waiting on the other side of the door.

Hah. There's no time to do anything with my hair, anyway.

***

Just breathe, Jam. I hate crowds, and crowds like this one are the worst. I don't know anyone here save for the wedding party. Thanks to the wedding prep, I now count Tara, Noel, and Trista as friends. And the guys, of course. *It's nice to have friends again. Friends who are good people.* Her sisters are great too, but I haven't had much time to get to know them, and they'll fly home tomorrow.

When Fern found out about my crowd problem, she insisted on inviting my parents and sister so I'd have someone here to distract me, but they live too far away to make it on such short notice. *I can do this.*

Trista and Ryan, the first pair to walk, make it three-quarters of the way down the aisle. That's the cue for Noel and Darren to go. Then, it's Nicole and John followed by Chris and me.

I just have to make it to the arbor, and no one will look at me anymore. Everyone's focus will shift to the next couple down the aisle—Tara and Gabe. *It could be worse. I could've been first.* Or, even worse, I could've had to walk with Austin. Ivy is stuck with him, though.

"Jam?" Chris whispers. He pats my hand where it rests on his arm. "You okay over there?"

"Yeah," I whisper back, but I barely make a sound. I peel my eyes away from the crowd to look at him. I try to smile, but I don't think he's buying what I'm selling today.

He drops his chin and fixes me with a look I've seen him give his son, Keaton, when he's caught in a fib. "You're shaking. And you're digging your nails in."

I duck my head to hide my blush. My hand relaxes, and I stretch my fingers out wide to alleviate the ache from clenching them so long. I'd let go, but I need to hold onto something to keep me steady. "Sorry!"

"It's alright," he says softly. "It didn't hurt through my jacket. Don't like crowds?"

"Hate 'em."

He pats my hand again. "Just smile, okay? But not that manic smile you were just wearing. Pretend it's just you and me, like rehearsal last night."

That's easier said than done, but I'm willing to try. He moves forward, tugging me along with him because the alternative is me being dragged behind him like a child acting out for not getting their way in the store. "Did I tell you what Keaton did last weekend?"

"No." *This ought to be good.* That little boy is hilarious. He's always getting into some sort of trouble, and one of his honorary uncles usually puts him up to it. Mason is surprisingly good at coming up with things for Keaton to do considering he was a single father for a while. One would think he wouldn't want to make Chris's life more difficult. Fern tries to intercede, but Mason insists Chris brought it upon himself.

He grins. "Oh boy . . . So, you met Becca last night, right?"

Becca . . . The name is familiar, but I met so many new people last night. "Yeah," I say anyway, eager for the rest of the story. I'll figure her out later. If she was at the rehearsal, she'll probably be at the reception.

"Well, we've sort of dated for a few months now, so I decided to let her meet Keaton before we get in any deeper." *Smart move.* Dating when you have a kid has to be like walking a tightrope. And in addition to the trampoline underneath, there are also bear traps and spikes. "She rings the doorbell. I let her in, call for Keat . . . He comes running out of the bathroom, buck naked, covered in crap from the waist down. He didn't tell me he had an accident and took his Pull-Up off by himself."

I can almost see it, that sweet little cherub face smiling and so excited to meet his daddy's friend—too excited to wait to be cleaned up. "Oh, my gosh. What did she do?" I can't imagine what I would do in her shoes. Run, maybe? I like kids and all, but man . . . That's a lot to handle when you're first meeting a guy's kid. *A make or break moment.*

"She helped me clean him up," he says. There's something different in his voice when he says it, so I glance over to find him *glowing*. Pride? Happiness? Love? All of the above, maybe? Whatever it is, the guy has it bad. "See you on the other side."

What? I glance around. The arbor is directly in front of us. Mason stands under it, grinning at us. Chris used his story to distract me long enough to make it down the aisle without me freaking out. I hope Becca is good to Chris because he seems like a good guy. I might have to join the butt-kicking committee if she does him wrong.

I take my place next to Nicole and watch Tara and Gabe finish their walk. Sage and her brother-in-law, Scott, come next. Ivy and Austin bring up the rear of the bridal party. *Dang it.*

I thought my placement in the lineup was pretty good. I didn't have to go first, and I didn't have to walk with *him*. But no! I have to watch him walk the whole way, looking like the best sort of sin in that tux. *This isn't helping!*

There must be something in the water these guys drink because not one of them is in bad shape. But none of them make my fingers tingle with the desire to reach out and touch him like Austin does. I don't know what it is about him that gets to me, but I wish it would leave me alone. It should not be possible for such an obnoxious twat to be so attractive.

Next to the others, he looks like a teenager who has finally reached his height potential but still has some filling out to do. Ryan calls him wiry, whatever that means. He's the runt of the litter, which is fitting since he seems to charge into everything with the optimistic abandon or curious determination of a puppy and isn't smart enough to stop when he's in over his head. *Comparing him to a dog doesn't make him less sexy, Jam.* That doesn't mean it's not accurate, though . . .

He smiles at someone in the crowd, and he's close enough I see him wink. *Ugh.* Can't he wait until the reception to flirt with his next conquest? How disgusting! *I wonder who she is?* There are too many people to single one out. It doesn't help that they're all facing the opposite direction.

He stops at the end of the aisle to hug Mason. Then the kids are coming down the aisle, and their cuteness drives all thoughts of *him* from my brain.

Austin

Over the crowd, I get a glimpse of Jamaica. She looks gorgeous today, not that she ever doesn't. I like that they left her hair alone instead of trying to tame it into some fancy configuration like the others are wearing. *Did she bring a date?*

Why do I care?

Ivy and I go our separate ways. Before I take my place, I stop to hug my brother. This is a big day for both of us. Once the marriage license is signed, I am off the hook. Chambers Freight International will never be my problem because his daughter will officially be next in line for that throne. He and Ronni are more than welcome to it.

More importantly, it's good to see my brother happy again. I can't take all the credit, but I do like to pat myself on the back for helping him pull his head out of his ass and realize how special Fern is. I'll be there to plug it with a boot if things ever get rocky and they start throwing around words like "separate" or "divorce" too. They're not splitting up on my watch. And our sister will be right there with me.

I turn and watch a gaggle of kids trooping up—or is it down?—the aisle, while Ronni does her best to keep them all in line. Nicole's eldest daughter, Mallory, walks in front of the others, liberally scattering white rose petals as she goes. Her little sister, Charlotte, clings to her flower girl basket with one hand and to Ronni's skirt with the other. And Chris's son toddles along on Ronni's other side, holding her finger and dragging the ring bearer pillow by the ribbons the fake rings are supposed to be tied to. *Thank God Ivy and I decided to hold onto the real ones.* When they stop in front of Mason, Charlotte turns her basket upside down, dumping the petals within in a heap at his feet while the crowd politely stifles a laugh.

Grandmothers hurry forward to wrangle the small ones, but Ronni goes to her father. She's sunshine and smiles today because she's as excited as they are. The music changes, and she bounces on the balls of her feet. Ivy whispers and beckons for Ronni to join her, but she holds her ground. She can stand wherever she wants as far as I'm concerned. This is her day too.

I move a bit, shifting to the side until I can see Mason properly. I want to see the look on my brother's face when he gets his first glimpse of his bride. I hope the photographer gets a good picture. His eyes go wide, and he must be holding his breath because his chest stops moving. The grin he's worn all day stretches into the smile I've spent years trying to copy. Women go nuts over his smile, but I can't see what's so special about it unless he's smiling at "his girls" like he is now. *I wish Dad were here.*

Someone must be cutting onions out here because I am *not* getting all emotional and teary-eyed. This is a happy day. Dad would be ecstatic. He wouldn't want waterworks.

Blinking rapidly to clear the excessive wet stuff from my eyes, I step back into line and watch my new sister and her dad walk our way. They don't seem to be in any particular hurry. Every now and then, I catch a gleam on her dad's face that makes me wonder if he's crying. Fern is absolutely radiant, but there's a nervous edge to her smile. They need to hurry up. She'll relax as soon as Mason takes her hand. It's a strange and beautiful thing to watch, the way love affects those around me.

Nicole and John have their little quirks. So do Tara and Gabe. I've even noticed some of Ivy and Scott's in the past few days. Makes a man think that there might be something to the whole relationship thing . . .

But it's a lot of trouble too. I mean, I'm in hot water up to my ears with Jamaica, and we're not even dating! I don't see myself ever being comfortable in a real relationship. My family and my buddies all think I just haven't found the right one, but the truth is, I'm not looking. As beautiful as this love thing is from the outside looking in, I don't think I can do it.

I've seen what they all went through to get where they are now, except Ivy and Scott. I'm sure they have a story that's not so happy too. That's the problem—it's not all happy-happy joy-joy. Shit gets real, and I don't do that. That's when I make a joke at the wrong moment, and everyone gets pissed at me because they think I'm not taking it seriously. I *am*, but I can't handle the heavy stuff.

Nope. I think I'll stay a free agent. No one gets mad. No one gets hurt.

Chapter 4
Jamaica

Miss Lola flags me down on my way out of the tent, yelling my name to make herself heard over the throbbing pulse of the music. I dodge through the crowd and lean close to hear her better. "Could you sign this for me, dear?" she asks, brandishing a clip-board with one hand and passing me a pen with the other. "We'd like to include some of the pictures in the CFI employee newsletter and maybe on the website."

"Sure," I reply automatically. I carefully sign the line on the release waiver she is holding and hand back her pen. It's officially over. They said their "I do's," the ink is dry on the marriage license, the pictures are taken, dinner was delicious, the cake is cut and served. Time to take a walk before I get roped into the bouquet toss. Fern's DJ friend, Desi, already put out the call for all the single people in the crowd to gather. That's not my scene.

Safety is a few steps away when Austin shouts, "Jam! Where are you going?"

Are you kidding *me?* Other voices shout for me to join them. I turn and look for Fern, but she's talking to Desi and Mason, oblivious to what's going on. She'd give me an out. Her other friends won't. People who like this stuff don't understand how anyone could hate it.

Austin opens his mouth to say something as I storm past him, but I keep walking. I don't want to hear it, whatever it is. I won't make a scene at Fern's wedding, so I will join the herd of women hoping to catch the bouquet and be bequeathed with the magical flower dust that ensures their own wedding will soon follow before they drag me. *If I catch it, I'm beating him with it.*

I plaster on a smile to be a good sport and fall in at the back of the pack. They shout a countdown. Fern launches her beautiful throwaway bouquet of white roses and lilies over her shoulder, then quickly turns to watch the madness. Predictably, a few guests make fools of themselves, jumping and lunging for the stupid bloody thing. It sails right over their heads and nearly smacks poor Noel in the face. She barely brings her hands up in time to stop it.

Trista cheers for her, and Tara quickly joins them while the others clear off, shooting sulky looks her way. She doesn't move, staring at the arrangement of flowers in her hands as if she's never seen such a thing before and can't quite imagine its purpose. It's just a guess, but I don't think she wanted to participate, either.

The guys are up next. Since my suffering is over, I stick around to watch. Poor Fern's face is the same red as a traffic signal before Mason finishes removing her garter with his teeth. She's nicer than I am—I would've kicked him in the head for trying that.

Men are strange creatures. All of the single ones flock together for this time-honored tradition, but unlike the ladies, they actively avoid the garter if it flies their way. They will risk life and limb to dodge whatever magic that little scrap of lace and elastic supposedly holds. It's like a play park game of cooties, but someone always takes one for the team for the sake of the bride and groom.

Grinning, Mason takes careful aim and shoots it in his brother's general direction. I laugh along with everyone else when Austin throws himself to the floor, exaggerating the action to be funny. It flies over his head and smacks Ryan in the chest, and the game is over because the spell is broken. It touched someone. Ryan is the loser. As a consolation prize, he gets to take a picture with Noel perched on his lap, though neither of them seems pleased with the situation. Not that I blame them. Yeah, they're friends but still . . . It's probably weird. At least they're not total strangers, though. That would probably be more awkward.

Entertainment over, I make my way to the nearest exit, which is just about anywhere because the reception is taking place in a big open-sided tent on Mason's grandparents' land, not far from the ceremony site. There's nothing for me to run from anymore, but I need a break from people. I can't go too far—the bridal party will have their dance soon—but I can recoup a bit of sanity before I have to smile for the crowd again.

The last party I went to didn't end well for anyone. I know this one won't be a problem. No one would dare ruin Mason and Fern's day, and several people present are more than capable of handling anyone who gets out of line. My anxiety missed that memo, though.

The evening air is cooler away from all the bodies packed into the tent. Almost too cool. It's nice, though. Just a bit farther out and—

"Jam! Wait!"

I keep walking. I don't want to talk to Austin right now. Or ever again. I will suffer his presence when necessary for Fern's sake, but that's it.

I'm almost far enough away for the low buzz of the crowd to fade into nothingness, but I'll still hear Desi call for the bridal party to gather on the dance floor.

"You're going to miss their first dance."

Bloody hell. He knows what to say to get me to stop. I do want to see it, though. They've practiced for weeks—Mason's idea, not Fern's. I'm sure someone will record it . . . No. That's not good enough. I don't *need* to be there—Fern would forgive me for missing it—but I want to be. I want to watch my new best friend and her husband dance and smile at each other in that way that restores my faith in happily ever after.

I make a wide turn to avoid Austin and stomp back to the tent, imagining the ground under my feet is his face every step of the way.

Austin jogs after me; the sound of his shoes slapping against the ground warns me of his approach. He slows when he catches up to me, matching my pace. "I'm sorry."

I want to ignore him, but my mum would be ashamed of my rudeness if she found out. "For what?" I ask through clenched teeth. He would be much easier to tolerate if I could pretend he never said what he did, but I can't. I can't forget that my lack of breasts apparently means I'm less of a person to him, and he treats it like a joke. I thought I'd heard all the jokes before that night. Maybe that's why it hurts so much more.

That and I actually *liked* him. I thought he was funny and charming and, occasionally, incredibly sweet. He's great with kids, he loves his family and friends fiercely, and he's quick to step in with a joke to break the tension when his friends are at odds. But I know the truth now.

It was all an act. *Just like with Jordan.*

He clears his throat. "I thought you didn't hear Desi or something. I didn't know you *wanted* to miss the bouquet toss. Though . . ."

I wait a beat for him to finish that thought, but he doesn't. "Though what?"

"Never mind," he says quickly. "I'm sorry I shouted after you. I know how some women are all about catching that bouquet, and I didn't want you to be upset that you missed your chance."

His apology thaws my frigid attitude a bit. Enough to appreciate that he wasn't *trying* to be a jerk. This time. "You should thank your lucky stars I didn't catch it."

"Oh?" he asks, a hint of a smile in his voice. "Why's that?"

Unable to resist, I turn my head to catch a glimpse of that smile. A kaleidoscope of butterflies takes flight in my stomach. *I'm hopeless.* "'Cause I woulda beat you to death with the dumb thing."

His laughter echoes through the fading twilight. "Fair enough."

I managed to make it farther than I thought before he stopped me. We walk the rest of the way together, and some stupid part of me hopes he will take this opportunity to offer an apology for the things he said that night. To prove that he's different than my ex, because Jordan never apologized for anything. He never acknowledged that he did anything wrong. It was always my fault.

But he doesn't, proving that the things I said about him are true. The butterflies all land or leave to find somewhere with more flight time then they'll get with me.

Stepping into the pool of light spilling from the tent breaks our tentative truce. I walk away from him and hurry to Fern's side to keep myself from crying for the lost opportunity. I won't let myself drag her down on the happiest day of her life.

Austin

Jamaica walks away and straight to Fern's side without looking back even once. I thought we were making progress, but I need a little more time to figure out what to say to her. She's not going to accept a generic apology; she just proved that. She'll ask me what I'm apologizing for. *Must be the lawyer in her.* But what happens if I don't have a suitable answer?

I try not to dwell on it while my brother and his bride take to the dance floor, but I can't think of anything else. Maybe it's time to heed the advice of men more experienced in the art of appeasing an angry woman. When the song ends, I get my bearings and am halfway out of the tent again when Desi calls for the bridal party to join Mason and Fern on the dance floor. That plan will have to wait. Jamaica isn't going anywhere for a few hours, and neither is her anger.

***

I hurry across the lawn, skirting the house instead of going through it. I don't *think* anyone is inside, but I don't want to risk it. I don't want to answer questions. *This is ridiculous.*

I've bought flowers for plenty of girls before, but for birthdays, the odd first date, and—once or twice—to melt panties, but I've never snuck into Grandma's garden in the dark, praying against all odds that some flower is still open after sunset so I can *apologize* because she took something the wrong way. I have a better chance at finding a pot of gold and Lucky the Leprechaun at the end of a rainbow than I do of finding a flower right now. I'll probably have to wait until tomorrow and order flowers, then track her down to apologize. That might be better, anyway. How could one or two flowers I scrounge up here compare to a bouquet arranged by a professional?

Still, I round the last corner into the garden. I'm not ready to give up, even if I don't understand why I'm doing this. Maybe it's better if she doesn't like me. I like her a little too much. Relationships and I don't mix. But no, I was in the wrong. I need to fix this.

"Oh, holy shit." I stop short. There are flowers *everywhere*. "Lucky, if you're out here, man, I'm not after your gold." Better safe than sorry. I've heard Leprechauns can be scrappy little bastards.

I knew some flowers bloomed at night, but I didn't know Grandma had a whole garden of them. I move through the flowerbeds, taking care not to trample any of the plants. Grandma will know. Grandma always knows. And she'll know it was me, too. I'm in enough trouble; I don't need two of them mad at me. My luck, they'll join forces and turn making my life a living hell into a tag team event. And with the pair of them feeding each other's anger, it'll go on forever. A fumbled attempt to appease one of them will only anger the other worse. *No thank you.*

I take my time, examining each different type of flower, wondering which she'll like best. I settle on one that looks like it might be pink, but it's hard to tell in the dark even with the light of the waning moon. It's simple and pretty, and I like it. There are a lot of them too. Grandma won't miss a couple of them and come after me for desecrating her garden. I select two that show no signs of wilt and hurry back the way I came.

I hover outside the tent, contemplating the flaw in my plan. I have to get these flowers into the tent and find Jamaica without anyone seeing them. The guys know what's going on, so they won't think anything of it. But the girls . . . They'll take it all wrong. They'll put two and two together and get six million. The rumor mill will spin up. They'll have Jamaica and I walking down the aisle inside an hour for sure.

Ain't *nobody* got time for that.

I just want to make amends before Fern figures out I hurt her new bestie's feelings and she decides to practice her Muay Thai on me. I can't believe she doesn't already know. I am *not* fast enough to outrun her. I fucking hate cardio, unless it's horizontal naked cardio. I'll do that kind all day.

I can't call Jamaica and ask her to come out here because I don't have her number. I can't ask Fern for her number; she'll get suspicious.

Mason! Nope. He won't give it to me. He'll tell me some bullshit about humility being good for me or something like that. *Easy for him to say.* He's not the one walking the gauntlet of women high on the success of one wedding and ready to plan another.

I might as well be strolling through a lion's den naked with a raw steak strapped to my ass.

But it's not like I have a choice unless I want to stand outside waiting for her to go for one of her random walks because she can't sit still. She's worse than Fern in that regard. Both of them always *have* to be doing something. For all I know, I just missed her requisite walk, though. I could stand here for another hour.

Just do the damn thing. I don't have to walk in and go right to Jam. I can play it cool . . . Talk to some friends, then *happen* to walk by her. This does not have to be awkward. I don't even know why I'm thinking about it so hard. It's not a big deal at all. No one will notice if I walk in there with flowers. There are flowers *everywhere.* I swear Mom ordered the whole damn flower shop when Fern put her in charge of procuring the bouquets. What's two more?

I take a deep breath, stand up straight, square my shoulders, and march into the tent like I own the fucking place, holding the flowers down by my side in hopes they go unnoticed.

Chapter 5

Jamaica

Someone stops next to me, close enough their sleeve brushes my arm. I look over and up at a profile I know too well from many stolen glances. Austin isn't looking at me. He's watching the dancers too. Silently, he raises his hand, showing me two flowers clutched in his fist.

"What's this, then?" I ask, eyeing the blooms. I'm not allergic to flowers—not like I am grass—but I sense a catch. His head is still turned toward the dancefloor, but he's watching me from the corner of his eye.

"They're for you. I uh . . ." He stops, and his shoulders rise and fall with a sigh. "I know they're not as pretty as the wedding flowers. I went up to the house and picked them for you, though."

Awww! He picked them for me? My naïve little heart melts into a pile of goo. I'm a sucker for gifts. The house isn't that far, but he left his brother's wedding reception to do this. For me. Maybe he isn't a total jerk after all. I take the flowers from him, and his shoulders heave again.

"I wanted to apologize for our misunderstanding a few weeks back."

Or maybe he is. "Misunderstanding?" He insulted me. There's not much to misunderstand about it.

"Yes . . . I didn't realize you were so sensitive about . . ." He gestures toward his chest.

Sensitive? The hope that things might get better between us drowns in a wave of anger. First, he makes fun of me. Then, he acts like I'm in the wrong for being upset about it?

"See, I heard you and Fern joking around that day, and I thought you had a better sense of humor about . . . it."

"It?" My chest is now an 'it.' That might be even worse. To top it off, he's insinuating I don't have a sense of humor. Again. I wanted him to apologize so bad, to explain himself and make it better. This isn't helping, though. It's only making everything so much worse. He makes it sound like it's all my fault when I was sitting there, minding my own business, until he came up and started teasing me for something I can't help.

I get that we can't help whom we're attracted to, but I'm very disappointed in myself. It's a good thing he's pretty because that's all he has going for him. *I pity whoever ends up stuck with him.*

I step in front of him and reach to tuck the flowers' stems between his tie and his collar. He covers my shaking hands with his but doesn't stop me.

"Jam?" he asks, scowling down at me.

"Just stop talking, Austin." Every time he opens his mouth, I feel like more of an idiot for the silly, school-girl crush I've harbored since the day we met. I knew he would never be interested in me. I'm not the perfectly coiffed, bubble-headed cheerleader type he flirts with when we're all out together. *Maybe he noticed and this is his way of discouraging me.*

He didn't have to be so cruel about it, though. It's not like I was throwing myself at him. I wouldn't do that. I wouldn't do *anything* because I'm too gun shy. Putting my heart out there for a guy didn't end well for me last time. I won't make that mistake again.

His fingers wrap loosely around my wrists. His barely-there touch is a balm for my anger, but it doesn't soothe the pain. "Those are for you," he says.

"Thank you, but I don't want them." I should take my hands back and walk away now, but I can't find the will to move.

"Jam, I'm trying to apologize here. I didn't know about—"

"Generally, when someone apologizes, they don't make things worse."

"How am I making things worse? You just don't understand—"

I grab a fistful of his shirt and tug him down to eye level. My eyes land on his lips, which are slightly parted but still curved up at the corners in his perpetual smile. I could kiss him. Lord knows I've thought about it plenty of times. It would be so easy with him this close. It would only make things worse for me, though. And he doesn't want me to. "Leave me alone, Austin. We can play nice for Fern's sake, but leave me alone."

"You want to kiss me, don't you?" he asks, his voice heavy with self-assured confidence. He knows he's cute, and it makes him a little arrogant. Somehow, that makes him even cuter. Sometimes. What little space there is between us is suddenly charged with tension, making it hard to breathe. My whole body throbs in time with my heartbeat. The urge to touch him— run my fingers through his hair and trace the little scar that barely peeks out from his collar to find out if it's rough as it looks to be—has that tingle spreading through my hands.

I swallow hard. How does he know I was thinking about doing just that? Why do I want to do it even more now? And not stop there . . . "No, I don't."

Especially not here. It doesn't matter that we're not in the thick of the crowd. Anyone could be watching right now. I'm not helping my case by holding him here, so I open my hand and step back. He doesn't let me go, though. And he stays on my level.

"Then why are you staring at my mouth?"

"Just wondering if you could still wear that cocky little smile if you have a fat lip."

"Liar."

"Prick."

Surprise flashes across his face, and he laughs, releasing one of my hands to rest his on his chest. "That's not a denial."

Shoot! "Didn't feel the need to repeat myself," I say, shrugging carelessly. "I thought you were resorting to insulting me again."

His lips part and his eyes go wide. "I wasn't *insulting* you!"

"Shut up, Austin," I say to stop him before he can dig his hole a little deeper. "You don't get to tell me what hurts my feelings."

"That's not—Never mind. Why do you hate me?"

What I feel and what I do are completely out of sync. I'm so irritated with him that I wish I could throw a fist like Fern and find out if he actually *can* smile with a fat lip. Instead, my head darts forward, and I seal his lips with mine. The sweetness of chocolate cake and champagne from the toasts clings to his soft mouth like a promise. Lust's familiar siren's song of pleasure sends heat coursing through my veins to pool low in my belly. Austin's eyes widen for a split second before they drift closed and he reaches for me.

What am I doing? I snap out of it, tearing myself away from him though it's the last thing I want to do, and stepping back before things get any more out of control.

"I said shut up," I tell him, panting. "I don't hate you! You're just an asshole!"

Oh, my gosh. I just *kissed* him. I glance around, but no one seems to be looking our way. They're all too busy visiting or watching the dancers. *Thank goodness!* I don't want to deal with our friends teasing me about this. Or worse, trying to set us up or something. We'll never work.

My face flares hot. Not knowing what else to do, I walk away, escaping out of the nearest side to get lost in the moonlit night, the trees, and eventually the silence of being so far from humanity.

How am I ever going to face him again? I just handed him more ammunition to use against me. I must seem so stupid to him. He made it clear he doesn't find me attractive, then I go and practically force myself on him.

No. That's not right. He could've stopped me if he didn't want it too. He *reached* for me. I will *not* feel guilty. Stupid, yes, but not guilty. It's just another thing for him to tease me about and hold over my head. I won't fall for it this time, though. I know that game. He'll offer me little scraps of attention, then find cruel ways to tease me once he reels me in.

A warm, firm hand closes around my wrist and pulls me to a stop. "Jam, stop."

"Let me go!" I yank at my hand. He lets go, and I smack myself in the face. "Ow!" *Because I haven't humiliated myself enough tonight!*

"You okay?" He doesn't really care. There's a smile in his voice. He wouldn't smile if he was concerned.

"Oh, go ahead and laugh. You know you want to."

He sighs. "Forget this," he mutters. *Good. Go away.* My face is engulfed by two big hands. Warm breath tickles my face, then his lips ghost across mine.

"W-what are you doing?" I sputter. I should back away, but his touch— so much gentler than I expected—holds me in thrall.

"I wasn't done kissing you when you ran off," he says, following through with another soft kiss.

Lust flares to life again, burning hotter than the sun. *This is daft!* How can I want someone like him so much? We don't get along at all. He's the last person on earth I should want, but my body doesn't agree. It's not particular about the whos and wheres right now, just the when. And the sooner, the better.

At least he can't talk if he's kissing me. My lungs burn, reminding me to breathe. Another barely-there kiss makes me dizzy. Or maybe it's that I forgot to breathe again. My hands tingle, but this time it's different. I don't just want to touch him. I want to grab him and pull him closer, feel his body against mine, and hold him tight while we move together to find the bliss of release.

His lips brush mine again, and I forget why I shouldn't want this. My fingers glide through his dark hair. It's even softer than I thought it would be, almost silky. He moves one hand to my neck. The other goes to my hip and squeezes, making my thighs clench. He pulls just a bit, inviting me closer. I go willingly, pressing myself as close to him as I can get from hip to chest. Any doubts I might've had about his interest are erased by the hard length of his dick digging into my belly. *But what's the catch?* I'm not sure I care.

"Closer." The word is growled more than spoken, and more of an order than a request. I hate being told what to do but in this situation . . . I'd let him boss me around all day. I *want* to listen. I want to make him happy because his order carries the promise of pleasure. I hike my skirt up a bit and sling one leg around his hip. Our lips meet again. His hand on my hip slides around to squeeze my bum, and I moan into our kiss. "Closer," he says again. "Jump."

I don't move. How is jumping going to get me closer? He sighs and crouches a bit, lifting my other foot off the ground when he straightens. *Oh.* With both of my legs wrapped around him, he walks farther into the timber. Trees loom overhead, quickly blocking out the lights from the tent. The sound of rushing water is louder with every step, warning me of the river's proximity.

He wouldn't throw me in, would he? It's the sort of thing he'd find funny, and it would serve me right for trusting him. I cling to him as tightly as I can. I won't go without a fight.

"Jam," he says, purring in my ear. "I'm in a hurry here too, but if you choke me out, neither of us are going to get what we want."

"Oh . . ." I relax my arms a bit, but not my legs. I won't risk it.

"Better," he says. He walks around a tree trunk that's wider than I am tall and leans his back against it, putting it between us and anyone coming from the direction of the tent.

"Why'd you freak out?" he asks.

"Who says I freaked out?" I don't want to tell him what I feared he was planning. He doesn't need something else to tease me about.

He frowns. "You tried to choke me out, Jam. Change your mind?"

"No, I didn't change my mind." *Not that you asked what I wanted.* I suppose he did, in a way. I'm the one who pulled him closer instead of pushing him away. "I don't want to talk about it."

If I tell him my fears about the river, he'll laugh at me. Or he'll do it. *Jordan would've, but only after I was convinced he wouldn't.*

The moonlight shining through the canopy of the tree casts shadows across his face, making it hard to tell, but I could swear he rolls his eyes. "Whatever. I like you better when you're not talking, anyway."

Oh, no, he didn't! How can he be so *insufferable* and still make me ache for him? I can't deny the thrill I get from arguing with him, though. "Same here. So shut up."

He lunges forward and nips at my bottom lip. "Gladly." His lips brush mine again, but I'm done with his teasing. I sink my fingers into his hair and press my lips to his so hard it hurts. He groans and pushes harder. I didn't mind the pain anyway, but his approval—his *response*—makes it almost enjoyable.

We both gasp for air when we separate. "You like it rough, huh?" he asks.

A thrill runs up my spine. Something tells me I wouldn't mind Austin's version of rough. He might be a complete jerk, but he's not heartless. I shake my head, too breathless to laugh. "No. But . . ."

I'm used to it. That's not something I'll tell him, but I don't know how to put what I want to say into words that will make sense to him. I like the warning of the pain in this case. It reminds me not to get complacent with him. He's still Austin.

"I get it," he says before I can find a way to explain. "If it *hurts,* say so." He lets me slide down his body, holding me steady until I find my balance once my feet are back on the ground. Then, he grabs a handful of hair at the base of my skull and gently pulls, tipping my head back for another kiss. Another thrill shoots from the roots of my hair to my center, followed by a rush of heat. "Okay?"

"God, yes," I say, panting. I like that he's careful in his assertiveness. *You shouldn't.* I'm not supposed to like anything about him.

"Good. Do your worst, Jam," he whispers while he nuzzles my neck, sending little shockwaves of need through me. "You're not going to hurt me."

Uneasiness cuts through the mad rush of desire. "You get off on pain?" Maybe this is a bad idea. *Ya think?* I brush that voice aside and focus on the specifics. I already know shagging Austin is a bad idea in general. No matter how often I'd like to pop him in the mouth for being an idiot, I couldn't really hurt him. Not even if he wants me to. If that's what he needs to enjoy this maybe it's best if we walk away now.

Austin shakes his head. "No. It can be fun in certain situations. I just get the feeling you're holding back because . . . never mind. Just don't."

I'm not sure what to make of that, so I change the subject. "I want to touch you," I say, stating the simple truth. If this is actually happening, I'm going to satisfy my curiosity.

He chuckles. "You *are* touching me."

I shove at his shoulder. "No, not your clothes."

He shrugs lightly. "Whatever gets you off, but we're keeping our clothes on. Would be hard to explain grass and leaves stuck places they shouldn't be."

That's a good point. I'd rather avoid the awkward situation that will surely come about if our friends find out about this. How would I explain something I don't understand myself?

"I can work with that." Undo a few buttons, and I can get to plenty of him.

He grins, the moonlight glinting off his perfectly straight teeth. "Good. Now, shut up." He pulls on my hair again, tugging my neck to the side, and nips at my earlobe. While I make my shaking hands work enough to un-button his jacket and a few of the frustratingly small buttons on his shirt, he nips and licks and sucks at my neck, triggering a rush of heat low in my belly. It's so hard to focus on the buttons when I want to go for his zipper instead, but I don't let myself. I'm not wasting this chance.

I slip a hand through the opening in his shirt and slide it up his abs. If he were anyone else, I'd stop him and insist on a look because he actually has abs. With the way he eats, he must log a lot of hours at the gym. They may not be as well defined as some, but they're there. Instead, I lightly trace my finger up and down the faint dips between them, making him shiver.

"Damn. Do that again," he whispers in my ear. I do, and he grabs my bum to pull me closer and grinds his dick against my hips. "I can't wait to be inside you."

There's a rushing in my ears, like the river is flowing right between them, and I get light-headed. I want that, too. Soon. Now. There's no need to wait anymore. Let's do this so we can get back to hating each other in peace. *Whoa.* The insanity of what we're doing cuts through the frenzy.

"Are you sure about this?" My hands don't stop, though. I'm not sure about this, but I want it. I will explore every inch of him I can get to with his clothes on until he stops me.

"Mmhmm," he hums into my neck. "The sooner we fuck each other out of our systems, the better off we'll be. We might even get along better."

Interesting. "So, you've done this before?" As infuriating as he is, it's not surprising. It's actually reassuring to hear him acknowledge that we're on the same page about this. It's not about feelings, it's about satisfying this . . . whatever it is between us.

He straightens to look down at me, that cocky little half-smile of his nowhere to be seen. "That is one instance where I absolutely do not kiss and tell."

"I'll take that as a yes," I say, undeterred by his uncharacteristic seriousness. At least I know he's serious about keeping quiet.

"First rule of fight club."

I roll my eyes at him. "Got it. Shut up and—"

He lunges in for another kiss. "I get your panties, though."

"*What?*"

"You heard me. I get to take them off you. I get to keep them."

"What, for blackmail?" *How stupid can you get, Jam?* Even though I expected there to be *something*, I walked right into his trap. *Will I ever learn?* I push against his chest to get away, but his arms tighten, locking me in place.

"Nope. This will never be spoken of again. They're a souvenir. I piss you off something fierce, but I'm still getting in your panties."

"That's all?" That we're in this situation implies some measure of trust between us, but can I extend it that far? Would he lie to me? *No. Austin doesn't lie.* Too many people have too much faith in him for him to be a liar.

He nods. "That's all. I swear. Deal?"

Whatever, weirdo. I'm not here to judge his kink. I might care later, but if that's all it is, it's not a deal-breaker. I've done a lot of work to get back to a place where I'm comfortable in my own body and comfortable sharing my body with someone else again after the mental hell Jordan put me through. It sucks that Austin is the first guy I've wanted to get naked with since Jordan, but it is what it is. Right now, I'll agree to just about anything to get him so deep inside me, I can't tell where I end and he begins.

"Fine. Fair is fair. I get your boxers."

He grins, and his eyebrows twitch up and down. "Who says I'm wearing any?" I open my mouth to insist he is but I don't say a word because I really don't know. That deep belly laugh of his fills the night. "Deal. Shut up and earn them."

I can do that. I work a hand between us to tease him, squeezing his hard cock through his pants. "I want this," I tell him, smiling to myself. I never had a problem going after I wanted until my ex was through with me. He made me question everything I thought I wanted and made me too scared to ask for it. *It's good to be back to me. Mostly.*

Austin groans, tipping his head back to rest against the rough bark of the tree. It can't be comfortable, but he doesn't seem to mind. "You're going to get it, too. Show me how bad you want it, Jam."

Eagerly, I wiggle out of his grasp to give myself room to unbutton his pants. I want that cock free so I can see if he's really as big as he feels through his clothes. And then, I want that big cock deep inside me, and I want to ride him until I come all over him.

I push the waistband of his underwear down, and he springs free. His clothes *definitely* weren't padding him.

"You just gonna look at it?" he asks. "We don't have all day, babe. Someone will come looking sooner or later. You might up and wander off all the time, but I don't."

I grab his cock and squeeze. He gasps, but his mouth stops running. "Shut up and fuck me."

"Such a lady," he says on a laugh. "And so greedy. You ready for me to take those panties off you and fill you up?"

Bloody hell! That mouth! "Shut up and—"

He presses his lips against mine in another one of those painful kisses, cutting me off. I didn't mean it anyway. I want him to say outrageously filthy things until my panties are so soaked my wetness drips down my legs. "There's that sass. I thought you were starting to like me there for a second."

"Dick."

"Yep, that's my dick, alright." He slides his hands from my hips to my tits over my dress and smirks at me. "It's going to be so far inside you; you'll feel me in places no one else has ever touched. You're going to feel me tomorrow. Every time you walk, you're going to remember my dick."

His filthy promises leave my head spinning, but I don't want him to know that. I don't want him to know how much he gets to me. How much I like it.

"I've heard that before," I tell him, rolling my eyes. No one has ever said anything like that to me, but I'm not letting him have that win. This isn't some sexy bonding time. This is . . . hate sex.

"After tonight, you'll never believe it from another man."

I let him go. "Shut up and fuck me, Austin."

"Give me those panties. I'm ready to coat myself in your sweet honey and feel that pussy choke my cock." He pulls his boxers up, then grabs my hair again and pulls my head back to kiss his way down my neck. He reaches my collar bone and moves lower, kissing down my chest and between my breasts.

He looks up at me while he pushes one of my shoulder straps down my arm and shoves one side of my bodice out of his way. Staring me in the eye, he cradles my breast in his palm and sucks my nipple into his mouth. The heat is intense after the cool night air. Gasping, I thread my fingers in his head and throw my head back to hide my face from him. I'm not supposed to enjoy this so much, am I? I don't want him to know I am.

He sucks at me while his hands work to gather my skirt, and I regret choosing a long one. I should've at least gone for one with a slit, but I didn't plan to slip into the timber for a hate bang after the wedding. I'll plan better next time.

Austin comes off my nipple with an audible *pop* that makes me look down. He grins and sinks to his knees before ducking under my skirt. I gasp. "What are you doing?"

"Getting my souvenir," is his slightly muffled reply. His warm lips brush against my inner thigh, causing me to flinch. "Relax," he chuckles. "Damn baby, your panties are drenched."

"Just—"

His teeth scrape against my skin, and he tugs at my panties.

"What are you doing?" I ask him again.

"Shut up, Jam. Unless I'm hurting you in a bad way, the only words I want to hear from you are 'yes,' and 'Austin.'"

Teeth scrape against my skin in a different spot, and there's another tug at my panties. *He's taking them off with his teeth!* I think I get why Fern didn't stop Mason earlier. The tease of his mouth on me, so close to where I want him, drives me crazy with need.

More teeth on skin again, and a quick tug. And again. Roughened fingers skim across the sensitive skin just above my slit. "Hello! What have we here! You naughty girl. Are you completely bare?"

What? Oh! Part of the wedding week festivities . . . We all went to a spa, and I got a bikini wax to cross that off my bucket list. *Not sure it was worth it, but at least it's not going to waste.*

His warm, wet tongue teases the top of my slit and slides down, caressing my clit just enough to make me groan. "You like it when I tease you?"

"Shut up, Austin." As eager as I am to please him, I refuse to stroke his ego. It doesn't need to be any bigger.

He bites me where his fingers were moments ago.

"Oh!" I cry out at the sting.

"You like that?"

God yes! I bite my tongue to hold back a moan, and he does it again. "Do. You. Like. That?"

"Yes!" I pant.

He does it again. "Good."

One last quick tug and my panties fall to my ankles. "Damn, I wish I had a bed and a light. I want to see this pretty, bare pussy. I want to watch your clit pulse while I tease you."

I want that, too. I whimper his name, and he answers with a gentle kiss to soothe the sting of his bites.

"Austin!" His name is a plea for more. I *need* him.

"Good." He sucks my clit into his hot mouth.

My hips jerk forward. He moans his approval, and the vibrations set my hips to rocking again. "Yes!"

"Yes, what? You ready for me?"

"Yes!" So ready, I ache for him.

He ducks out from under my skirt and stands, pulling off his jacket. "Put this on," he says. "I don't want the tree bark to scratch that pretty skin of yours."

I do as ordered, and he picks me up to turn and put my back against the tree before putting me down again.

"Get that skirt out of my way."

I do while he frees his cock from his boxers again. Then, he picks me up again and settles my legs on either side of his hips. He reaches behind him and freezes. "Tell me you're on the pill," he whispers.

"No?" There's only one reason he'd be asking. Disappointment knifes through the haze of lust.

"Shot? Anything? I don't have my wallet. No condom."

The heat in my blood fades as quickly as it came. "Bloody *hell!*" I want to scream. This can't be happening.

He chuckles, and I wish again that I could get by with punching him. This is no time to laugh! "I'm not going to leave you hanging," he says. He moves a bit, and his cock slides against my pussy causing me to shake for want of it. "You're going to get yours, Jam. Just like this. I'm clean, and I'm hoping you would've said something by now if you weren't." I nod, letting him know that he's right on both counts. "Rub that pretty clit all over my dick until you come for me."

That mouth! It won't be the same this way, but it's better than walking away frustrated. If that happens, we might go back on our agreement about never doing this again.

He rocks his hips back and forth. "I'm not going to let you fall. You ride me just like this. This is my only chance to make you come, and it's going to be on my dick one way or another."

Foreplay and his filthy mouth had me close, but the undercurrent of desperation in the words he's growling in my ear push me even closer. He could hit his knees again and finish me with his mouth or his fingers. Somehow, his solution is so much sexier. More satisfying. I still get his dick, just not where I want it. I mimic him, rolling my hips to rub myself along the hard length of his cock. If I don't do what he wants, he might make me stop.

But it's not enough.

"Please, I need to feel you." It doesn't have to be for very long, just a moment so he can keep those promises. I know the risks, but what are the chances that a playboy like Austin is a two-pump chump?

He shakes his head. "Nope. This is as close as you're getting. I don't trust my self-control right now. Once I'm inside you, I might not leave."

Oh, my God. That shouldn't be so sexy.

I thrust against him for the friction I desperately need and shatter into a million pieces, only to be put back together again when he rocks his hips again, milking my orgasm to keep it going.

"Fuck, Jam. I would give anything to feel that," he whispers reverently in my ear.

His soft words are not what I expected. Gloating or derogatory comments about me being dirty or desperate for an orgasm would be more in line with what I'm used to. Neither would surprise me from Austin, either. But this . . . intimacy is wholly unexpected. And I can't let myself fall into the trap of thinking this was something it's not. No matter how nice it feels right now.

He slides himself against me until every last piece of me has settled back into place, and I sigh contentedly. Only then does he put me on my feet.

I hold out my skirts so I don't kneel on them and drop to the ground. He said this is our only chance, and I am not walking away without this arrogant, *infuriating* man getting off for me. Every time he sees me, I want him to remember how I made him come. Me. The one he insulted. The one who isn't good enough. I want that power over him, the same way he has it over me. We can't leave here unequal.

"Fuck, yes," he whispers.

I look up at him, meeting his eyes before I lick him from base to tip. He closes his eyes but doesn't turn his face away from me. *Oh no. You will watch me.* I work his shaft with one hand and take his head in my mouth, teasing the tip with my tongue. Austin's eyes fly open, and his hips buck, trying to fuck my face.

"Do that again," he says. It's not a request, but as long as his cock is in my mouth, I'm the one in charge here.

"Jam," he says, his voice taking on a steely edge. "Again."

Or what? If he likes that, he's going to love what's coming. I ignore him and take a little more of him in, readying myself to swallow him down. I take a deep breath. This isn't my favorite thing in the world, but it's worth it. I love the power that comes with knowing he's at my mercy. The mere anticipation of his reaction sends another rush of heat through my core.

His fingers slide through my hair on either side of my head, and I threaten him with my teeth in case he's forgotten who gets to say what goes now.

"Mmm," he hums. "I like that too."

His reaction causes my thighs to clench with need. I pull back and tease him with my tongue again, then suck him so hard my cheeks hollow out. He groans and rocks his hips, so I swallow him down and watch the understanding pass through his eyes.

"Really?"

I hum, which is the closest thing to a yes I can give him. It makes him shudder and groan. "More. Do that while I fuck your mouth, baby. I'll stop before I come."

No, you won't. We both know who holds the power right now, so I humor him and hum low in my throat. He holds my head steady and drives himself in and out of my mouth. I know when he's close because he breaks eye contact to look toward the sky and his strokes get shorter. I can't tell him to keep going, that I can take it, so I grab his bum and pull him in.

"Fuck!" His movements become jerky, almost savage. My eyes tear up, but I take a deep breath through my nose and will myself to be calm. I'm fine, just a little uncomfortable. This isn't the first time. There's no need to panic.

He cries my name into the night when he comes. *That's right. I did that.* A few more strokes and he pulls out to fall to his knees in front of me.

"I am so fucking sorry," he says. He throws his arms around my shoulders and pulls me into a hug. "Are you alright?"

I push against his shoulders, trying to get away from him. We just hate fucked. I don't think we're supposed to be hugging. "I'm fine. I didn't want you to stop," I tell him, guessing at his problem. "I can take it." Hell, that was easy. I've had worse.

He sits back on his heels to look at me, then wipes at my eyes where they were watering. "I'm so sorry."

I move away before I get stupid and lean into his touch. *Why is he being so . . . Sweet?* "Austin, shut up. I'm fine. Let's get back before someone worries."

Sighing, he stands and holds out a hand to help me up. "You're probably right," he says on a sigh.

He reaches to tuck himself away, so I turn around. Yeah, I just had his dick in my mouth, but there's still something awkward about watching while he puts himself to rights. As long as I don't have anything on my dress, I'm good to go. The buckle on his belt clanging lets me know he's done, so I take off his jacket and hand it back to him.

He takes it and shrugs it on, then walks around me and stoops. When he rights himself, he's twirling something on his finger. *My panties . . .* "I'll keep my end of the deal," he says over his shoulder, "at a later date. Not like you have anywhere to stash a pair of boxers, anyway. Unless you want to unevenly pad your top."

I suck in a breath and wonder again why I can't just punch him and get it over with. "Ha. Ha." *He just said we're never doing this again so how does he plan to deliver at a later date?* I don't even care anymore. I don't need them to remember what happened here.

"Speaking of your top . . ." He turns and walks back to me and tugs up the strap he pushed down before. My cheeks get hot. I forgot all about it in the heat of the moment. I can't believe I didn't notice the cold. "There."

I almost thank him but choke the words back at the last minute. I don't want him to misconstrue and think I'm thanking him for what we just did. I needed that, but I wasn't *that* desperate. "I guess I'll see you back at the party," I say instead.

He nods. "Before you go . . ."

His eyes slide up and down my body, making me squirm with a fresh wave of lust, but he doesn't finish that thought. "Yes?" I ask, fighting off a cringe when my voice comes out much huskier than normal.

"Fuck it." He cups my cheeks and swiftly leans in for a kiss. I smack him on the shoulder, but my heart isn't really in it. He nips at my bottom lip, and my body throbs in time with my heart again, already geared up for another go. I open for him, and his tongue rushes in at the invitation. His hands slide around my waist, and he pulls me close. I melt into him again.

We're both breathing raggedly when he ends it. "One for the road," he says. "I'll be up in a minute."

"Okay . . ." I turn around in a daze and walk in what I think is the way we came.

"Hey, Jam?" he calls after me. I stop and look back. "I like your tits. I think I can fit a whole one in my mouth if I try."

A wordless shriek rips from my chest. *That arrogant bastard!* His laughter follows me, my only company as I stomp through the night.

Austin

I sigh and watch Jamaica disappear through the trees. I need a minute before I go back. The not-quite-sex and that last kiss were both so hot I want to have her again. If the not-quite-sex was that good, the sex has to be mindblowing. Probably the best I'll never have. Hell, the not-quite-sex was better than some of the sex I've had.

But I'll never know how good it can be.

What I said while she was walking away was a dick move. I know she's still upset about the joke, but I had to do something to stoke the animosity. It's better this way, no matter how hard it'll be. Neither of us will get hurt. I need to irritate her just enough that she never wants to find out what happens if we have a few condoms, privacy, and an unlimited amount of time. Just because I'm the one who said we can never do this again doesn't mean I won't be tempted to say this round didn't count because it wasn't really sex.

Stop thinking about sex, dumbass. I adjust myself and try to will my hard-on away. At this rate, I'll never be able to go back to the reception.

Chapter 6
Jamaica

Bzzzt . . . Bzzzt . . .
B I blindly slap at my nightstand, searching for my phone to snooze my alarm. I don't even know why I set the alarm.

Bzzzt . . . Bzzzt . . .
It's Sunday. And I got home late. I have nothing to do today.

Bzzzt . . . Bzzzt . . .
The reception didn't break up until two o'clock in the morning.

Bzzzt . . . Bzzzt . . .
Oh, crud! I scoop up my phone and swipe to answer the call. "Hello?"

"Good morning, Jamaica," my mother greets me, her thick Jamaican accent filling my heart with longing for a place I haven't been since I was a toddler. I still remember chasing waves on the beach, though. The sand between my toes and the water lapping at my ankles. "How are you today?"

How am *I?* I'm sure she wants an honest answer, but I'm not ready to give her one. I haven't been awake long enough to evaluate how I feel about last night's questionable decisions in the light of day. I force some cheerfulness into my voice. "I'm great, Mum! How are you?"

It's true enough—for now.

A smile warms her voice. "I'm fine, thank you, baby. How was the wedding? I'm sorry we couldn't be there."

I'm overcome with a strong desire to reach through the phone and hug her. After everything I put her through with Jordan, she still loves me. I beat back the old memories with ones from last night. Sufficiently bolstered, I sigh happily and try to come up with the right words to describe it. None of them are good enough, though. "Oh, Mum, it was beautiful. I'll send you pictures. I wish you could meet Fern. She's so nice. So are all her friends, and Mason's." *Except for Austin . . .*

"Someday, baby. I'd love to see pictures, though. I miss your smiling face! You're going to make me learn how to use a webcam, aren't you? Or get one of those crazy phones that lets me video chat."

The day my mother actually gives in and embraces new technology will be the day I grow wings and fly to the moon. She'll carry a flip phone until her dying day, or until they stop making them and she has no choice but to get one of those "crazy new gadgets you can't really call a phone."

"I miss you too, Mum. Maeve will help you with a webcam. Or a phone," I throw in hopefully. Moving so far away from my family was hard, but it was the right decision for me. I had to get away from my group of so-called friends. Video chats might ease the ache of missing my family. "But I'm happy here."

"And that is what matters," Mum says. There's a catch in her voice I've heard too many times. She's holding back tears. It guts me to know that she's about to cry because of me—again.

"Aw, Mum, don't cry!"

"They're happy tears, Jamaica." She pauses to sniffle. "No parent wants to watch their child suffer as you have. You have a good heart, and you were wasting it on people who only wanted to hurt you."

"I promise you, Mum, no one here is mistreating me. My new friends are great."

"I'm glad to hear that." She pauses, and I catch Dad's lilting Irish accent in the background. "It's time for church, though. I'll ring you later, alright?"

"Okay, Mum. Tell Father Barns 'hello' for me, please."

"I'll do that, baby. Your dad sends his love. Have a good day."

"You too, Mum. I love you. Tell Dad for me, yeah?"

"Of course. I love you too."

The call ends, and I fall back into my pillows. How *am* I today? That's a loaded question. I close my eyes and take stock.

Physically I'm great. Better than I've been in a long time. Every cell in my body is humming in absolute satisfaction. Still.

Mentally . . . What happened with Austin last night was beyond stupid. Saying "I've never" doesn't mean much at my age, but I've never wanted someone as badly as I wanted him at that moment. Regardless, I can't believe I did that, even though it's something the old me would've done. Mum always told me that I'd learn to look before I leap someday and she was absolutely right. I leaped for Jordan and landed in a viper's nest. So why did I leap again with Austin?

Chapter 7

Austin

Four weeks later . . .

I take stock of the cars parked outside Gabe's new house. *Gang's all here.* They'll excuse me for being late, though. I grab the bag of steaks and the ridiculously expensive bottle of whiskey I bought to go with them and cut through the grass, dodging puddles and hoping Gabe opens a window to yell at me for it so I can tease him about being old. *Not that I need an excuse.* He's not as easy to rile up now that he goes to therapy every week, though. I'll take the openings I'm given, and the four-year age gap is fair game.

Someone in the neighborhood is taking advantage of the first day of sunshine after a week of rain to grill. Clouds of acrid smoke drift lazily down the street. My stomach growls in response. I hope Gabe read my mind and has his grill heating up because I'm starving. It's been a whole three hours since I last ate. I could've sent him a text, but where's the fun in that?

I open his front door and stroll on in like I pay the mortgage. "Honey, I'm home!"

"Uncle Austin!"

What the . . .?

No one here should be calling me that. "Rice Monster!" I call back because I'm never *not* happy to see my niece. She comes running from the family room and collides with me, wrapping her arms around my middle and squeezing like we didn't recently spend two weeks tormenting each other while her Dad and Fern were off on their honeymoon. "How're you?"

"I missed you!" she says on a happy sigh.

"I missed you, too, Shrimp, but I was at your house like two days ago. And I came to visit every day while your dad was gone."

"I know. That's why I miss you! Now that Mom and Dad are back, I don't get to see you every day!"

Mom . . . Kid always gets me right in the damn feels with that. I'm so happy she can finally call Fern by the title she's more than earned. And if sucker-punching me with the Mom thing isn't enough, she's gotta make me feel like shit for not visiting often enough.

"Sorry, kiddo. You didn't get to see them for two whole weeks. I thought you might like some time with them."

She rears back and looks up at me. "Yeah . . . Good point. Thanks, Uncle Austin. I love you."

Tears sting my eyes. My uncles live three states away. They weren't around to teach me how to be an uncle, so it's nice to know she thinks I'm killing it. "You're welcome, Shrimp. I love you too."

She crooks her finger at me—something she picked up from Fern—so I bend over to kiss her on the cheek. Four women in this world can rightfully claim to have me wrapped around their little fingers, and they all call me uncle. *One of my siblings better give me a nephew soon, though.*

Ronni scampers away, shouting something about a movie. I straighten up and look right into Fern's soul-stealing green eyes. She came home from their honeymoon a whole new person. I thought paper white was her only setting, but she actually has a tan—a good one. And her brown hair is streaked with blonde from the sun. She and Mason are now more relaxed than I've ever known either of them to be. *I hope it lasts.* I've already worn out the "must be nice to have nothing to do but fuck for two weeks" jokes, so I give her a break. At least until one of them says something to provide me with new material.

"Hey," I greet her, noting the pink tinge to the whites of her eyes. She must've heard Ronni, because that "Mom" shit gets her, too.

"You're a good uncle," she tells me, shoving off the doorframe she's leaning against with her shoulder. Her eyes drop to the bags in my hands. "What did you bring?"

"Thanks . . ." I say. Her praise makes me antsy. I don't like to be recognized as being good at things. People expect more of me if I'm good at something. "Steak and whiskey." I grin at her and raise my voice so everyone here can hear me. "It's our first meeting since Mason strapped on the ball and chain, so I thought we should celebrate in style."

Fern rolls her eyes, but she laughs. "We're all in the kitchen."

I toe off my shoes since I walked through the grass and follow her to find five adults and a toddler packed into Tara's kitchen. Ryan, Chris, and Keaton are leaning against the only bare expanse of wall in the room, which won't be empty for long because Gabe is having cabinets made to go there. Mason and Fern are seated at the little table on the other side of the room. He is intently tapping away on his phone, probably dealing with some "crisis" at work. *New joke material! Did he actually stop working long enough to consummate the marriage?* Tara is at the counter, throwing things into a big bowl, and Gabe is next to her, cutting up tomatoes.

"What the he-eck is this?" I ask, catching myself before the bad word can defile poor little Keaton's ears. "Last time I checked, this was a guys-only thing. They don't have the right equipment for this shindig," I say, pointing to Fern and Tara. "And that one," I swing my finger toward Keaton, "isn't old enough."

Laughing, Tara leaves off stirring her big bowl of something to take the bags from me, so I steal Chris's kid and pull up a bit of wall to lean on between him and Ryan. "Oof! What's your daddy been feeding you, little dude? You weigh a ton. I think you've grown a whole foot since I saw you last."

Keaton kicks his feet. "Nope. Onwy gots two foots, Uncle Austin."

I love kids. I don't laugh, though, because I don't want him to think I'm laughing at him. "My bad, little dude. My bad!"

Motion catches my eye, and I look over to see Chris rubbing the back of his neck. His pale skin quickly turns red, the shade somehow clashing horribly with his coppery red hair. "Sorry. I couldn't find a sitter."

I'm not surprised; his go-to sitters when his mom and sister are busy are all here.

"Mason was going to bow out to spend time with Ronni," Gabe adds. "So, we made it kid- and wife-friendly, so we aren't missing anyone."

I tip my head side to side, pretending to think it over. His logic is sound. It's better to have a few extras than to miss a couple friends. "I'll allow it."

I toss Keaton into the air and catch him, loving that little kid giggle. "But only if I'm not on diaper duty."

His laughter cuts off abruptly. He scowls at me, a miniature version of his father. "I use da potty now!"

I hold up my hand for him to smack it. "Way to go, Keaton! The girls like a housebroken guy."

His little nose scrunches up, and he tips his head to the side. "You funny, Uncle Austin."

"Thanks, kiddo." I kiss the top of his curly head and set him free to run, ignoring Chris's pained groan. Chris won't turn him loose because he worries about Keaton breaking something, but Tara and Gabe need a trial run of that. Their little house breaker will be here before the year is out. *Speaking of . . .*

I turn to Tara. "How's my kid?"

Gabe is too far away to make contact, but he swings at me, anyway. "Fucker," he mutters under his breath.

I can't resist the wordplay. "Maybe I did . . . Maybe I didn't. I'm just saying, if the kid comes out with dark hair, you can't say I didn't warn you."

He lunges at me, but I'm not too worried. He knows I'm just messing with him. The worst he'll do is pretend to punch me in the gut. Sure enough, he stops after his initial jolt and goes back to cutting up tomatoes. I swallow the urge to call him whipped and a number of other unflattering things. Mostly because, from the outside looking in, what he has is nice. Teasing him about it only paints me jealous.

Tara shakes with laughter, but she bites her lip to hold it back. "Arabella is doing great," she says when she gets herself under control. She caresses her growing belly in that loving way expectant mothers have. "Still not letting me keep much of anything down, though."

Gabe rounds on her. "You are *not* naming our kid Arabella. Besides, we're having a boy."

She rolls her eyes. "Mmmhmm, you keep telling yourself that."

They devolve into bickering about whether or not their kid's genitals will be an innie or an outie.

Ryan rolls his eyes and goes to the fridge. He comes back with two beers and hands me one. "The others will be here soon," he tells me, cracking open his can.

I glance around to double-check, but I didn't miss anyone earlier. We're all here. "Others?"

"Tara's tribe," he says, meaning Noel, Trista, and possibly Madi, her new business partner.

"Oh, joy. A full-on invasion!" I open my beer and take a swig. I was looking forward to a guy's night, but this works too. I guess. *At least Jam isn't coming.*

Mason puts his phone away and rolls his eyes at my sarcasm. Fern stifles a giggle. "Jam too," she chimes in.

I choke on my beer. Sputtering, I double over and cough into my elbow.

"Wrong pipe," I manage to cough out. I put my beer down and wipe at my eyes, which are leaking all over the damn place, while I try to catch my breath.

Ryan pounds on my back. "Stop talking and breathe, dumbass."

"Love you too, man." He thumps me again with a little more force to shut me up. This will be my first encounter with Jamaica since our not-quite-sex. *This should be fun . . . Not.* I just know she won't be able to handle it and things will get awkward fast. It would be bad enough to run into her when it's just us, Mason, and Fern. This is just too much.

"Why don't you invite your girlfriend?" Mason asks me, pairing it with a pointed look. The asshole knows the answer to that question. The last time I invited a girl into my personal life, it didn't go well. She got mad that I didn't put her first when my brother's life was on the line.

Fern shoots me a wink, her signal to me that the next words out of her mouth are not to be taken to heart. "Because Austin has commitment issues."

I know she's joking, but the comment hits a nerve I didn't know was exposed. I can't let any of them know that, though. If they think I have a problem, they'll try to help me fix it. I'm fine the way I am. I do *not* have commitment issues.

I roll my eyes. "I can totally commit. I bought a car. I'll buy a house when I find one I like better than my apartment, though there's a lot more space to clean in a house, so . . ."

She scoffs at me. "I've committed to hairstyles that last longer than any of your girlfriends," she says.

"You want proof I can commit? Fine, I'll get a tattoo."

Ryan snorts. I survey him from the corner of my eyes, taking in the ink decorating his arms from his wrists on up. His tee hides most of it, though. "Are you seeing anyone?"

My jaw clenches, grinding my teeth together. The truth only proves their point. I haven't gone home with anyone since the wedding. No one has caught my fancy lately. I can't seem to get Jamaica out of my head. So, technically, I'm seeing Jamaica after a fashion.

"In a manner of speaking," I say, flashing a triumphant smile at Ryan. I know how everyone here will take that. They'll assume I have a beneficial arrangement with a friend.

"What?" Fern cries. "For how long? Do you like her?"

"Uh . . ." I scramble for answers to questions I wasn't expecting. "A few weeks. And . . . It's complicated."

"Meaning he likes what she does in bed," Chris mutters.

Do I ever . . . I elbow him in the ribs. "Thanks, asshole."

"Happy to help," he says with a grin.

Fern frowns and drums her fingers on the table restlessly. "But have you actually taken her on a date?"

"I don't think bringing her home from a bar counts as a date," Ryan tells her. He dodges my elbow.

"Austin?" Fern makes my name a question. I make the mistake of looking into her eyes. I can't even fib my way out of this one with her looking at me like my answer could make her whole day.

Mason's grin gives me goosebumps. I've seen that look before. This isn't going to end well for me. "I dare you to face your fears and take this woman on a real date."

Sonofabitch! He *knows* I can't say no. Backing away from any sort of challenge isn't something I do. There's a video of me singing "Call Me Maybe" on a stage to prove it. And he'll never buy a fake relationship, not after what I convinced him to do with Fern. And look how they ended up.

Fuck. There has to be some way around this. I can't just grab some random woman at a bar and ask her on a date now. I backed myself into a corner when I fibbed about seeing someone.

"Oh no, that's not facing his fears. That's just . . . adding dinner to a booty call. He needs to spend real time with her" Gabe says, raising the stakes.

Whoa, wait. I hold up my hands in the universal gesture for stop. "Why are you all ganging up on me?" I ask.

"What's wrong? Can't commit?" Mason asks, eyes wide with false innocence.

"It's not that . . ." I pick at the label on my beer bottle while searching for a way out of this that doesn't involve backing down.

"You're fibbing," Tara says. "You bit your cheek before you said it. That's your tell."

Fucking hell! "Damnit, woman! You're supposed to be on my side!"

She shrugs, just the barest twitch of her shoulders. "Maybe I am? Maybe what you need is to give a girl more of your time than just the time you spend in bed with her?"

That is the *last* thing I need. But none of them know what happened with my most recent attempt to date. I told Granddad because he asked, but no one else gave her a second thought after the disaster that was Thanksgiving. Not that I blame any of them. I try not to give her a second thought, either.

"Good point," Mason says, nodding to Gabe. "New plan, Austin, I dare you to fully commit six weeks to this woman and actually *try*."

I push off the wall and pace, agitated with him for pushing me when he *knows* why I don't date. "That's not a dare! That's a challenge," I argue for the sake of arguing and to buy me more time to find a way out.

Mason shrugs. "Splitting hairs, but a challenge implies you can or cannot do something. I know you *can* do this; it comes down to whether you will or not. Therefore, it is a dare."

Growling, I shove my hands into my pockets. "Consequences?" I ask. Whatever the alternative is might be worth it. It's not *quite* the same as quitting. It's . . . rerouting. I'm still accepting the dare, just on my terms.

Ryan, Gabe, and Mason exchange looks while thinking it over. It's Chris who speaks up, though. "You have to cook for yourself for the rest of the year."

Gabe barks out a laugh. "Oh, that's good." He stops what he's doing to fistbump Chris for his genius.

"No, that's evil incarnate," I grumble as I continue pacing. I *hate* cooking. I always burn everything. There's another way to meet their terms on my own, though. There's always a loophole.

Mason didn't lay down any ground rules aside from the six weeks of effort. He didn't say I have to have a *romantic* relationship or even sleep with that woman. I just have to try . . . So I can *try* to make amends with Jamaica, which is something I want to do anyway—I'm only killing two birds with one stone. And I have a deadline. A friendship is a kind of relationship. I'll just have to be careful not to cross the line from one to the other. *Hopefully that's not easier said than done.*

"No," Mason says, that evil little smirk on his stupid face again. I tense, bracing for whatever bullshit he's going to come up with now. "After six weeks, we get to meet this woman. If you gave it your all—and we'll know if you did—well, congratulations, you have a relationship. If not, you can't drive your 'Vette for a year."

What? No! My loophole still works. He still didn't specify a romantic relationship. However, there's no guarantee Jamaica and I will ever get along again. My heart pounds. You don't screw with my car. I *love* my car. "That's not even right, man!"

Ryan barks out a laugh. "Instead, you have to drive a 1980 Yugo."

I don't know what that is, but Ryan's smile says it all. It's not good. And they're not going to back down now. They know they've found my kryptonite. I've probably done something to deserve this, but *damn.*

Mason's brow wrinkles with his frown. "That's . . . oddly specific."

Ryan grins at him. "Had someone try to sell me one to resto yesterday."

"Fine," I say, spitting the word like a bad taste in my mouth so they don't realize I've already found a way to cheat and try to change the rules. *Even if we don't get along, she won't be able to say I didn't try.* That eases my panic. I've got this in the bag already.

"Shake on it," Ryan says, holding out his hand. So I shake with the four of them to complete our pact.

The doorbell rings. *Where was that five minutes ago . . .?*

Tara and Gabe look at each other. "Who could that be?" Tara mutters because any of the stragglers will probably come on in as I did. She makes it two steps toward the door before we hear the sound of the latch working to open.

"You don't ring the doorbell here, silly," Noel's voice carries back to us. "They're expecting you. Go in."

"But—" Jamaica's voice argues.

"But nothing. Don't overthink it. It's like Olive Garden, okay? When you're here, you're family." Noel bursts into the room, practically dragging Jamaica by the wrist behind her.

"Sorry I'm late," Jamaica says. I try not to, but my eyes fly to her like metal to a magnet. I take in the jean shorts and tiny white top she's wearing, but every time I blink, she's back in her bridesmaid's dress. Half of the top pulled down because I wanted to see the tits that got me in trouble. The skirt gathered around her waist. Her pinned against that tree, pleasuring herself with my dick. *I can still feel her.*

My pants are suddenly way too tight. I don't want the memory. I want *her.*

"You're right on time," Gabe tells her, cutting through my dirty little daydream.

Deep breaths. Think about something else. I shift around, trying to find a position to hide my raging hard-on until I can distract myself enough for it to pass.

"Tris is in the car," Noel says. "Her mom called . . . Was unhappy about something."

Moms. Perfect. Nothing kills a hard-on like talking about someone's mother. *Unless we're talking about a MILF.* Trista's mom is cute, but she's definitely not a MILF. She's too controlling to even think about going there.

"Of course she is," Tara mutters.

When isn't *she unhappy about something.* That list is probably shorter. Could fit on half a Post-It note. That's one of the first things I learned about Trista. She has no mind of her own, and her mother is always worried or upset about something. Ryan is the only person I've met with the patience to wait for Trista to make up her mind about anything, and I swear it's only because he likes to make her squirm.

Time to change the subject before Trista walks in on Tara and Noel complaining about her mother. She knows her mom pioneered the helicopter side of the parenting spectrum, but it's her mom. That's not her fault, and I'm sure it still hurts when Trista catches one, or all, of us talking about how she needs to stand up to her mother. "Well, if someone had warned me, I would've brought enough steak for everyone. But no one did. So I didn't. So what's for dinner?"

"Burgers," Gabe says. "I bought a new grill last week and haven't gotten to try it out because of all the rain."

Perfect. Another chance to torment him! "Pffft. Real men grill in the rain."

He raises a fist and glares at me, so I laugh. We both know it's an empty threat, but I'd laugh anyway. It's another sort of challenge.

The door opens and closes again. "Sorry I'm late!" a vaguely familiar voice calls.

Madi bustles into the room. Most of the time I've spent in her presence was passed watching her run around their store like a reverse tornado. I look forward to getting to know her, though. My eyes drift toward Jamaica without requesting my permission. I look away quickly. I don't want to be the catalyst for things going downhill.

Madi locks eyes with Tara and asks, "Why is Tris sitting in her car?"

"Her mom called," Noel says.

Madi nods her understanding even though they only started hanging out a couple months ago. "Should've known. Why are we all in the kitchen? It's a little crowded in here."

That is an understatement. Tris *might* fit when she joins us, but only because she's fun-sized. I salute Madi with my can. "Because there's beer in the kitchen."

"And food," Ryan adds. "But, the grill is out back."

"Do the burgers need pattied?" Fern asks. Knowing her, she's probably offered to help twenty times since she got here and is just *looking* for something to do.

Tara shakes her head and motions toward the back door. "Nope. Thank you, though. We did that already. Let's go enjoy the sunshine!"

"I'll be right there," Ryan says to no one in particular.

"Alright, bring the kids when you come, please," Chris says.

"Sure." Ryan pulls out his phone and taps the screen a few times while the others file past him. I move to lean on against a recently vacated stretch of counter and pretend to be finishing my beer while watching Ryan from the corner of my eye.

The door closes behind Madi, leaving the two of us alone save for Keaton and Ronni, who are both completely engrossed in whatever they're watching on Gabe's big screen. *"And I would've gotten away with it, too . . ."*

Whoa. *Scooby-Doo. Good choice.* Maybe I'll hang out with them instead. I won't have to worry about random, Jamaica-induced hard-ons if I'm hanging out with the kids.

"Tara know you've got a thing for her friend?" I ask Ryan under my breath. It's a rhetorical question. Trista is probably the only person here who hasn't picked up on it because she's intimidated by the broody bastard. He hid it well for a long time, but he gave himself away one night at Easy Speak. And now, I'm going to make him squirm for his contribution to the dare.

The smug bastard smirks at his phone. "Fern know you went for a very long *walk* with her friend after the wedding?"

Oh fuck. I knew there was no way absolutely no one noticed us leave, but since none of our friends said anything at the time, I thought they were all distracted. I shrug, trying to play it off. "Nothing wrong with a walk. I was afraid Jam would get lost."

A slow, deadly smile spreads across his whiskered cheeks. "I never named names."

I shrug again. "Not that hard to figure out who you're talking about. Jamaica is the only one who randomly wandered off in the dark, in unfamiliar territory, near a river." They are all three excellent points and put together, they're the trifecta of excuses.

Ryan pockets his phone and smirks at me again. "Uh-huh. Sure. Wonder whose version of that story Fern will buy?"

I do my very best to keep my face completely blank. I *think* Fern would take my side, especially if Jamaica can keep it together long enough to back me up, but I don't want to find out. "There's only one version of the story."

He scoffs. "Whatever. She's the one, isn't she? I've caught you watching her more times than I can count."

It takes me too long to come up with a suitably vague answer, and his smile takes on a knowing edge.

"Nothing is going on between Tris and me. I'm not even sure I'd call us close," he says, changing the subject. *Fuck.* He knows he's caught me. But Ryan is good at keeping secrets. He won't tell anyone.

You just fell into your own damn trap, dumbass! "I didn't name names," I say, throwing his words back at him.

"Not that hard to figure out who you're talking about," he says, playing my game. "Tris is the only one who's single."

"Wait, what?" We can come back to him and Trista later. I know Madi is in a rocky relationship, but I thought Noel and Trista were both free. "Who's Noel with?"

"Tara's brother," he says, smiling at me again. If Tara can handle her brother dating one of her friends, she can deal with Ryan dating another. She calls him her brother, anyway. It's practically the same thing.

"Which one?" I ask because Tara's got four and only one was married last time I checked. I don't keep tabs on them, though. They're a fun bunch, but they are all older than the rest of us, so they have their own things. They were all out of high school when Tara and her parents moved here because her mother got a better job.

"Colton," he says, naming her eldest brother.

"Whoa. Did *not* see that one coming." Noel is high maintenance and puts super-models to shame. Colton beats people to a bloody pulp for funsies. Talk about opposites attracting. Seth, the youngest, seemed more likely to me.

"I don't think anyone did. Even them."

"Since when?" I can't get my head wrapped around this one. It has to be a new thing. But Colton and Gabe don't get along well anymore, so I can't see the four of them hanging out here.

"Rehearsal dinner."

Wow. Very new.

The front door opens and closes again. "Hello?" Trista calls.

"In here," I call back to her, beating Ryan to it. Her face betrays nothing when she walks in and sees him. She wouldn't be able to hide it if there *was* something going between them.

"Where is everyone?" she asks.

"They went out back," Ryan says. "One of my clients got hurt today, so I hung back to check on her."

"Bad?" I ask. Ryan's clients regularly work with hefty hunks of metal, sometimes lifting them over their heads. There's a lot of room for injury there.

He shakes his head. "Landed badly after a kick and sprained her ankle. She'll be alright in a day or two."

"Good." He'd feel bad if it were serious, even if it isn't his fault. Underneath the tough, broody, badass-y exterior, he's a total marshmallow. "I'm going to round up the midgets and head out."

I stuck around to rake Ryan over the coals about the Trista situation and backed myself into a damn corner. Time to exit gracefully, stage left, before I get my ass in deeper. And Jamaica is here. I can get a jump start on this stupid dare. Carefully.

Chapter 8
Jamaica

J follow Noel into the yard. Despite the oppressive heat that doesn't seem to bother anyone else, I breathe freely for the first time since I saw Austin in the kitchen. Avoiding him forever isn't possible, but why did we have to meet up again in front of *everyone?* There's no margin for error here. One look that lingers too long and it's all over. The others will figure us out.

Would it be so bad? These people aren't Jordan and his friends. When they tease one of the guys for sleeping around, there is no malice to it. No one here will call me a slut and mean it. They won't presume they have the right to proposition me because "friends share."

"Aw, come on. You do it for him! I've heard all about what you can do with that mouth when it's not running."

"I'm not your girlfriend, JT."

"Jordan won't mind sharing. He'd want you to! Come on, girl. On your knees."

Loud laughter behind me dispels the memory. The heat doesn't stop the chill that starts in my gut and rapidly spreads. As horrible as it was, that was the night I found my freedom. Sometimes I wonder if JT knew what he was doing—knew the fight he was asking for—and did it on purpose to help me get away. He was so mean, though, it was hard to tell. I still can't imagine him putting himself in danger for me.

No, these people wouldn't do me that way. They'll rib the hell out of both of us for a day or two and then move on. Still . . . We broke some unwritten rule. It's better if no one ever finds out.

I finally have friends who don't judge me based on someone else's opinion of my body or my choices. Even if they don't mean anything by it, their jokes will re-open a wound that has just started healing. That would hurt more than the original damage.

Noel grabs my arm when I don't move fast enough for her. "Come on you! Before all the good seats are taken!"

I pick up the pace to make her happy. "Good seats?"

She doesn't look back. "Yeah! Gabe bought a projector. Once it's dark, we're going to watch a movie."

"Cool."

I like Noel. She's fun, and, as uncomfortable as it can be, she doesn't let me hang back. She'll drag me into the center of anything we're invited to, kicking and screaming, if she must. She has a good heart, and, in my opinion, she does it because she knows how it feels to be an outsider. It could also be that she's so used to forcing Trista to do more than sit on the sidelines that it's second nature to her now. Either way, it's good for me. It's what the old me would've done before Jordan wrung the confidence out of me.

Gabe and Tara have added to their collection of lawn furniture since I was here for their baby shower. They have four rows of chairs set up to accommodate us all, two up front for the kids, then a row of three, and two rows of four. Noel proclaims the row of three to belong to Tris and the two of us.

"I'll grab cushions," she says, and then she's gone. She comes back with three from a stack I hadn't noticed on the patio and arranges them in the seats to suit her. "There. Ours."

"Cheaters!" Chris calls. I smile across the yard at him and count the chairs versus the number of people here.

"Is Becca coming?" I ask Noel under my breath.

She shrugs. "Hope not, but you'll have to ask him."

"Why do you say that?" I ask. I didn't meet her again at the reception and still don't remember her from the rehearsal, but Chris was smitten.

She wrinkles her delicate nose. "Just got a bad vibe off her. I swear she only paid attention to Keat for show."

My heart breaks for Chris. I hope Noel is wrong. Either way, I'll feel awkward asking him now. Maybe he'll bring it up . . . It's weird. I hardly know him yet, but I really want to see him happy. He's been through a lot. *Like me.*

She narrows one eye at me. "Do you have a thing for him or something?"

Huh? "What? No!"

Her face splits into a bright smile. "Oh, come on! You two would be cute!"

I shake my head in hopes of driving the point home. "No, nothing like that. He's just a really nice guy, and I hoped he found his happily ever after with her."

Noel's face falls. "Yeah," she whispers. "He is. He'll find someone." Smirking, she pokes me in the side. "You sure it's not you?"

I hold up my hands to ward her off. "Oh, no. I wouldn't date any of these guys. I mean, obviously, Gabe and Mason are off-limits, but the others are too. That would be weird, don't you think?"

She gives me the universal 'are you serious right now?' look, chin down, eyebrows up. "Three single guys, with steady, high paying jobs, who know how to treat a lady, and I have my theories about how they are between the sheets, and you think dating one of them would be weird? Honey, that's like prime real estate there."

My eyes roll of their own accord. "If they're prime real estate, why are they single?"

Noel puffs out her cheeks. "Hang around long enough, and you'll figure it out. Let's see. Ryan just doesn't date." She shrugs. "Something to do with his parents, but he doesn't talk about it. Chris is super selective because of Keaton, obviously. Austin can't handle relationships because they're serious and that's something he doesn't do. Ever. And to top it all off, all three of them have to deal with fake bitches throwing themselves at them for various reasons. That's just my take on it, though—an outside-looking-in type thing."

Her assessment is shockingly direct. I don't know them well, but as far as I can tell, she's spot on. "So why didn't you date any of them?"

She shrugs dismissively. "Didn't want to ruin a good thing. Tara's my best friend. They are Gabe's best friends. We run into each other a lot. If things didn't work out, it would be awkward."

I grin and poke her in the ribs this time. "But you think I should date one of them."

"It might've been different if I'd clicked with one of them or something, but that never happened, and there was no sense in trying to force something because they're conveniently located."

"I get it." That doesn't justify me dating any of them, though. "I'm not ready to date again anyway," I tell her.

Noel tips her head to the side, a wrinkle forming between her blonde brows. She doesn't give voice to the question, but it's written all over her face. *I am stronger than my demons.* It's not a secret; it's just hard to talk about. Surprisingly, I *want* to. It's what friends do. They trust each other with the dark parts of their lives, not just the bright, happy bits, and in doing so, they become closer.

But maybe not everything. Not yet, anyway. A little at a time.

"My ex was . . . abusive." *That's like calling the ocean a bit damp.* I need to figure out how to change my type before I try dating again because, so far, I seem to be attracted to jerks. And not even well-meaning jerks. Just the everyday, average, mean-for-fun pricks. The ones who are good at hiding their true colors until they know you're caught in their web.

I need to learn to like genuinely sweet guys with no hidden agenda, not guys who put on a front in public and brainwash me in private.

Noel's eyebrows knit together and she grabs my shoulder and squeezes. "Oh, honey."

I know that look. Fern gave me the same one. They want the whole story. I don't blame them. I'd want to know if our roles were reversed. Someday, I'll tell them everything. The wounds are still too raw to expose them completely.

"Noel, I made your favorite!" Tara calls, inadvertently coming to my rescue. She holds up something small and chocolate-brown and waves us over.

Noel's lips twitch to one side, but she smiles and squeezes my shoulder again. "That better be what I think it is," she calls back. She gives me a little nudge toward the others. "C'mon. You've gotta try these. They're life-changing."

"These" turn out to be chocolate-covered cheesecake balls. I bite one in half and moan in delight because it's the best thing I've ever tasted.

"Right?" Noel asks.

"That's the best thing I've ever put in my mouth!"

Someone to my left chokes on a laugh. Then, the guys devolve into a fit of giggles. Five fully grown, muscle-bound men giggle like school girls. I pop the other half in my mouth and turn to face them. Austin is using the hem of his shirt to mop beer off his face, presumably because he choked for real, while the others try not to spill their drinks from laughing so hard. But are they laughing at *me* or at his reaction?

"That's what she said," Ryan says between peals of giggles.

"Literally," Chris adds.

"I doubt any of *you* have ever heard that," Noel shouts, cutting through the noise they're making. The laughter abruptly halts.

"They might've said it, though," Madi says. She and Noel laugh and hip bump.

Austin looks at me and says, "I can definitely think of an instance where I should've said that."

My cheeks blaze hotter than Gabe's grill. *He did* not *just go there in front of all these people.*

He smirks. "Fern makes the best sheet cake in the universe."

"Here, try one." I grab another of the confections and throw it at his head, hoping it drills him in the forehead.

He catches it left-handed and shoves the whole thing in his mouth. He chews slowly and swallows. "Fern still takes the prize for best sheet cake, but Tara wins best cheesecake," he says.

"A diplomatic answer if I've ever heard one," his brother mutters.

Austin lightly backhands him in the chest. "Hey, I'm not stupid. You don't insult the people who feed you."

"Should've remembered that in the kitchen," Gabe says. "I believe I'm the one feeding you tonight, shithead."

Austin shrugs. "I brought steaks. I ain't scared. Burning a steak is like sacrilege to you four. Someone will save it."

***

After sunset, we move across the yard for the movie. Noel takes the far seat in our row, so I turn to look for Tris to ask her if she wants the middle. But she's hovering in the back row with Tara and Gabe. I go ahead and sit, figuring I can move if she wants me to. I don't want her to think I'm hogging Noel's time tonight. Someone falls into the seat next to me, and I look over, right into Austin's smiling eyes.

Oh, crud. What is *he* doing here?

"Tris took Ryan's seat, so Ryan took Chris's. Chris took Madi's, so she took mine," he says. All the names make my head spin. I repeat it to myself, slowly, until I think I've got it. Tris was the first domino in a chain reaction that leads to Austin sitting next to me. *Lovely.*

"Austin, I can't see through your big head," Chris says. "Deflate your ego or move over a bit."

Austin sighs, stands, grabs his chair, and shuffles it closer to me. "My ego is just fine, thank you very much," he says over his shoulder.

"I meant the other way, but that works. Jam can just beat you with a shoe or something if you bug her."

That he's breathing bugs me. Does that count?

"Me? Bug someone? I would do no such thing! I'm an absolute delight. Right, Jam?"

"I'd absolutely delight in beating you with a shoe." I turn in my chair to look at Chris while Austin sputters indignantly. "Does it have to be the shoe I'm wearing, or can I borrow one of Tara's heels?"

Chris purses his lips and strokes his beard like he's thinking it over. "I did not specify," he finally says.

"Yous not s'posed to talk while da movie's on," Keaton shouts from in front of me.

"Sorry, Keat," we all three say in tandem.

Austin is so close now his arm brushes mine. The skin-on-skin contact gives me goosebumps. I hope and pray he doesn't notice. Every time he moves, I hold my breath, afraid I'll make a noise and give myself away. My body remembers the last time he and I were skin on skin and disagrees with my brain's decision that it'll never happen again.

A few minutes into the movie, he leans over to whisper in my ear. "I take issue with the statement you made earlier."

I swallow hard, afraid of where he's going with this. It's impossible not to remember the taste of him on my tongue. "Oh?" I ask, managing to keep my voice normal.

He breathes out a chuckle. "Yeah," he whispers. "You haven't tried Fern's sheet cake."

My sigh of relief is automatic and amusing to him. "Shut up and watch the movie, Austin."

I swear he moans softly, but a loud crash in the movie is timed perfectly to cover it. The mere suggestion of it makes my thighs clench and raises goosebumps on my arms despite the heat of the evening. "What did you think I was going to say, Jamaica?" he asks, somehow sounding innocent when he is anything but.

I move my arms, crossing them over my belly, to hide my reaction. "Watch the movie, Austin."

I take my own advice and ignore him like it's my job though my body is vividly aware of his nearness and is of the opinion that he's much too far away.

***

The skin on the back of my neck prickles as I follow Trista to her car. Tension slowly seeps through my whole body. It's not the same sensation as being so close to Austin. It's a sick feeling, like something bad is going to happen—the same sensation I used to get when Jordan was in one of his moods and a fight was brewing. I glance around the quiet, empty streets of Tara and Gabe's neighborhood and give myself a little shake. Jordan is in prison. It's all in my head.

"Did you have a good time?" Trista asks while we're buckling our seatbelts.

"I did," I tell her, smiling at memories of collective silliness. Things were never this easy—this fun—with my old friends. "Did you?"

She smiles back. "Oh, yes."

"Thanks for the ride. I really appreciate it." I need to quit dragging my feet and buy a car. I can afford it. I just don't know much about them, and Dad isn't here to help. But maybe one of the guys would have time to go with me some weekend.

"Anytime! I don't mind at all!"

I force myself to ignore the urge to check behind us when she pulls away from the curb. There's no one back there except a memory that I refuse to let haunt me.

Chapter 9

Austin

My phone rings, causing the song pouring from my car's speakers to cut out. *Damnit, I like that song.* It's been a long day. I just want to listen to loud music and drive.

"Call from Fern," my automated assistant says.

That makes it better. Fern is allowed to interrupt good music and bad days. I answer the call with a push of a button. "Hello?"

"Austin!" she greets me much too brightly. Fern is always bright and bubbly now, but this is a little extra. Something's up.

"What do you want?" I ask warily. It doesn't matter. The answer is yes. I don't know if she knows that. She wouldn't abuse it if she does. That's just not Fern. My exit is coming up, so I change lanes and slow down.

Her sigh comes through loud and clear. "You caught me. I hate to be a pain in the ass, but would you run an errand for me in exchange for dinner? I'd do it, but I'm a little swamped here."

I don't doubt that at all. Mason and I had hoped she'd slow down after the wedding, but that doesn't seem to be the case. Now that they're back from their honeymoon, she's busier than ever.

"What's for dinner?" I ask, not that the menu matters, either. It's food. I'll love it.

"Roast and—"

"I'm in. What hoops do I have to jump through?"

She giggles. "I have something here I need taken to Jam." *Fuck.* I hold back a groan. Of *course*, it's something for Jamaica. *I'm not sure food is worth it.* I'm not in the mood to tiptoe through the minefield of Jamaica's problems with me. "She's sick."

Damnit! I can't say no to that. That would be letting them both down. And if Fern is calling me for this, she's really out of options. She hates to ask for help.

An old clunker cuts me off. "*. . . A 1980 Yugo.*" *The dare!* I shudder and pat my steering wheel. How could I forget? *Two birds . . .* Three in this case. It's one step closer to repairing our friendship, thus completing the dare. And Fern will be happy.

I blow by my exit, picking up speed before I change lanes again. At least traffic isn't bad this evening. "I'll be right there."

***

I ring the buzzer for Jamaica's apartment, take a breath and ring it again to be annoying. Then I ring it again for good measure. *It's the little things in life.* It's been a whole week since I got to pick on her, after all. I have lost time to make up for. Yes, I need to land myself back on her good side, but I'm still me. And I don't want her to like me *too* much.

"What do you want, Austin?" Somehow, the intercom makes her sound like one of the Chipettes. But which one? Eleanor? Brittney? Jeanette? Surprise keeps me from laughing about it, though.

"How did you know it was me?" *Jeanette. Definitely Jeanette.*

"Because you're the only adult I know who can make ringing a bell *that* annoying. Go away."

It's so damn hard to take her seriously with that squeaky little voice. "No can do. This is Fern's version of making me sing for my supper. She sent you food."

Her reply is a long time coming, but I finally hear the signal that the door is unlocked. "I'm sick. Leave it outside my door."

Not likely. I save my breath, though. I'd rather talk to her face-to-face because I'm going to laugh if I have to hear that Jeanette voice again. Plus, making her open the door will annoy her. Annoying Jamaica is my new favorite pastime. *I'm walking a fucking tightrope here.*

I pound on her door loud enough for the neighbors to hear. "Strip-o-Gram!" I shout. *Go big or go home!* I pull out my phone, open my music streaming app, and queue up Genuine's *Pony*. Regretfully, my phone isn't capable of any real volume. No one opens their doors to shout at me. Or watch.

It has the desired effect, though. Jamaica's door opens just far enough for her to stick her head out and glare at me through red, swollen eyelids. *Holy shit.* She really *is* sick. Her cute little nose is all red too.

"Are you *daft?*" she asks. Even if I could take that look seriously, her voice ruins it. The crappy intercom isn't to blame for the shrill chipmunk squeak she's got going on.

"Turn that off!" she says, reaching for my phone.

Grinning, I jerk it out of her reach. "But I like this song. Could you and the other Chipettes do a cover for me?"

She shrieks, but it's more of an adorable little squeal . . . Like a pissed off kitten. "Shut up, give me the food, and go away."

"Shut up and fuck me." I shiver. Her words conjure up a replay of our not-quite-sex, just like they did at the barbecue last weekend. I kill the music before it can lead my brain deeper into the gutter. "Don't tell me to shut up," I tell her.

"Or what?"

How can I put this without saying 'because it makes me want to fuck you again?' "Let's just say you telling me to shut up sends me on a trip down memory lane. And if I take too many of those trips, I might want to visit again in person."

"Oh . . ." Her cheeks darken. She swallows hard. Her eyes drop to my mouth. "G-give me my food and go away!"

Interesting. I'm getting the feeling she won't hold me to the whole "we can never do this again" thing. *What can I say? It was good.* Sleeping with her again is out of the question now more than ever. It would feel like I'm manipulating her to accomplish this dare. *But after . . .* And this is why she can't like me too much. I'm only a man. "So, the food comes with instructions. Ready?"

She nods. "Let's have it, then."

I hold out the bag, and she opens the door all the way to take it, revealing the cutest pair of unicorn-print flannel pants I've ever seen, and I have four nieces. "She said to leave it in the fridge overnight. When you wake up in the morning, put it in the Crock-Pot, on low, with three cups of water. Stir occasionally, and it'll be ready by dinner. Got it?"

Jamaica bites her lip and holds the bag out to me. "I don't have a Crock-Pot yet."

Well, shit. Ignoring the bag, I turn on my heel and hustle to the stairs. "I'll be back," I call over my shoulder. Fern will chew my ass up one side and down the other if I report back with the food in my possession. And then she won't cook for me this week. I'll have to cook for myself. No one will be happy.

A quick trip to the store makes everyone happy and works toward getting Jamaica to like me again. And! Jamaica won't expect me to be so generous. She'll be suspicious. Waiting for the other shoe to drop will annoy her. Mission fucking complete.

But where the hell do I go to buy a Crock-Pot?

I grab my phone and punch one of the speed dials.

"Yo?" Chris answers. I don't want to ask Mason or Fern because I don't want Jamaica to think it was their idea. I'll be amazed if Ryan knows what the fuck a Crock-Pot is. Tara isn't sleeping well at night, so I don't want to call her or Gabe in case she's napping. Chris will know, though. He's a dad. He knows everything.

"I have a question, and you can't laugh," I tell him while I dash down the stairs two at a time.

"No promises," he says. There's a smile in his voice. He's already ready to laugh at me.

"Where do I go to buy a Crock-Pot?"

His chuckles rolls across the line like thunder. "Any Superstore will have them. Or you could hit one of the department stores."

I can do this! There's a Target a few blocks away. "Thanks, man!"

"Why do you suddenly need a Crock-Pot?"

"Don't ask questions you don't want answered!" I end the call before he can pry more. It's no great secret, but life is more interesting when I keep everyone on their toes.

Jamaica

My buzzer rings to the tune of the old Shave and a Haircut bit. *Austin* . . . Sighing, I roll off my couch and stumble to the door to buzz him in. While I'm up, I open the door a bit so he can let himself in. Benadryl is kicking my butt. He's lucky I'm still awake.

I shuffle back to the couch and roll myself up into a blanket burrito. Maybe I can fall asleep before he makes it upstairs. He can talk to himself because I'll be dead to the world. *I hate allergies.*

"Jam?" The hinges squeak when the door opens. "Jam?" he repeats.

I grunt so he'll stop calling for me. I hate the way he says my name. It makes me think of *that* night.

"You okay?" Gentle hands pull back the blanket where it's covering my face. I grunt again. "Do you need a doctor?"

"No. Jus' allergies."

"I brought you a Crock-Pot. I'm going to put it in your kitchen, okay?" His hand brushes over my forehead, smoothing back one of my curls I missed when I wrapped my hair. From anyone else, the touch would be soothing. But this is Austin, which renders it mildly unsettling. I'm too tired to do more than open one eye and glare at him.

"'Kay." What happened to him while he was gone? He's being *nice. He's the one who needs a doctor. He's clearly ill.* "T'anks," I say because manners are important, even with Austin. He *did* go out of his way to bring me food and a Crock-Pot. I'm sure I'll appreciate it more in the morning when I'm not high as a kite on Benadryl.

"Purse is in da bedroom. I have cash."

"Are you sure you're okay?" he asks, ignoring my offer to repay him. "Do you need anything else?"

"Jus' lock da door behind ya." I'll be down for a good twelve hours. I'm a lightweight. Someone could walk in and take everything I own, even this couch, and I wouldn't know until I wake up. I fall asleep to him carefully brushing that stubborn curl back again.

***

Consciousness comes back to me slowly, one sense at a time, beginning with smell. *Coffee?* That doesn't make sense. There's something else, too. Something savory. *At least my nose is clear enough to work.* My brain begins to process the signals my ears are sending it. There's water running in the kitchen, and I can hear my coffee maker doing its thing.

Wait! My apartment shouldn't smell like anything. My coffee maker and the water shouldn't be running. Did Fern stop by to check on me and let herself in? I roll to my feet and immediately trip and fall face-first to the ground. My arms are bound too tightly by the blanket to catch myself.

"Jam?" a masculine voice calls.

Adrenaline surges through my body, propelled by my pounding heart. There shouldn't be a man here. *What do I do?* I need to get out of here and call the cops.

"Stupid. Blanket," I mutter. There's no point in being quiet. Unless the intruder is deaf, they heard me hit the floor. Even if they are deaf, I hit hard enough for them to feel it.

Feet pad into my line of sight.

I scream and fight harder against the blanket monster. *Why. Won't. This. Thing. Tear?* "Leave me alone!"

"Jam!" he shouts. "Jamaica! Chill out!" Hands grab at me. I try to roll away, but he pins me down with his body.

"No! Go away! There's cash in the kitchen drawers!" There isn't, but that might buy me time to untangle and run.

"Jamaica, shut up," he growls in my ears. Those words cut through my panic to another primal part of my brain. I freeze. Brief flashes of memories from last night come back to me—Austin bothering me about something, me rolling up in my blanket like a big idiot burrito. That explains the face-plant, but not why Austin is here. Again.

"Good," he purrs, just like *that* night. And, just like that night, I really wish I could punch him. It's cheating for him to use sex against me. "I'm sorry I scared you."

"What are you doing here? How'd you get in?" If I ask enough questions, I can distract us both from the elephant in the room because between those words and the way he's holding me down, my mind is going places it shouldn't. I wiggle a bit, hoping he'll get the hint and let me up.

"Sorry," he says. His weight disappears, and he helps me find my way out of the blanket so I can sit up. I quickly wrap the blanket around me again because a smiley face tee and unicorn print pants don't exactly scream "screw off to where you came from." I'm already a joke to him; no need to make it worse.

He smiles, and I regret leaving my blanket burrito haven. I couldn't see him there. I was safe from that smile. "I never left . . . You scared me when I got back, so I sat down to keep an eye on you until I heard back from Fern and I dozed off watching shitty *Gilmore Girls* reruns."

"So, you were here all night?" I clutch the blanket a little tighter. I was more or less in a coma for hours, and he was here the whole time? The man has been all up in my business, but his revelation triggers a sense of vulnerability. Why would he do that? He's made it clear he doesn't care about me.

His eyes track the movement, and his smile fades. "That's what I said. What do you have for breakfast? I'm starving."

He's always *starving.* I sigh. For some reason, I feel like I at least owe him breakfast. It's ridiculous—I don't owe him a thing!—but my gut says it's the right thing to do. He stayed when he didn't have to because he was worried about me. It's oddly touching. "There should be a box of microwave breakfast sandwiches in the freezer. I haven't made it to the store yet this week, so I don't have much."

He blinks at me. "'Breakfast sandwiches' and 'freezer' should never be used in the same sentence without the words 'don't belong.'"

I shrug. I tried. It's not my fault if he rejects the offer. They're not horrible. I actually like them. "We can't all be Fern. I'm not a morning person. Cooking before lunch isn't happening. If you don't like it, you know where to find the door. Don't let it hit ya where the good Lord split ya."

He blinks again and doubles over laughing. "You come up with the most creative things to say to avoid cussing."

And you frequently exhaust my ability to do so. "Well, if you wouldn't give me so many reasons to cuss, I wouldn't have to be so creative."

He stands up. "Don't eat that shit. I'll be back with something that doesn't taste like freezer and broken dreams."

I close my menu and lay it on the table. "I think I'm getting the shrimp alfredo," I tell Jordan, happy with my decision. It's one of my favorites, but it's not too expensive here. I didn't want to pick something too expensive for our first real date since he's paying.

He looks at me over his menu. "No, alfredo is gross. You'll have the eggplant parmesan."

I think back on what I said, wondering if I made him think I was open to suggestions. I don't even like eggplant. "But alfredo is my favorite. That's what I want."

"No, it isn't. I'm paying. You'll order what I want, or we're leaving."

I'm not letting another man tell me what I do and do not like. "I'll eat whatever I want!" I snap at Austin with more anger than the situation really calls for. "There's nothing wrong with those sandwiches!"

He ignores me and shoves his feet into his shoes. "What kind of pancakes do you like?"

"I don't like pancakes!" That's an outright lie, but I will defend my choice of breakfast sandwiches until the bitter end just because he belittled them and had the nerve to boss me around.

He stops tying his shoe to look at me. "Now you're just being difficult. Everyone likes pancakes."

I cross my arms and glare at him.

"Fine," he sighs. "I'm sorry I don't like your stupid breakfast sandwiches. There's an IHOP a few blocks over. I saw it while I was buying your Crock-Pot last night. It's not Fern's cooking, but I will bring you whatever you want, my treat, just tell me what you like!"

"Just tell me what you like!" I replay that sentence in my head a few times. That changes things. He's still rude and insufferable, but he's not trying to deprive me of a choice.

My face must betray my wavering because he grins. "What'll it be?"

"Surprise me," I say, surprising myself. After Jordan's manipulation, I enjoy making decisions for myself. So why am I giving this one away?

His grin becomes that smile that makes me think stupid thoughts. "You got it."

He walks out, pulling the door closed behind him, but stops and sticks his head back inside. "Hey, Jam?"

"Yeah?"

That ever-present smile disappears. "I should've asked sooner. Are you feeling better?"

I bite my lip to keep myself from smiling. Just because he asked doesn't mean he really cares. It doesn't mean that he's not like Jordan. "Yes, thank you. For now, anyway."

Austin frowns. "For now?"

I do smile at that because I didn't expect him to ask. "In an hour or two, the congestion will be back." It doesn't matter what the doctor gives me; I'll be miserable for days. I'm grateful I held out until the weekend this time.

"You go through this a lot?"

I nod. "Every year about this time. I'm allergic to grass."

His eyes widen. "Seriously? Grass?"

"Seriously," I answer, stifling a sigh. That's the typical reaction, usually followed by questions about why I don't move to Arizona. What the desert lacks in grass it makes up for in temperatures. Allergies are only a problem for a few days every year. The desert heat is perpetual. The choice is clear to me.

His mouth pulls to one side in a thoughtful little half frown. "Can I get you anything else while I'm out?"

I bite my lip. I hate to ask him for a favor, but I forgot to stock up on tissues.

His eyes move to my mouth. "What is it, Jam?" he asks.

I sigh and give in because I don't want to venture out myself if I don't have to. "I'm down to maybe half a box of tissues."

"Say no more," he says, nodding like a man on a mission.

I stand up and shuffle to the back to get my purse. "Let me get you some—" The door closes, cutting me off. "Money."

Chapter 10
Austin

rass? I can't wrap my head around it. Allergies are bad enough, but fucking grass? That shit is everywhere. Jamaica can't go anywhere without mother nature trying to kill her. It's like one giant fuck you from the world. How can she live like that?

I'm glad I stayed last night now, even if it was an accident. I don't like the thought of her being miserable, alone, and subsisting on something that barely passes for food.

Jamaica's dislike for me runs deep enough that I don't have to worry about her trying to fan this spark of interest between us into anything more if I help her out today. In fact, she'll probably be suspicious of anything nice I do for a while, just like the Crock-Pot. So I'll take this opportunity to show her that, even though we don't like each other, we can still be perfectly friendly when the situation calls for it. Because as my sister-in-law's best friend, the situation will call for it a lot. And, eventually, *hopefully*, it will cease to be for Fern's sake.

Since I have to wait for our order anyway, I wander the aisles of the pharmacy department at Target, searching the shelves for anything else Jamaica might need. More Benadryl, some VapoRub, something called a Neti Pot, distilled water, and some lozenges for a sore throat, just in case. I also grab a bottle of scented bath salts because the website I consulted about allergy treatments recommended inhaling steam. What better way to inhale steam than a hot bath that'll also help her feel better? Another site suggested a mixture of hot water, local honey, and lemon juice, but I doubt I'll find local honey here.

I'll ask Mom and Grandma. One of them will surely know where to get some local honey. It seems like the sort of thing they'd know anyway. Before I can forget, I whip out my phone and text them both, explaining it's for Fern's friend so they don't attack me with a million questions about my random inquiry.

I still have time to kill, so I find the appropriate aisle for bottled lemon juice and head to check out. *She'll be so surprised. And suspicious.* It's almost like a prank—completely harmless but still satisfying because it's not what it seems.

***

"What's all this?" Jamaica asks in her Chipette squeak. Her prediction about when the congestion would return must've been off.

She reaches to take some of the bags from me, but I turn, putting my body between her and them. "Sex toys."

"From Target?" she asks, skepticism heavy though her voice is hardly recognizable. I lead the way to her little kitchen, fighting off her attempts to help the whole time. I wouldn't be surprised to find that Target does have a selection of sex toys, but probably not enough to fill this many bags.

I search through my haul for the Neti Pot and the distilled water I picked up to go with it. "Here," I say, pushing both items into her hands.

She looks the box for the Neti Pot over good, then asks me if I'm crazy with her eyes.

"I had time to kill," I explain with a shrug. "So, I did an Internet search for remedies for allergies, and that was one of them."

"I think you're secretly hoping I'll drown myself."

Now why would I want that? You're too fun to pick on. "If I wanted you dead, I'd let Mother Nature finish the job. Not buy you things to make you feel better."

Her lips twitch into the beginning of a smile, but she quickly presses them together to stop it. "Thank you, Austin. If you're not careful, I might think you actually like me."

Yeah, I do . . . when you're not accusing me of being a grade-A douche. I wink at her. "Nah. I just don't want Fern to be sad."

Jamaica's laughter follows her out of the room. A door closes—presumably the bathroom, but I'm not going to follow her to verify. Instead, I unpack the rest of the goodies I picked out for her.

To kill more time, I stir the soup I started for her this morning with the spoon she left next to the Crock-Pot, then snoop through the drawers for her flatware. It would be easier to ask, but I'm nosey. And it might annoy her. Win-win.

"Godiva?" she asks from the doorway, startling me because I didn't hear her come out of the bathroom. The Neti Pot must've helped because she sounds like herself again. I glance back to see her eyes fixed on the little golden box of chocolates I picked up at the checkout counter. Growing up with Nicole, I quickly learned that chocolate solves almost every problem in a woman's life. And if it doesn't solve it, it at least makes it more bearable.

"Breakfast first." I check the to-go boxes and pass her the appropriate one.

Styrofoam squeals when she opens it to appraise my choice. "Strawberry pancakes?"

Grinning to myself, I nod. There's more to it than that, but I'm not going to spoil the surprise. "Mmhmm. I had a hunch. Did I do good?"

She doesn't answer right away. I turn around to find her staring at the contents of her box with a faraway look on her face. *Aw, shit.* "Don't tell me you're allergic to strawberries, too?" The thought crossed my mind, but I figured she'd warn me if she was. I edge past her and head for the door. "Throw those out. I'll go get you something else."

I don't know if strawberry allergies get as bad as peanut allergies. There's a guy at work who can't even be in the same room with someone who ate a peanut. I don't want to find out the hard way. I've dealt with enough anaphylactic shock to last me a lifetime, and Fern isn't here to tell me what to do this time.

Jamaica grabs my arm to stop me. I could swear there are tears in her eyes, but they could be watering from her allergies. "No! I love strawberries. This is perfect, thank you."

"Are you sure? You didn't look very excited . . ."

She smiles at me the way she used to before the bachelor party—the way she still does for our friends. "I am. Really! It was just a surprise. I figured you'd play it safe with plain pancakes or something."

I grin again. In a way, I did. I ordered chocolate chip for myself so I could trade her if she hates strawberries or something. But her face when she looked inside that box made me want to go back and order a stack of every variety of pancakes they have just to make her happy. I'll take that to my grave, though. "When do I ever play it safe? Let's eat."

Before I sit, I shuffle the neat stacks of papers and a handful of pens with bite marks on the back end out of the way. I can picture her sitting here, bent over a book, nibbling on a pen while she studies. Judging by the number of pens I've noticed in odd places, she misplaces them like Nicole and Fern do hair ties. *Why is that cute?* Probably because I don't live with her. It would be annoying to deal with all of the time, I'm sure.

I say a silent prayer and lower my ass into one of the spindly chairs at her table. It's one of those dainty little things that I always assume is more for looks than functionality. It takes my weight without the slightest creak, so I relax, pop open my to-go box, and dig into my steak and eggs, saving my pancakes for last in case she changes her mind. Jamaica strikes me as more of a scrambled-eggs-and-bacon kinda girl, so that's what she got to go with her pancakes. The best part is, I get to clean up whatever she doesn't eat—another win-win.

Jamaica sits across from me and cuts into her pancakes first. I watch through my eyelashes while her first bite slips past her lips. The memory of those lips sliding up and down my dick in the moonlight follows quickly. *Deep breaths, Austin.*

She chews a couple times, then moans. *Fuck. My. Life.* I *felt* that from all the way over here. My dick stirs in my pants in response. I've heard that sound before while she used me to pleasure herself.

She quickly chews and swallows to ask, "Cheesecake?"

I nod and swallow hard so I can speak. "Thought you might like that since you appreciated Tara's cheesecake balls so much."

She smiles, but it doesn't reach her eyes. "It's delicious, thank you." *Is it that hard for her to admit it?* I guess that means everything is going according to plan.

I clear my throat while shifting in my chair, trying to find a way to relieve the tightness in my jeans without her figuring out what's happening. "You're welcome." *I'd still rather hear you say that my dick is the best thing you've ever had in your mouth.*

Get it together, man. It's only five more weeks. *It was easier to ignore how much I want her when I still had the option of sleeping with someone else.* Technically, talking her out of her panties again wouldn't violate the dare . . . But that would be manipulative and we have an agreement. It can't happen again.

Chapter 11
Jamaica

"I didn't know rich boys knew how to wash dishes," I say purely to goad Austin, who is at the sink washing our forks from breakfast.

I shouldn't tease him so. At least not today. He's not being an obnoxious twat. I'm actually enjoying his company again. I survey the odd mix of items he brought back from Target and smile. *Proof he* can *be sweet.*

It was probably Fern's idea. Even if it was, he still called her and followed through instead of deciding I wasn't worth the trouble, so I can't give her all the credit.

"The Chambers boys do," he says. I glance his way in time to catch him smiling at me. He grabs the towel off the hook over the cabinet door and turns around to lean against the counter while he dries his hands. "No joke, the summer before my freshman year, Mom gave the maid a paid vacation, and Nicole, Mason, and I had to take over for her. Mom said that she would not send her children out into the world not knowing how to take care of themselves or their homes."

Fighting a smile, I say, "But you still didn't learn how to cook."

He tosses his head back and laughs until a tear runs down his face. "No," he says, wiping at his eye. "I tried, but the others got tired of eating burnt food really fast."

"It's not that hard!" I might favor frozen dinners because they save time and I have a lot of studying to do, but I enjoy cooking. I'm not as good as my mum or Fern, but I can hold my own.

He rolls his eyes at me. "That's what everyone says! It just doesn't work out for me. I can clean. I can do laundry. I can wash dishes all day long. I can't even make grilled cheese without burning it."

I cross my arms. I'm not buying this. Grilled cheese isn't that hard. It's one of the first things I made for myself. *He probably messes up on purpose.* "What do you do, forget about it?"

Austin drapes the towel over his shoulder and mimics me. "No! It just goes from not done to too done too fast!"

"Maybe don't turn the burner on high?"

"But it takes too long if I don't!"

Why am I not surprised that he can't wait? I have first-hand experience with his penchant for instant gratification. "But it doesn't burn!"

"It's hard to be patient when I'm hungry!"

"You're always hungry!"

"You're right. Got any ice cream?"

"Seriously?" I throw my hands up in defeat and let them fall, my palms slapping against my flannel-clad thighs. *This guy is a bottomless stomach.*

". . . Maybe."

"You *just* ate! And you ate part of mine too! How do you stay so skinny?"

He preens like a peacock, puffing out his chest and stretching every last millimeter out of his height. "Just lucky, I guess. Or it could be all the time I spend at Chris and Ryan's gym."

My fingers itch to explore the smooth skin of his torso and retrace his abs. *Bad idea, Jam. Focus!* "Has anyone ever told you it'll catch up with you someday?"

He takes his time looking me over from head to toe, and a rush of heat follows his gaze. *Is he remembering too?* "You're one to talk."

I shrug and badger my brain into concentrating on the here and now instead of escaping to that night behind a tree and his lips on mine. "Genetics, I guess. I'm built like my dad."

Austin suddenly clears his throat and pushes away from the counter. "You never said on the ice cream?"

My brain glitches, trying to catch up with the conversational U-turn. "Uh." A whisper of a laugh slips out. "Yeah. I think."

The lips I was just thinking about kissing turn down into a frown. "You *think?* What kind of woman are you?"

Oh, yay. Austin *is back.* Once again, I am less of a woman because I don't meet his preconceived notions of what constitutes a real woman.

He strides the short distance to the fridge and yanks the freezer door open. "Ooh, Rocky Road!" Carton in hand, he closes the freezer and goes to the drawer to get a spoon. "Want some?" he asks, pulling the lid off.

I cross my arms defensively to hide my chest as if that'll protect me from further scrutiny. *Why is it so easy to forget what a jerk he is sometimes?* "No, thanks. I'm still full."

"Hey, wanna watch a movie?"

Do I what now? I blink at him and open my mouth to ask him what the heck he's on, then close it because I'm not going to stoop to his level again. "Did Fern assign you to babysit me or something?" I love the woman, but if he says yes, she's gonna get a piece of my mind. I'm not an invalid. Sure, I wouldn't mind some company, but not *Austin.*

He frowns at me while his eyes flick back and forth across my face. "Nope. I don't like being alone when I'm sick. I thought maybe you were the same but too stubborn to say so since you haven't told me to get out yet."

"Is that an option?" I'm not sure if I actually mean it or if I'm only joking, but the words roll off my tongue easily. "I mean, you bought me breakfast and all that stuff from Target. I was beginning to think you're capable of being a decent human being. Kicking you out seemed a little extreme after that."

His expression hardens to a full-on glare. My body stiffens, ready to move. *I know that look.* Jordan never hit me, but nothing good ever came of that look on his face. Heart pounding, I shuffle back a few steps, putting myself out of range on instinct. I don't think he'll hurt me—he doesn't seem to be the sort—but neither did Jordan.

His eyes drop to the floor, taking in the space between us, but the glare is gone when he looks up again. Sighing, he stabs the spoon into the ice cream and rubs his jaw with his empty hand. "I *am* a decent human being," he says softly. "Same as I've always been, and we used to get along fine. You're the one who got pissed off over a joke and lashed out at me, Jamaica. I was trying to show you that we *can* get along for Fern's sake, even if we don't particularly like each other."

My arms slip around my middle, and I hug myself tightly. There's no trace of that anger in his voice, but it could be an act. I don't trust myself to know the difference. "I think you should go now."

I need space. I don't know how to handle him right now. I don't know how to handle *me*. I swore I'd never cower again, but the first sign of hostility has me back in the self-preservation mindset. I'd love to say that the Austin who fell asleep watching over me last night would never physically hurt me, but Jordan proved that the cruelest people are also capable of being tender.

Shaking his head, he breathes out a laugh and turns away from me. "So that's how it is, huh? Can't even try to have an adult discussion about our differences? I say something you don't agree with, and you either shut down or fling insults."

I can't win here. If I try to explain, he'll turn it all around on me. That's how it always goes. It's always my fault. I'm always the one in the wrong. Defending myself only leads to more strife. Shouting. Snide comment. Insults. Slammed doors. It's best to keep my mouth shut.

"Unbelievable," he mutters. "See you around, Jamaica. Hope you get to feeling better." He puts the ice cream back in the freezer, the spoon clatters in the sink, and he storms out of the kitchen. I brace for the slamming of the door, but he closes it so softly, I creep out to make sure he didn't leave it standing wide open.

Austin

I make it to the ground floor before I stop. *What is wrong with me?* I get frustrated with her, and I want to kiss her. That is not normal. Or sane. *We can't fight when we're kissing, though.*

Growling to myself, I reach to open the front door and stop. Once I walk through that door, there's no coming back. She won't let me in again. This will remain one more unresolved issue between us, and I don't even know what I did to set her off! Everything was fine until it wasn't anymore. And I hate that.

I should go back upstairs and refuse to leave until she explains. No. She asked me to leave. I will honor that. I clench my fists, digging my nails into my palm as if the dull pain might cut through the craziness in my brain. I should want to get away from her, not closer to her. I'd like nothing more than to go knock on her door and kiss her when she opens it. I can't do that, though. We agreed. Never again.

But that *look . . . Has someone hurt her?* She doesn't act like an abused woman in my limited experience. She shrunk away from me and slammed the metaphorical door between us in a heartbeat, though.

Now, I know what Mason means when he talks about how Fern used to be. Fern wasn't abused, per se. *Who are you kidding? Yes, she was.* Mason's ex mentally and emotionally abused Fern because she was jealous.

So, what is Jamaica's story? There has to be a reason for this behavior. She plans to be a lawyer, so I doubt she's afraid of confrontation. Not if she ever intends to set foot in a courtroom. She only gets that way with me, that I've seen anyway.

She only gets that way with me. Why me? She wasn't like that before the bachelor party and the joke that we can't talk about without her getting all defensive and telling me I'm making it worse. I've tried apologizing. I picked her flowers. I've done everything I can to make it up to her, but she still behaves as if . . . As if I've abused her.

Who hurt her?

It's the only logical explanation. Someone put that fear in her. I have no right to pry, though. And I can't ask Fern without her asking too many questions.

What do I do?

Chapter 12

Austin

*M*ason's front door is wide open, so I let myself in. "Knock, knock!" I call, but no one responds. I check the ground floor, braced to run into Jamaica each time I enter a room. She's bound to be here somewhere since Mason, Fern, and Ronni are leaving for vacation today. I haven't seen or heard from her since our little tiff four days ago. I'm not sure if she's still pissed at me for no apparent reason and I don't want to find out today.

Fern and I meet at the top of the stairs. Wide-eyed, she stops just shy of bowling me down. "Gimme," I tell her, reaching for the handle of the suitcase she's pulling. The damn thing is almost as big as she is. She doesn't need to drag it down the stairs when I'm here to help. Yes, she can do it. She is strong enough—and stubborn enough—to get it done. That's beside the point.

She bats her eyes at me and clasps her hands under her chin. "And they say chivalry is dead. Thank you, Austin."

"You know," I call on my way down, "I could swear you have a husband to do this for you." I don't know where my brother is, but I know he heard me. He hears *everything*. And, if Fern takes her cue, this will be fun.

Her giggle follows me. "I married the wrong brother!" she shouts loudly enough for anyone, anywhere in the baby mansion they call home, to hear.

She remembers! I stop at the bottom of the stairs and turn around. Hands on my hips, I follow her lead. "Damnit! I knew I should've objected!"

"You did once."

Yes, I did, and I wasn't so sure my brother wasn't going to kill me for that joke. "Oh, I remember. No one listened to me, though. No one ever takes me seriously."

I shouldn't joke about that. It's not funny because it's the truth, and it sucks sometimes. *Maybe that's why Jamaica and I can't get along.* Everyone else assumes I'm joking when I'm not; Jamaica does the opposite.

Fern's body shakes with the fit of giggles she's holding back. That laughter glitters in her eyes as she presses the back of her palm to her forehead and throws her head back like something you'd see in an old movie. "I've made a terrible, terrible mistake! Oh, Austin! Can you ever forgive me?"

There's no annoyed growl. No slamming doors. No thundering footsteps heralding impending doom. *What the hell is going on here?* I can always count on Mason to be . . . Mason. He chooses today of all days to let me down? "Where the hell is my brother? You got him tied up somewhere?"

She straightens up and her smile switches from happy and playful to something seductive that only Mason should see. "Do you really want me to answer that?"

I open my mouth, hoping something halfway intelligent and witty will find its way out, but nothing happens. I'm at a loss for words. *That's a first.*

She dissolves into giggles, leaning against the wall for support. "Oh, my God. Your face!" she somehow manages to say. "He's with Ronni. She's convinced she's going to be bored out of her mind and is trying to pack everything she owns."

"You're joking, right?" How can she think she'll be bored in California? They're taking her to a beach. Fern is going to teach her to ride a horse. There will be new places to explore, new things to try.

"Nope. Go see for yourself," she says, waving over her shoulder toward her step-daughter's room.

I run up the stairs again so I can say I got some cardio in today and stroll down the hall to my darling niece's room. I open the door slowly in hopes neither of them will notice. It's better to know what I'm walking in on than to blindly walk into the crossfire.

"Veronica Anne, you don't *need* another suitcase." *Uh oh, he two-named her. She better watch it.* There's no mistaking the sound of my brother's seemingly infinite patience—at least where Ronni is concerned—on its last legs.

"But Daddy, what if there are no other kids there?" I know the exact look that goes with that wheedling tone. I've fallen prey to it more times than anyone needs to know about. And she gives her cousins lessons.

"I said no, and that's final. One suitcase is more than enough. We're only going to be gone for two weeks."

Uncle Austin to the rescue! But who am I rescuing, Mason or Ronni? Or both . . . I swing the door open wide and take two running steps before I stop short because every inch of her bed is covered in clothes, toys, games, and books. There's nowhere for me to land safely if I jump as I planned on. "Whoa. Does your bookshelf have a cold, Ronni?"

Mason growls softly at the interruption, but that could mean anything from fuck off to thank God you're here to save me.

"Uncle Austin, it's a bookshelf. It can't get a cold."

"Are you sure? 'Cause it looks like it sneezed all over your bed, Pipsqueak. So did your toy box. And your game shelf. We better get out of here. It might be contagious."

Ronni anchors her fists to her hips and tilts her chin up, a perfect copy of her stepmother when she is set on something. "I've changed my mind, Daddy. *I* don't need a suitcase. Uncle Austin does. I want him to go with us."

Well, shit. "Not this time, Ronni," I say so my brother doesn't have to be the bad guy here—again. "I have to do your daddy's job better than he can."

She scowls at me. "Daddy is working on this trip. So is Mama."

Damn, she caught me. Mason didn't want to take off again so soon after his honeymoon, especially not since he, Fern, Grandad, and Grandma are wrapping up planning the company Fourth of July picnic which will take place a few days after their return. "Not the whole time. They can't do everything via video chat. I have to help get ready for the party."

Funny how I didn't want his job, but I keep doing it. It's not all that bad, though. And I like being here to lighten the load for him. He's finally happy, and I want him to enjoy it. This is their first family vacation. I'd do a lot worse than helping to coordinate vendors and planning tent placement.

"Will you come with us when we go back for grape harvest?" she asks.

"Wouldn't miss it for the world." She'll never know how much I mean that. Fern inherited a *vineyard.* I want to see this. I want to get out of this city. I haven't traveled in years, not since Mason graduated, and Mom stopped planning family vacations for all of us. I have no one to travel with, and it's no fun to go alone.

"And you're going to show me around then, right?"

"Yes!" she says with a decisive nod.

"Good. Then, you don't need all this stuff. You'll be too busy learning everything there is to know about the place so you can play tour guide when I'm there with you."

Ronni purses her lips. She turns to survey everything on her bed. "Maybe just two books," she says.

Mason sighs audibly. His shoulders sag for a moment, but then he smiles. "Alright. Pick two and get packed. We're waiting on you, Rice Monster."

I follow him out of the room and close the door behind me.

"Thank you," he says, leading the way down the hall to his room. "I couldn't convince her that it isn't some stuffy place where she can't touch anything for fear of breaking it."

That surprises me. The place is awesome from what I've seen, but I'm also not nine years old. "She saw the pictures, right?"

"Yep. Says it all looks expensive and refuses to believe a kid has ever set foot there."

"Pfft, expensive." I make a show of looking around as if to take in their home, though there's really nothing to see from where I'm leaning against his doorframe. He can't see me anyway because he's wandering around, searching for something. There's no expensive art on the walls, though every photo is priceless to Mason and Fern. No stuffy vases to knock over and break.

"She lives here," he said, understanding what I'm getting at. He disappears into his closet, still talking. "And I learned early that anything glass isn't a sound investment. Where the hell is my suitcase?"

I smile. *Game on.* "Oh, you missed it. I carried it downstairs for Fern, and she realized that she made a mistake."

Mason moves back into my line of sight and frowns. "And that would be?"

"She married the wrong brother."

He rolls his eyes and moves on to whatever is next on his list.

"That's it?" I ask. "You're not going to threaten me? Tell me to keep my ass away from your wife? Anything?"

He holds his left hand up at face level. "Mine."

"What, you put a ring on her finger and stop worrying?"

"Nope. The ring on her finger is for the rest of the world. I knew she was mine the day I died."

His callousness makes me shiver. *How can he be so . . . matter of fact about it?* I still have the occasional nightmare about him lying in the grass in Mom's back yard while Fern works to keep his heart beating until the EMTs arrive to take him away. Only, in my nightmares, he doesn't make it. And he acts like it was just another Thursday? "Don't talk like that, man. You didn't die."

He stops digging through the top drawer of his nightstand to look at me. "Yes, I did. I was dead for approximately eleven minutes and forty-three seconds based on the time Fern told the dispatcher she couldn't find a pulse."

I shove away from the wall and hurry across the room. The absolute stupefaction on Mason's face when I collide with him for a hug is something I'll smile about later. When I'm not reflecting on how close I came to losing him. "Don't forget your EpiPens."

"Love you too, little brother."

"Whatever." I thump him on the back and let him go. "Finish packing. I've gotta go hug your wife now."

Thanksgiving will never be the same for our family. It will forever be a reminder of how fragile life is; how quickly it can end. We came so close to having another empty chair at the table, figuratively speaking. It's something that haunts me. I've already lost my dad; I don't want to lose my brother, too. He's as much of a father figure as Granddad. There'd be a huge hole in my life without him.

I find her in the kitchen. She's busy unloading the dishwasher but looks up when I walk in. Something makes her stop, so her hands aren't full when I hold out my arms to her. Without a word, she steps around the dishwasher door to hug me.

"Thank you," I whisper.

"For what?"

"My brother. Everything."

She squeezes me harder and sniffs. "I'd say anytime, but if I have to save him again, I might kill him for putting me through that."

"Then you'll have to revive him again so I can."

"Yeah, let's just not. That sounds like a lot of work."

"I agree. Are his EpiPens packed?"

"Yes. So are mine. So are the spares."

"Good."

"Will you do me a favor while we're gone?"

"Name it." There isn't much of anything I wouldn't do for her.

"Check on Jam for me, please? She's taking online classes, and she forgets to eat sometimes when she's focused."

Anything but that . . . She doesn't know what she's asking of me. I haven't forgotten that betrayed look on Jamaica's face when we parted ways last, nor the way I wanted nothing more than to kiss her until it went away. "You bet." I give her one last squeeze and noisily kiss the top of her head before I let her go. "Thanks for understanding. You always do."

She smiles at me because she understands. Again. We're not the same. She hits things when her emotions are more than she can handle. I make jokes. She's always got it, though, even before when she was only Ronni's nanny. I know there were times she didn't understand what was on the line for me while I was making light of the situation, but she rolled with it even if she wanted to beat me over the head with whatever she could get her hands on.

"Ronni's packed!" Mason calls. A heartbeat later, the *whir* of suitcase wheels on the hardwood floor precedes him into the room. "I think we're about ready to get this show on the road."

"Can I tag along?" I ask. I hate good-byes, and I really missed them last time they were gone. And this time, they're taking Ronni, too. I'll take all the time I can get with them before they go. Especially now that I can't stop thinking about last Thanksgiving.

"Sure," Mason says.

"I need to finish unloading the dishwasher first!" Fern says. "And is Ronni's room picked up?"

Mason takes a deep breath. "Sweetheart, it's not going to be our problem for two weeks." The way he says it leads me to believe they've had this discussion before, probably before their honeymoon. They don't argue; they discuss.

"I don't want to come home to a messy house and have to start cleaning the second we walk through the door!"

"If you'd let me hire a new cleaning lady . . ."

Fern purses her lips. "I can do it!"

"I didn't say you *can't;* I said you don't have to."

Ronni comes clomping into the room. She looks at me and rolls her eyes. "Here they go again," she says, confirming my suspicion that this is a common discussion.

Fern lifts her chin, and I bite my tongue to keep from laughing since Ronni *just* did that to her dad. "There's no reason. I've cleaned this house for years."

"That was before, when it was all you did. Now, you're getting your degree, learning the ropes of managing this new estate, helping Grandma shoulder her load with the company events, you're already up to your ears in scholarship applications, *and* you're trying to clean the house and spend time with your family."

"Fern," I say before she can deliver what I'm sure is a compelling argument in her favor. Not. "Just give him this one. Lighten your load. Enjoy life. We know you *can* do it all. You have nothing to prove."

She opens her mouth and closes it, then lightly punches me in the arm. It doesn't hurt at all. I rub the spot anyway to humor her. "Ow! What was that for!"

"For taking his side!"

"I didn't. I'm on yours. But to be on yours, I have to agree with him."

"I do too, Mama. We don't get much time to play anymore."

"Rainbow! I—"

Mason crosses to her in two quick strides and engulfs her in a hug. She hides her face in his chest, and her whole body heaves. "You're not failing," he says, though she didn't say a word. "I hired you because I couldn't do it all by myself. Your only job for years was to take care of her and this house. That isn't true anymore. Hiring a new cleaning lady isn't replacing you, Fern. It doesn't mean you're failing as a wife or a mother. It means you have a little more time in the day and one less thing to worry about."

Fern nods, keeping her face hidden. *Is she crying? Oh, please, don't let her be crying.* I can't handle tears.

"I'll put Darren on it. We can conduct interviews together once we're home."

"You don't need t—"

His hand rubs slow circles between her shoulders. "Hush. No one will be good enough in your eyes. I've done this before, remember? I tried to find a reason you weren't suitable and look at what I would've missed out on."

Why does my life always seem great until I witness little moments like this? It's hard to tell myself I don't want someone permanent to share my life with when I'm surrounded by rock-solid relationships. Watching Nicole and John navigate their way through three small children and still love each other, or Gabe turn into a child himself when he talks about the baby, and seeing these two figure out how to settle into life as husband and wife makes me want to follow their lead. If they can do it, so can I. I just have to be like John, Gabe, and Mason.

But I'm not them. They're great men, but I'm me. I'm Austin. I'm the goof that can't quite get it right.

"I'll make sure everything is perfect when you get home, Fern," I promise. We might have different definitions of perfect, but I can empty a dishwasher and clean Ronni's room. "You go enjoy your trip and don't worry about anything here. It's all under control." I bite my tongue to keep from smiling. She has no idea how much I have this under control.

Chapter 13

Jamaica

*K*nock-knock-knock. I jump and somehow knock a book and a stack of notes off the table. *The downfall of preferring physical copies.* Digital textbooks and notes are easier to hide, though. I learned the hard way when Jordan decided my schooling was taking too much time away from him.

No one buzzed to be let in. Whoever it is must be on the wrong floor or something. Though, how could they forget the apartment number between the door and here? Picking up my mess will give them time to realize their mistake. If they're still there when I get to the door—*knock-knock-knock.*

Maybe they're not lost? Or convinced they're not. I hurry to the door and lean in to check the peephole. And I groan. *What does he* want? I take a deep breath to clear my head, then another to make him wait—one more for good measure.

"Jam?" his voice carries through the door. "Do I need to play *Pony* again?"

No! My neighbor still asks me who sent me a stripper. And if he was any good. And if she can come over next time. She's old enough to be my grandmother! I turn the lock so hard I'm surprised I don't break it and yank the door open. "What are you doing here?"

We didn't part on the best of terms last time. I'm not sure this is a friendly visit.

Austin raises his eyebrows, hooks his thumbs through his belt loops, and rocks back on his heels. "Nice to see you again, too."

I refuse to fall for that trick and feel guilty. I didn't invite him here. I cross my arms and do my best to fill the doorway, hoping he'll get the message that he's not welcome. "I'm studying."

His head bobs once. "That's why I'm here. Fern was worried. You didn't—"

My insides plummet toward the center of the earth. *That's* today? "Fern! Oh, no! I'm supposed to meet her for lunch! Did I miss it? Are they gone?"

His face softens a bit. "Yeah. She asked me to check on you and tell you she'll call tonight."

"Thank you," I mumble. I can't believe I lost track of time and missed our lunch. What time is it even? I grab my phone, but it's dead. She probably tried to phone to remind me. She knows how I get when I have a test coming up. But now, I won't get to see her for two weeks. And that's probably why he's here. I step back and wave him inside. He won't leave until his mission is complete. "Was she upset?"

Austin scoffs as I shut the door behind him. "We're talking about Fern, Jamaica. No, she wasn't upset. She knew exactly what you were doing. Thus my presence here."

"Why does she always send you?" I ask as I brush past him on my way back to the table. Why can't it be one of the girls? Or even one of the other guys? Heck, I'd be happy with Mason's assistant, his scary driver-slash-security-guy, or some random schmuck she found on the street.

I sit and turn in time to see him shrug. "Beats me. She knows I'll do it?"

That only raises more questions. We don't like each other, so *why* does he do it? "But why? Don't you have better things to do?"

He shrugs again. "I've got time. But I owe Fern a lot. I'd walk naked through rush hour traffic if she needed me to."

The mental image does a number on me. I've only seen bits and pieces of him in the moonlight, but it's enough to construct a fairly accurate picture of him in my head. I wouldn't mind checking that against the real deal, though. I force myself to laugh to cover the momentary lapse in judgment. To distract him in case he noticed, I ask, "Because of your brother?"

His stare jumps from my lips to my eyes when I speak.

"Because of my brother." He hesitates and adds, "Mason was my first best friend. He's still my best friend."

My throat ties itself in a knot, making it difficult to speak. "I get it. My sister . . ." Words fail me. Fern told me about the Thanksgiving incident. I never want to know what Austin went through. "Anyway, I'm okay. Thank you for checking, though. I appreciate it." Oddly, his dislike of me, specifically the way we left things last time he was here, makes that even more true.

"When did you eat last?" he asks.

"What time is it?" The words roll off my tongue without a thought. I cringe. It was the wrong answer to give if Fern sent him on a mission. *Darn it! He's got me.*

He exhales heavily. "Three o'clock."

Lying to him will get me nowhere, so I think back. I know I ate before class yesterday, and I grabbed lunch after. But class is online Wednesdays, so it's harder to keep track. "Uh . . . I might've had breakfast. No! That was dinner last night." My stomach rumbles on cue. *Et tu, Brute?*

"Uh-huh . . . When did you shower last?" he asks me with a smirk.

My cheeks get hot. *Do I smell?* No! Wait! "Last night, after dinner."

He lifts his chin like he's sure he's got me again this time. "And did you sleep?"

Hah! "Yes."

His smirk becomes a smile. "In your bed?"

Shoot! ". . . No."

He consults the mini-computer strapped to his wrist. "Grab a snack, Jam. I'll be back later with dinner."

"What? No!" I don't want him to come back! I don't need him to babysit me! I know Fern wouldn't tell him to do that.

He makes a shooing motion. "Then get your shoes. We'll go get something now."

"I don't need a keeper, Austin," I tell him, crossing my arms. I will *not* let him order me about like some kid who doesn't know any better.

He mimics my stance but leans closer and lowers his voice. "Last time I was here, your refrigerator was empty, and your freezer was nearly the same. When was the last time you went grocery shopping?"

That's a good question . . . "I can take care of myself!"

"I'm not saying you can't. I'm saying Fern told me you get focused on studying and forget the little necessities in life, like food, water, and sleep. I promised her I'd check in on you. This is me keeping that promise and ensuring you have the things you need to take care of yourself. So, are we going now, or will I see you later?"

I usually hitch a ride to the supermarket with one of the other girls since I don't have a car. I've figured out they all have a set day each week they take care of their shopping—all I have to do is text and ask to tag along. I was afraid of being a burden at first, but they all seem to enjoy the company. With Fern gone, I've missed all of my chances this week, though.

I roll my eyes to let him know I'm relenting under protest. This really is my best option now. "Just drop me off at the store, and I'll get a rideshare home or something." Maybe I'll find a friendly driver who will help me carry everything in. Stranger things have happened.

Austin gives me a *look*. It's almost like the anger he displayed last time he was here, but not as severe—maybe just minor annoyance. "Just get your shoes, Jam. I'm not going to make you rideshare with a bunch of groceries."

I wave him toward the couch, though he probably doesn't need an invitation to make himself at home. "I'll be right back," I say as I retreat to my room to find a clean shirt and shoes. Maybe some shorts that won't show half of my bum if I bend over too. "I need to change."

"Take your time."

"Because I'm sure you have *nothing* better to do today," I mutter. He already doesn't like me. I'm sure this isn't helping matters. Not that I *want* him to like me.

"I really don't," he says quietly.

Even my ears burn this time. "I didn't mean for you to hear that."

"I know you didn't."

"Is good hearing a genetic thing with your family?" I ask. Mason heard me practically whispering to Gabe before the wedding.

"Nope, you just weren't as quiet as you thought you were."

***

"Can I drive?" I ask Austin as we approach his beloved bright yellow Corvette. I want to ask him that every time I see it, but I've never worked up the nerve before.

"Another time," he says after a brief hesitation. "We'll head out of town so you don't have to deal with traffic."

I stop. "Seriously?" I was only joking—sort of. Yes, I want to drive it, but I didn't think there was any way he'd consider it. In my experience, guys are ridiculously protective of their cars.

He doesn't stop walking or look back. "Yeah. I figure you want to live, so you're not likely to get stupid and cause a wreck."

"You're not worried I'll graze a parked car or something? Back into another car? Hit a light post?"

He shrugs and opens the passenger side door, so I hurry to catch up. "I'm not worried about fender benders. I've got insurance."

I slide in and wait until the door is closed behind me to mutter, "You've got *money.*" The song says mo' money, mo' problems, but, near as I can tell, it's possible to reach a level of rich where there *are* no problems. Austin's family is there, but none of them act like it until they say something like that.

He stops in front of the car to get his phone. He checks the screen, swipes, and holds it up to his ear, then resumes walking.

"Yeah," he says, folding his lanky frame into the low-sitting car. "I think I'll have to pass," he says. "I'm taking Jam to run some errands."

I reach for the door handle. I'm not going to be a burden. There's no reason for him to miss out on whatever it is. I can order a pizza or something and figure out groceries tomorrow.

The voice on the other end clearly says, "Bring her along." I stop. *Gabe?* "No reason she has to be left out just because Fern isn't here. I was going to call her anyway."

"I'll call you back," Austin tells him. He hangs up before Gabe can reply.

"If something's come up, I can—"

"Gabe and Ryan decided they want to go to an escape room and get dinner."

"An escape room?" I swallow hard. Locked in a room with Austin? That might be a bad idea, even with the others to act as buffers. If he starts in on me, I might not care who is around to hear what I have to say. I won't let another man walk all over me.

"Wanna go? Ryan's treat."

It would be good to get out for a while and spend time with people instead of textbooks and stacks of print-outs. But . . . "I have a test Monday . . ."

"What's the square root of pi?"

What? "A. There isn't one, really. It's an irrational number. B. Not that kind of test; I'm pre-law, not an engineer or anything. It's a political science test."

He fires up the car and turns in his seat to watch where he's going as he backs out. "I'm sorry, if you can tell me the square root of pi off the top of your head, I think you can ace anything they throw at you. And your test is *Monday*. It's currently *Wednesday*. You can take a few hours off and still have plenty of time to study."

He does have a point. This will be good for me. I can't live with my nose in a textbook. I'm presentable enough, and I can eat later. I've made it this long. "You're right. Let's go."

The car stops. He puts it in park and shuts it off in the middle of the parking lot. "I'm sorry, could you say that again?"

"Let's go?"

Grinning, he shakes his head at me. "Nope. That first part. I didn't hear you clearly."

I narrow my eyes at him, doing my best to imitate my sister Maeve's perfect "screw you" glare. "You're right," I growl out between gritted teeth. If he gloats, I'm out. "If you're going to—"

He turns the motor over, throws it in gear, and takes off. "I should've recorded that."

"That's it! Stop the car! Let me out!"

I'm only joking, but he casually reaches down and pushes the button to lock the doors.

I stick my tongue out at him. "They were already locked."

"Just making sure." He glances my way. "We have plenty of time to get you a snack and groceries before we meet the others if we hurry. I've always heard not to grocery shop on an empty stomach, but I think maybe you should."

"What's that supposed to mean?"

"I've been to your place twice now, and your fridge was empty both times. Maybe you should over-shop."

Two visits and he thinks he knows me? "Don't tell me what to do."

"Funny, you didn't mind it at least once that I can think of."

I don't have to think about he means. I know exactly what he's referring to. My fingers tingle with that same annoying need to touch him. "Shut up."

He looks over. One side of his mouth turns up in a smirk. "Say it again. I dare you."

I cross my arms and angle my body away from him to look out the window.

"Chicken."

The word is spoken so softly, I'm not really sure I hear anything at all. Imagining it or not, I ignore it. I won't let him bait me.

Chapter 14

Austin

The others are already waiting in the lobby of a ramshackle old apartment complex that sticks out like a dandelion in the middle of the grass that is this gentrified neighborhood. I hold the door for Jamaica, then follow her in, trying to look anywhere but at her ass.

I can do this.

Damn, she looks good in those shorts.

Is she even wearing a bra?

I don't think she is.

What I wouldn't give to find out.

But I won't. I will be the perfect gentleman. We are *friends*.

I swear she was baiting me in the car.

"Sorry we're late," I tell the others while Tara and Jamaica hug hello. "We knocked out errands first."

"Errands?" Tara asks.

"Groceries," Jamaica says. "I forgot to ask to ride with one of you this week. Fern sent him by to check on me, so I figured he could make himself useful."

That's right, Jam. Just play along. The others don't have to know we can hardly make it through an hour without bickering about something. Grocery shopping with her was torture. I wanted to shove my tongue down her throat to shut her up so many times. *How can "do you need bread?" be taken the wrong way in a* grocery store?"

Ryan's smile catches my eye, reminding me that he thinks Jamaican and I have a secret. "That was nice of you, Austin."

I shrug it off like it's no big deal. Because it totally isn't. And it's definitely not what he thinks it is. "I didn't want Fern to spend her entire vacation worried no one would remember to make Jam stop and eat."

Fuck! I'm slipping. I can't believe I actually forgot about the stupid dare. I don't care about it so much anymore, not after the way Jam and I left things last time. I'm worried about her. Whatever is going on with her is more important than anything—especially the stupid dare.

"I don't need a babysitter!"

Here we go again.

"I'm sorry, who forgot to eat for nineteen hours?"

"Jam!" Tara cries.

Jamaica shrugs. "It's no big deal. I wasn't hungry."

Before anyone can push the issue, Tara's phone chimes and an older woman steps out of a room to my left. "Is one of you Ryan?"

He steps forward. "That's me."

She smiles brightly. "Is this everyone?"

"We're waiting on two more."

"Actually," Tara says distractedly while she rapidly taps on her phone screen, "I just got a message from Noel. Tris had to bow out, so Noel is going to stay in with Colt."

Ryan smiles at the woman, who eyes him up and down like a rottweiler checking out a juicy steak. "I guess this is it, then."

The woman returns his smile. "Alright, then. I'm Sharon North, and I'll be your game master today. I need everyone to turn off their cellphones and tablets. We do not allow any pictures or videos to be taken once you're inside, but we don't require you to leave your phones at the desk unless someone breaks the rules."

She continues on about the rules of the game, how we will be monitored the entire time, hints, and so on, but I stop listening. Jamaica is frowning at her phone, which is operable again because she charged it in my car.

I sidle closer to ask, "What's wrong?"

"My sister phones in the evenings when she has time to talk. I don't want to miss it . . ."

As someone who has two busy siblings, I'm confident that hers will understand. She only needs to know that she isn't being ignored. "Gimme that," I say, reaching for her phone.

She hesitates but lets me take it.

I grab her arm and pull her closer to the others. "Group photo before we go in!" We can text it to Fern and Jamaica's sister, then everyone is happy because they know Jamaica is out, having a good time, and well cared for.

We all huddle together, me on one end and Gabe on the other. He helps me hold the phone steady. I slip my arm around Jamaica's shoulder and press my cheek to hers. It's the closest we've been since that night. I swear my skin remembers hers and wants to know it better.

"Smile!" Tara says.

I'm hard in the millisecond it takes for her phone to capture the photo after I push the shutter button. *Down, boy.* This is not going to be good.

"Thank you," Jamaica says when she takes her phone back.

I shrug it off. "No problem. A picture's worth a thousand words. That should tell her all she needs to know. You can send it to Fern too, so she knows you're alright."

She smiles, then looks down at the screen to send the picture in a text, adding the caption, 'Escape room time! No phones allowed.' Then, she powers it down and pockets it. "Let's do this."

We follow the others down a hall until Sharon stops outside a door and waves us in. I push Jamaica ahead of me, more for an excuse to touch her than anything else. Hugging Fern was the most action I've had since the wedding, and thinking about it in those terms is just strange. She's *family*, and now, I feel icky, but that helps diffuse the situation in my boxers.

"Alright," Sharon says. I turn to look at her. "Good luck! Your time starts now."

Jamaica

"Your time starts now." Sharon shuts the door behind her. I hope the others are up to getting us out of here because my brain has a lot in common with a scrambled egg right now. My cheek still tingles where Austin's was pressed against it for that picture. I know he was only trying to fit into the frame. He didn't do it on purpose. He doesn't know how he made my heart pound or how I want to grab him and find somewhere a little more private and get that close to him again.

"We're never doing this again." Never mind that I can't have him again, can't find out what he can do when we have a condom, I shouldn't *want* to. Maybe he's nicer about it than Jordan was, but in some ways, he's just like him. He's controlling and demeaning. Not only do I want someone I can't have, but I also want someone who isn't good for me.

"Alright! Let's do this!" Ryan shouts, snapping me out of my pity party.

I turn in a slow circle to take in my surroundings, remembering that Sharon said any and every detail might be important later. Stepping through that door was like stepping through a portal into the past and falling into a Victorian Era sitting room. I might have the timeframe wrong, but I *think* homes in that era were notable for the elaborate wooden trim. The furniture looks right, too. My historian granny would be appalled that I can't remember.

Ryan holds up a scrap of paper and reads, "Widely regarded as the world's first computer programmer."

"Ada Lovelace," Chris says without hesitation. The quickness of his answer doesn't surprise me; there probably isn't anything about computers Chris doesn't know.

"So what, is it an anagram or something?" Tara asks.

My eyes land on the doily draped artfully over the mantle, though—the lace doily. With hearts worked into it. Love lace. *Could it really be that easy?* Biting my lip, I mentally cross my fingers and approach the fireplace. They were nice enough to include me; I want to contribute *something*.

"What're you doing?" Austin asks.

Ignoring him, I move the vase placed in the center of the doily and find another folded scrap of paper. Excitement makes my hands shake as I reach for it. "Charles Darwin."

That one is easy. I go to the bookshelf opposite the fireplace. Gabe follows me, but while I'm browsing for one of Darwin's works, he seems to be staring intently at a pair of taxidermied squirrels locked forever in a boxing match on top of the shelf. Thinking he's merely fascinated with the morbid art of the time, I continue my search and find *The Origin of the Species*. Taped to the front is another piece of paper. "Jack Broughton," I read at the same time that Gabe says, "Florence Nightingale."

We all stop and look at each other. Two clues at once? Now what?

"Uhh . . . What's going on?" Austin asks.

"Hell if I know," Chris says with a shrug.

Ryan sidles up next to Gabe and examines the squirrels locked forever in a boxing match. He scratches at the scruff on his cheeks and shrugs. "Jack Broughton is considered the father of boxing." I'm not at all surprised he knows that.

"Florence Nightingale had something to do with nursing," Tara says.

"They call her 'The Lady with the Lamp,'" I add, thinking back to my days in London. It's not a common moniker for her here.

"So, Charles Darwin took us to the book. Jack Broughton took us to the creepy squirrels. So we're on Florence Nightingale then, yeah?" Gabe asks.

Ryan shrugs. "Seems reasonable."

"Did you pick this setting?" I ask. Not that there's anything wrong with it, but it doesn't strike me as his style. *Maybe he picked it because of the squirrels?*

"Nope. Since it was spur of the moment, I told them we'd take whatever they had available."

I nod. That makes sense. "So where do we go from here?"

"The Lady with the Lamp," Austin says. I look up at him and turn my head to follow his gaze to an old oil lamp. The clue there is Thomas Edison. That sends us to a wall sconce, which sends us back to the bookshelf. We run all over the room, puzzling out what each person is notable for since our only clues after the first are names, then connecting that to something within the room. Some of them are easy, others, not so much, but we find the key with a wee bit of time to spare.

Every cell in my body buzzes with excitement born of triumph. I can hardly breath while Ryan runs to the door to unlock it. *We did it!*

Sharon is waiting for us, leaning against the wall across from the door with a wide smile. She comes into the room while we're busy congratulating each other on successfully solving the puzzles.

"That's the first time we've ever had someone go for the squirrels from the Charles Darwin clue," she tells Gabe. "And almost everyone asks for a hint on the Jack Broughton clue."

Ryan shrugs. "I had anger issues as a kid. My parents put me in boxing to work those out."

"As a kid?" Austin asks, the corners of his mouth curving up more than normal. His cheek earns him an elbow in the ribs, but Ryan grins as he does it.

"I get paid to hit people now, punk. It's a double dose of happy every day. Works wonders for anger problems."

"Exercise gives you endorphins," Tara mutters. The movies she usually quotes are a lot older than that, but I actually get this one.

"Endorphins make you happy," I say. Together, we finish it, "Happy people don't shoot their husbands."

Gabe clears his throat. "Uh . . . As the only husband here, I'm suddenly concerned for my wellbeing."

"You should be," Austin says. "She's like the perfect storm. Sleep-deprived. Emotionally unstable. Torn because she's married to you, but she desperately wants to leave so we can raise our child as a family." He puts a possessive hand on Tara's belly. She allows it, but she's also laughing too hard to do much else. Though, when she grabs his arm for support, it looks as if she's backing him up.

I happen to glance at Sharon in time to see her eyes widen comically at Austin's "confession."

"He's joking," I whisper to reassure her. These silly little games they play are much more fun when you're in the know. If you're not, they can be mildly horrifying. Like the first time I witnessed Austin provoking Gabe, claiming to be the baby's father.

"And she can't exercise," Ryan deadpans.

That part is hard on Tara, who was very active before. Since she struggles to keep food down and can't sleep, she's simply too tired to maintain her old routine.

"I'd watch it if I were you, bud," Chris says. "It's not looking good."

"I'm going to laugh so hard when the baby is born with brown hair," Ryan says, turning his teasing on Austin now.

Tara gasps for air between peals of laughter.

Austin guides her to a chair like a doting husband and helps her sit.

Gabe rolls his eyes this time since he and Tara are both blonde. "What're the odds?"

"About fifty-fifty," Austin says, unwilling to let the joke go.

"Would you stop!" Tara cries. "I'm dying over here."

"Breathe, honey!" Austin says, then mimicks the breathing exercises expectant mothers are taught. At least my sister was. I went to some of the classes with her since her boyfriend skipped when he found out about the baby. *Wonder where he learned that?*

Tara shoves his shoulder hard enough he rocks back. "Stop it!"

He looks back at Sharon and asks, "Can we get her a wheelchair?"

Gabe storms across the room, the scowl on the upper half of his face ruined by the slight smirk he can't seem to contain, and shoves Austin aside. "Come on, Princess. Lean on me. I'll save you."

Tara rolls her eyes skyward and takes his hand. "My hero!" she says in a falsetto.

Out of jokes, the others follow Sharon, who still seems a little shell shocked, out of the room. "To be honest, I thought that room would be more of a struggle for this group," she says over her shoulder. "The owner is a history fanatic and insisted on putting it together. We usually save it for other history buffs. It's the only one we had available, though."

"It's not the one I would've picked," Ryan admits, "but it was fun."

Outside, we all stop to power our phones back on. They all start beeping, singing, and-or vibrating. A text from my sister pops up on my screen.

Maeve: Who's the beefcake?

I grin and try my best not to laugh. She asks like there aren't four of them in that picture.

Jamaica: Which one?

She sends the picture back with a big red circle around Austin's face. *Of course . . .* The one beefcake I'd rather not talk about.

Jamaica: That's Austin. He's a less-practiced Jordan.

My thumb hovers over the send button. That last sentence doesn't feel fair. Austin definitely has some Jordan-like tendencies, but he also doesn't. I bite my lip and hold down on the delete button.

Jamaica: That's Austin. He's bad news.

That's better. He *is* bad news wrapped in a pretty package. He's the human equivalent of biting into a chocolate chip cookie, only to discover it's oatmeal raisin. There's nothing *wrong* with oatmeal raisin cookies, but when your mouth is watering for chocolate chip, it's a problem.

Great. Now I want a cookie.

My phone dings at me.

Maeve: Bad news how?

I tap my lip and contemplate an answer. He's not that easy to explain.

Jamaica: He's like swimming w sharks. U think ur safe. U relax. It strikes.

I'm not sure how I went from comparing him to a cookie to swimming with sharks, but both are good analogies for him.

Maeve: Ur doin it wrong. U gotta bite first.

Jamaica: Think I'll stay out of the water. He reminds me of Jordan.

The ellipsis that means she's typing pops up instantly. I cringe. She won't leave it at that. This is going to turn into a whole conversation, and this isn't the place for it.

Maeve: How?
Jamaica: Ring u later?
Maeve: Still w him?
Jamaica: Yes
Maeve: Don't forget
Jamaica: I won't

I pocket my phone and look up. The others are still huddled up, laughing about something. Chris slides over when I approach, making space for me between himself and Austin.

I step between them, keeping as much distance as I can between myself and Austin. Somehow, I bump Chris's shoulder and knock myself off balance. He quickly reaches out to steady me with a hand on my hip. "Easy there," he says.

"Sorry," I tell him. I didn't mean to crowd him; I just didn't want to stand too close to Austin and give anyone the wrong idea. I can only imagine how Austin will behave if he thinks I'm getting clingy.

"You ready?" Austin asks, a bit of a bite in his tone. I look his way to find his eyes trained on my hip, where Chris's hand rested to help me.

"Sure?" *What's up with him?*

"In a hurry to get to dinner?" Gabe asks him.

Austin blinks a couple times and turns to his friend. His usual smile appears. It should be a relief, but it doesn't suit the tense set of his shoulders. *What could he be upset about?* "Always. Where we going?"

"What sounds good to the little one, T-Bird?" Ryan asks of Tara. His eyes are fixed on her belly, a bit of a smirk quirking up one corner of his mouth.

Tara rolls her eyes. "Nothing sounds good to her. Ever."

He smiles widely. "What sounds good to you, then? If you're going to suffer for it later, you might as well enjoy it the first time around."

She steps into the circle to playfully slap at his shoulder. "That's gross!"

He shrugs. "But true."

"Raising Cane's?" she says, her voice rising at the end to make it a question. I'm excited. I've heard them mention this restaurant many times but haven't checked it out yet.

"Seconded!" Austin says quickly.

"It was already seconded," Gabe says. "She votes by proxy for the little one."

Austin grabs my shoulder. He's not hurting me, but I tense all the same. What is he thinking, touching me in public? *Relax. No one will suspect anything unless you act strange.* Chris just touched me, and no one gave it a second thought. Except for Austin.

"We'll meet you there," he tells the others before steering me towards his car. I'm too dazed to shake him off even though I planned to ask Tara if I could ride with them.

What just happened? If I didn't know any better, I'd think Austin was *jealous* of Chris for touching me. But that's ridiculous. We're not together. We barely tolerate each other.

It must be something else. Maybe he just feels responsible since he brought me, though using the word 'responsible' in any sentence directly relating to Austin is absurd.

He opens the passenger door for me, and I slide into my seat, my head still bogged down with figuring out what the heck is going on with him. I look up into his scowling face, completely at a loss as to why he's so unhappy. He closes the door, and I track him as he stalks around the car. He's still scowling when he yanks his own door open and wedges himself behind the wheel.

Chapter 15

Austin

The cashier repeats Jamaica's order and asks, "Will that be all?" I step forward, close enough that Jam's back brushes my front. The contact soothes the odd, angry feeling in my heart lingering from when Chris touched her. "I've got hers," I tell the cashier whose name tag reads Alexa. *I bet she gets sick of Alexa jokes.*

Her bored brown eyes slide from Jam's face to mine, and she blinks a few times. She smiles widely and bats her eyes at me.

In front of me, Jam stiffens. "Austin—" She turns her head to look at me—no doubt ready to argue that she can cover her dinner—but doesn't finish that thought. Her eyes drop to my lips like she's remembering another time we were this close too. *What would she do if I did it again?*

Stop thinking like that. We have an agreement. Never again. But what if she wants it too?

"My treat," I tell her. She opens her mouth but closes it and faces forward. I'm not even trying to confuse her anymore. I just want to do something nice for her. I don't want things to be awkward between us. I don't want to argue with her about things I obviously don't understand. There's a reason. I'm sure of it. But there's nothing I can do to make things right until she tells me except to not fuck up again.

That means no more plans to confuse her. No more jokes. *No more fun.* That's not true, though. The escape room was fun. *Is it worth it if I can't be myself?*

It would be easy to flirt with Alexa. She's pretty enough and on the right side of legal. Any other time it would be my automatic response to that coy smile just for the fun of it. But Jam's reaction just now . . . Flirting with this pretty girl would only make things worse between us, even though there's nothing there but one night and a promise.

"And what will you have?" Alexa asks, distracting me from overanalyzing the stiff set of Jam's shoulders and the determined way she's ignoring me now.

I give her my order and my credit card. "Why don't you go grab a table?" I ask Jam. This place is filling up fast, and the others aren't here yet. If one of us doesn't go now, we might not have a place to sit. Not that any of us would mind eating in the parking lot off the hood of a car like we used to on weekends when we were younger, and Ryan got his first car.

"Sure," she mutters, quickly edging away from me and hurries off.

The cashier hands my credit card back along with our cups, and I move aside to wait for our food. It takes real effort to keep my eyes forward and not turn to look for Jamaica.

Food in hand, I wade through the packed dining area to the far corner where Jamaica has two tables pulled together. Instead of sitting next to her, I take the chair across from her and push the tray between us. "I'll get drinks," I tell her when she reaches for the cups.

"Water, please," she says with a grateful nod, her eyes darting around the room behind me. I hate sitting with my back to a crowd, but not enough to give in and sit next to her. I'm not sure I can behave myself. The more time I spend with her, the worse it gets.

She hasn't touched anything on the tray when I return, so I grab my basket and push the other closer to her. Ryan, Chris, Tara, and Gabe all approach the table at once. I busy myself with tearing my chicken strips in half to cool so I don't snarl at one of the guys for getting too close to Jamaica. I don't know what the hell my problem is. I have no claim on her. But *fuck!* I hated seeing Chris's hand on her. It's not like he was even staking a claim. He was helping her, and I lost my shit. *What is wrong with me?*

The answer to that question scares me. What if my problem is that I *can't* have her? Like I only want the thing I can't have? That could be sex in general, though . . . Not necessarily with her. *A few more weeks.*

Tara takes the chair next to me. I fight to keep my face from betraying my disappointment. I should've expected it, though. It's easier for her to get to the bathroom from this side of the table.

Ryan drops into the seat next to Jamaica and smiles at me before he turns it to her. *You motherfucker!* Now *he's* baiting me. "I'm glad you came. Did you have fun?"

Her answering smile is a punch in the gut. She never smiles at me like that anymore. "Yes, thank you so much. It was nice to get out for a bit."

Tara nudges me with her elbow until I look her way. "Are you alright?" she asks softly.

I try to smile, but it doesn't feel right. "I'm fine."

Her eyebrows twitch upward. "You don't seem fine."

"I've just got a lot on my mind today," I tell her.

She frowns a little, her eyes searching my face then cutting across the table. One corner of her mouth lifts into a grin. "Well, if you need to talk . . ."

I grab her hand from where it rests on the table between us and kiss the back of it. "Thanks, T."

I don't need to talk. I need Jamaica to like me again because I want to be the reason for that smile. I don't know what to do to make that happen, though.

Jamaica

"You don't have to walk me up," I tell Austin on my way to the stairs. Having him behind me is making me twitchy. Maybe it's all in my head, but I swear he's close enough I can feel the heat radiating off him. Close enough that if I stop, he'll run over me. Hovering, like he did while I was unlocking the front door. Like he did at the register at dinner.

"Never let it be said that I'm not a gentleman," he says. It lacks the usual lightheartedness, though. Instead, it sounds more like the growl I heard at the river when he was definitely *not* a gentleman.

My heart races. Every nerve ending becomes hyper-aware. I can't think about that night with him so close. I'll do something stupid, and he'll have more ammunition. It's impossible to think of anything else, though. My head is consumed by memories of his hands, lips, tongue, and teeth on my skin.

"Jamaica?"

I blink my way out of the past to find myself stopped in front of my door.

"What's wrong?"

"Nothing!" I say too quickly. My voice is high-pitched and tight to my own ears. There's no way it's convincing him of anything.

"You're breathing like a winded racehorse, and you've been staring at that door for like, two minutes now. What's wrong?"

I quickly fit the key into the lock and wrench it around. "Nothing at all. Thanks for this. It was nice to get out." I open the door and nearly run inside without looking back, pushing the door closed behind me. Instead of slamming shut, there's a dull *thud.* He grabs my wrist, stopping me.

Yes! Pull me close. Touch me again.

"Jam? Calm down. What's wrong?"

My body throbs in time with my heartbeat. "Nothing's wrong," I repeat. *Nothing a few minutes alone in my room won't fix.* "What's wrong with you?" Maybe I can distract him by turning this around on him. He was acting oddly outside the escape room. And at dinner, come to think of it. He was quiet and standoffish. He barely interacted with our friends, and he wouldn't look at me.

He sucks in a deep breath and slowly lets it out. He releases my wrist and slips his arm around my waist. Holding me tight, he steps forward to press his body to mine. *So warm.* I don't keep it cold in my apartment, but his warmth is so welcoming. I'd love to snuggle closer and bask in it all night, but that can't happen. We have an agreement. And it obviously didn't fix anything the first time.

He grabs my hips in both hands and pulls me even tighter to him, letting me feel his hard length pressing into my belly like the most tempting invitation in the world.

A moan slips my control. It's not fair of him to tease me like that. The last time I saw that dick, I didn't get to do what I wanted with it, and he told me I'd never see it again.

Maybe we can alter our agreement. Last time wasn't proper sex, and that is what we agreed to, after all . . .

Austin lowers his mouth to my ear. He's breathing as heavily as I am. Each breath sends a wave of desire crashing through me, leaving me shaking with need. "I think we have the same answer to that question." His voice is low and gritty in my ear, just like it was that night. I shiver and fight back a moan.

"But you said—"

"I know what I said, but we weren't supposed to want this again. You drive me fucking crazy, Jamaica. The little head wants to do all the thinking when you're around, and, right now, I'm going to let it unless you tell me to stop."

I open my mouth, but no sound comes out. I don't *want* him to stop. I should. It's not smart. He hasn't exactly kept his promise to never mention that night again, but he hasn't publicly humiliated me for it, either. That gives me the confidence I need to make another leap with him.

Teeth scrape my neck, just below my ear. My knees buckle, but Austin doesn't let me fall.

"You want me too, baby?"

"Mmmm." I can't think straight with his lips brushing my ear.

His lips withdraw. "Say it."

His hold on me loosens. He backs up half a step, threatening to take away what I want again.

"Yes! I want you!" *No turning back now.*

"Good." He nips at my ear and shards of bliss cut paths through my body. It'll hurt tomorrow, but tonight, it feels divine. "Give me your key, go to your room, get naked, and wait for me on your bed. I'll be right back, and I won't mind if you start without me as long as you don't finish until I'm there for it."

I shudder, imagining touching myself while I wait for him—the look on his face when he comes in. Those eyes focused on my body while I work myself. Maybe he'll smile just for me. It's so . . . lewd. But so hot.

"Don't tell me what to do," I say, not because I don't intend to do just that, but because antagonizing him is so much fun. And I don't want him to know how much I want him.

"Shut up, Jamaica. I want you naked when I get back, or someone will have to wait for an orgasm, and that someone isn't me."

He's barely touched me, and I want him so much I'm about to come from his words alone.

His grip on my hips eases. He takes my keys from my hand and gently pushes me toward my room. "I'll be right back. I've got condoms in the car."

Condoms. Yes. Good. At least we won't have that problem this time. Maybe, just maybe, his theory about getting this out of our systems will work this time. The door closes behind me, jolting me into motion. I have more than enough time, but I don't want to risk it. He won't leave me wanting, I'm sure, but I have no doubt he'll keep me waiting. He's bossy, and I'd be lying if I said I hate it.

Chapter 16

Austin

I lock the door behind me, drop her keys and stick the ribbon of condoms between my teeth so I don't lose them, all while trying to control my breathing so I'm not panting like an over-excited schoolboy about to see his first pair of breasts in the real world. Impatiently, I toe off my shoes. My shirt hits the floor in the hallway. Her bedroom door is just barely open, blocking my view of her bed. I pause because, as fun as it would be to make her wait for her release, I don't want to. If I have to do that, I'm missing out, too. I've waited too long to feel her come on my dick.

I shouldn't be doing this. We had an agreement.

She wants this too. I'm not manipulating her. I didn't coerce her. I offered, she accepted. There's nothing wrong with this.

"Ready or not, Jamaica." I'm ready. It's been a long, *long* time. For me, anyway. Mason would laugh at me for whining about going without for seven weeks. Under different circumstances, I'm confident I could go longer. I do it more than they know. A lot of my so-called reputation is carefully crafted to make them think I'm happy. But with Jamaica occupying my every thought and wandering in and out of my life like a wet dream . . . My control is shot.

I unbutton my shorts and push the door open with my toe. My eyes fall on her naturally when the door opens, like I'm sure she knew they would. She picked her placement strategically, waiting at the foot of her bed, feet on the floor, legs splayed wide, and not a stitch of clothing to cover her beautiful brown skin. She even turned the light on.

The condoms slip from between my teeth, but I snag them out of the air without taking my eyes off her.

We lock eyes for a fraction of a second. I could look at her eyes all day, but I'll probably never get the opportunity to watch her touch herself again, so my gaze strays to her hands on her tits. They barely fill my palm, but that's alright by me. If they were any bigger, she wouldn't run around without a bra on, and I love to watch her tits sway when she walks. It's a fair trade, even if she disagrees. She smiles in my peripheral vision and slides one hand down her abdomen. Two fingers slide over her clit, then disappear inside her, exactly where I'm dying to be. My dick twitches, urging me closer.

I didn't think she'd do it. I wouldn't call her a prude. We got each other off behind a tree at my brother's wedding reception. That was a heat of the moment thing, though. This was pre-meditated. Calculated on her part.

Swallowing hard, I finish unzipping my pants and shove them off my hips, taking my boxers with them. I could stand here all night and watch her pleasure herself, but my dick has other ideas, and I did promise to let him do the thinking.

"You're fucking gorgeous." It's a good thing I don't need my eyes to open a condom or to put it on because I can't peel them off of her.

"You gonna stand there, or are you gonna come play, too?" *The invitation I didn't know I was waiting for.* She's had plenty of time to change her mind. Yeah, she's sitting here, finger fucking herself while I watch, but even the little head is smart enough to wait for permission to touch.

Grinning, I take a step closer. Then another. She doesn't move. "I'll watch you later. You can play with yourself while I rest. Give me a show to inspire me for the next round." Her cheeks darken and those long legs I've fantasized about wrapping around my head inch closed.

I cross the scant distance between us and kiss her, parting her lips with my tongue while I push her onto her back. She's already invited me to play, so I position myself over her and wrap her legs around my waist. I'll have her heels on my shoulders later, but that might push her boundaries, so we'll work up to that. This time, we have light, a bed, condoms, and all night. "Don't be shy around me. Take what you want, because I promise I'll do the same. If you're not getting what you want—what you need—

out of sex, you're doing it wrong. Or I am, and if that's the case, you better tell me so I can fix it. I'm an overachiever in the bedroom."

Her lips twitch, but she wins the fight with a smile and tries to hide that the battle ever happened with a roll of her eyes. "Shut up and fuck me, Austin."

Why is that so hot? The only time she cusses is when she's mad or telling me to fuck her. I can analyze later, though.

I know she's wet for me. I can smell it. Anticipation makes me breathless. I didn't get to feel her last time, but I know she'll be amazing. I line up and ease in just a bit, then give her what she wants in one quick thrust.

So tight. I suck a breath between my teeth and freeze, afraid to move again until I'm sure I'm in control. She feels too good, and it would be too easy to give in and go too fast. She cries out. Her arms wind around my neck, and she clings to me tightly, pressing her chest to mine.

"Don't stop," she breathes in my ear. "Oh, God. Don't stop."

"Gimme a second." I just started, and she feels so much better than I imagined. I just need a moment to get ahold of myself. Why would I stop? *Unless . . .* "Jam . . . Did that hurt?"

"Good hurt," she whispers. "Shut up and fuck me."

"Remember to tell me if that changes." I don't mind playing rough, but it should never *hurt*. I know some people are into that, but I'm not one of them. And I don't think I could be with someone who is. Intentionally hurting someone doesn't do it for me.

I'm still too close. I don't want her to get the wrong idea and think I can talk a big game but not deliver, so I set an easy pace. She makes the sexiest little whimpering noises with each stroke, clinging to me tighter and tighter.

"Let go," I tell her, reaching for one of her arms.

She shakes her head and holds tighter still.

"Jam. Let go."

She shakes her head. "So close."

Just like that? I groan and will myself not to move. I guess this *is* a big step up from rubbing herself off on my dick against a tree, but this is just a warm-up. "Let go."

She ignores me, so I pull out. "You want that back, you listen."

"Shut up and fuck me." Her arms fall away, though.

I shudder. Yes, those words from her lips do things to me, but I'm here to give her the best orgasms she's ever had in her life. That's what I do. She can do this boring shit when she's married to some dull minute man who doesn't care if he can make her come so hard she gets dizzy, so long as he gets what he wants and can get back to his day.

Stop it. I'm not thinking of someone else putting their hands on her while I'm with her. I grab her waist and push her up the bed to make more room for me. Kneeling over her, I anchor her heels to my shoulders and thrust in again, easily bottoming out at this angle. My fingers tighten around her ankles like I can hold myself back by holding onto her. I will *not* go before she does, but *fuck* . . . She feels amazing.

"Oh, my God!" she cries. "Austin!"

"Good. That's what I want to hear." I slip out all the way and take her again. Sheer force of will is the only thing that keeps me from blowing my load. *Not. Yet.* "Tell me how good it feels."

"So deep," she gasps. "Good hurt."

"Good." That's what I needed to know. I stop holding back and show her what she was missing out on before when she didn't want to let me go. She gets tighter and tighter, and I expect each stroke to be the one to send her over the edge—to send *me* over, no matter how hard I'm fighting against it. Still, she holds it back. Any other time I wouldn't mind, but I *need* her to come so I can. "Come for me, baby. Let me feel you."

She shakes her head. "Too good. Don't stop."

"Jam," I say, making her name a warning. I'm only a man. I can't hold on forever. "Get yours so I can get mine. Then, we'll do it again. And again. I'll fuck you so many times you can't walk tomorrow if that's what you want. But you've gotta come for me, baby."

She screams wordlessly as she comes undone around me. The pulsing of the walls cradling me pushes me into mine, and we have one of those rare instances where we come together. I let her legs down and push myself as deep into her as I can get, letting her ride her orgasm out and work herself down, and enjoying every second of it.

"Oh, my God," she gasps again.

I fall over next to her and pull her into my arms. "You're beautiful when you come," I whisper. *What the* hell *am I doing?* I don't do the pillow-talk, sweet-nothings bullshit. I don't make love. I fuck. My tongue has a mind of its own, though. "You're always beautiful, but God, when you come . . ."

I prop myself up on one elbow to see her better. "Absolutely gorgeous," I whisper again. I drop a kiss on her shoulder and roll out of bed to take care of the condom before I can say any more stupid shit.

Chapter 17

Austin

I find the ribbon of unused condoms I dropped on the floor and move it to the nightstand, tearing off a fresh one so it's close for our next round.

She watches me climb back into bed, her eyes roaming over my abs, occasionally dipping down to my dick for a second before snapping upward again. I try to fight a smile and lose. She's shy about looking at me after the things we've done to each other?

I stop and sit back on my heels, posing for her. "It's okay, you can look," I tell her.

She hides her face behind her hands. "You caught me."

Laughing, I grab her wrists and move them. "So why are you hiding? Look. I don't care. I look at you. I don't care if you know. And, let me tell you, I like what I see."

She rolls her eyes and moves her arms to hide her chest. "Yeah, right."

Sighing, I curse myself for that stupid joke. *Would she still doubt me if I never said it?* I grab her wrists again, careful not to hurt her, and pull them away so I can suck a nipple into my mouth, melting her resistance. I swirl my tongue around the little bud, enjoying the way it stiffens for me. She moans beneath me, and I feel the vibrations where we're joined. I don't want one boob to feel left out, so I switch sides.

"Your tits drive me crazy," I tell her. Predicting her argument, I cut it off at the pass, "I love it when you don't wear a bra. It just kills me knowing how easy it would be to get one in my mouth. Just pull your shirt up and . . ." I open my mouth wide and take in as much of her tit as I can like I teased her about last time we did this. Only I was serious.

She moans again and arches her back for me. "Tell me something," she says lazily.

"Hmm?" Until I have to speak it's not worth stopping. There might be a lot of time left on the clock, but it's ticking.

"What was up with you tonight before dinner?"

"Dunno what you're talking about," I lie. I slide down the bed and spread her legs, hoping like hell to distract her by putting my tongue to better use than talking.

She slips her fingers into my hair and pulls, fighting to stop me. I could win this fight, but I let her have her way, even knowing it'll cost me. "When Chris grabbed me to help me get my balance."

"Nothing." We're *not* talking about what came over me then. I had no right, and it won't happen again. It doesn't need to be discussed. I'm blaming lack of sex and seeing him touching what I couldn't. It was a fluke. It'll never happen again. "Just a stray thought about work." The lie is bitter on my tongue. I free myself from her hold and lick the length of her slit to replace the taste with something much better.

She gasps and seemingly forgets our not-discussion because she stops talking. *Mission accomplished.* She whispers my name and slides her fingers into my hair again, scratching my scalp. It's as far from an erogenous zone as can be, but damn, I'm hard again.

"Austin! Oh!" She gasps and wiggles out of my reach, but I follow her and grab her hips so she can't run away again. "Too much!" she cries.

"Take it," I growl, ignoring the blood rushing to fill my dick and the urge to drive into her again. *Soon.* "Don't fight it."

She thrashes her head and bucks her hips but stops struggling to escape.

"Good." I suck the pulsing bud of her clit into my mouth and tease it with my teeth. She unravels beneath me again much faster than I expected. *So fucking responsive.* Or maybe, I'm just that good. "You needed that, didn't you? You wanted my mouth."

"Yes," she whispers breathlessly.

"Good." I kiss my way up her body to nibble at her bottom lip. "I miss yours. I've dreamt about it." They weren't nice dreams at first. I dreamt of hurting her—of her passing out because she couldn't breathe. That didn't stop until I let myself remember every little detail of that encounter and understood that she never tried to stop me. She urged me on. She knew what she was doing.

"You're in luck." Her voice is a sultry purr that sends shivers down my spine. It's much different than her growled orders to shut up and fuck her. I like both, though. "Me and my mouth are right here, and I think we owe you one."

"I don't want to hurt you," I whisper. God yes, I want her mouth again, but not if it'll cause her pain. That's too high a price.

"You didn't hurt me, Austin."

"I know I didn't, but what if—"

She kisses me to cut me off. "Shut up, Austin, and let me blow your mind."

God yes. She's a grown woman. She knows what she's doing. And I can always stop if I think she's hurting . . . "Please."

She pushes at my shoulders, so I "let" her roll me over. She straddles me first and rubs her pussy on my dick again, making herself shiver, and I groan for want of her tight, wet heat.

"I'm not done with you yet," I promise her.

"No talking," she says.

I want her lips on my dick more than I want my next breath, so I close my mouth. She eases her way down my body, doing as I did and kissing random places until she gets to my abs. Grinning, she locks eyes with me and traces each one with her tongue. The muscles involuntarily flex like they're just dying to show off for her. No one's ever had the patience to do that before. Sure, girls touch and fawn over my body—that's the best reason to dedicate the time I do—but no one ever devotes the time that Jam is. The rest of me is just . . . the opening act. Others are just here for the D.

"Like that, do you?" She said no talking, but I can't resist asking. I want to know everything that turns her on. I want to know what makes her tick. *But why? I shouldn't care.*

"Mmhmm," she hums without stopping.

"I do, too," I tell her, enjoying the buildup to the moment I feel the wet heat of her mouth wrapped around me and she swallows me down. She can tease me as long as she wants, though. For tonight, my body is her playground. And hers is mine. The clock might be ticking, but there's no rushing perfection.

She moves down and licks around the base of my dick. Then stops. "Just like last time?"

Moonlit memories of her lips wrapped around the base of my dick stream through my head, making me so hard it hurts.

"Can I?" She might've known what she was getting herself into then, but that doesn't mean she enjoyed it. How could she? She was *crying* about it.

"Sure. Come with me." She gets off the bed and moves to an empty spot on the wall. She turns her back to it and kneels in front of it.

"What are you doing?"

"The wall gives us both something to brace against," she says. "I don't have to hold onto you to keep myself close enough, and you don't have to worry about keeping yourself upright."

I guess that makes sense. I roll off the bed and stand in front of her, letting her move me where she wants me with her hands on my hips. "You do this a lot?"

Something in her eyes changes, like a door slamming shut. "Let's just say I discovered this method through trial and error."

I want to ask questions, but I'm smart enough to know that's the end of the discussion. If this is how she wants to do it, so be it. I'm the one who gets to put my dick in her mouth. I'm not going to push her for answers.

"Give me that dick," she says in that purr from earlier. "I know you want to. Give me all you got, baby. Fuck my face."

Oh. My. God. Jamaica's got dirty talk. I love it. "Jesus, I'm going to come before I pass your lips if you keep doing that."

She grabs my ass and opens her mouth wide. I hold my breath until her lips are wrapped around me again, surrounding the head of my cock with my other favorite hot wetness. "Oh, fuck," I whisper, reaching to tangle my fingers in her hair because I *need* to touch her.

I don't move unless she guides me, giving her time to adjust. She moves her lips up and down my shaft, taking a little more each time until I feel the back of her throat. I suck in a breath and fight the urge to move. She squeezes my ass and makes eye contact, humming to let me know she's ready. My dreams didn't disappoint. Her mouth is as good as I remember.

As good as it feels—as much as I want to do this again—I'm scared. She *cried* last time.

"Baby . . ." I hesitate, unsure of how to word what I want to tell her. She sucks until her cheeks hollow out, silencing my fears.

"Jam!" I tip my head back and groan, holding onto control by a thread. "Please, don't let me hurt you," I whisper, sliding my fingers deeper into her lovely curls.

Jamaica slaps my ass, a clear order to get on with it. *Well, alright then.* If that's the way it's going to be . . . She squeezes with both hands and pulls me in deeper, then sucks hard again. My grasp on my control slips. I give myself over to my baser instincts again. *I warned her.*

My toes curl. Every muscle in my body tightens. Somehow, she sucks harder still. I feel her moans more than I hear them because the sound is lost to the rushing in my ears. I look down to watch myself pumping in and out, loving the way her lips look wrapped around me, but the tears rolling down her cheeks slice through the haze of pleasure.

I freeze. I'm so close to coming that stopping is torture, but it's not worth it to hurt her. There's no enjoyment in it for me if she's miserable.

She narrows her eyes at me and squeezes my ass, digging her nails in.

"Fuck! Jam! I don't want to hurt you. Let me go."

She takes a deep breath through her nose and takes over. One hand releases my ass, and she cups my balls.

"Jam!" *Fuck that's good.*

She squeezes, and I bust so hard the world tilts. She brings her other hand to my shaft and works it up and down while she sucks the crown, swirling her tongue around and around until I've given her all I've got.

I'm quickly sinking into the warm, fuzzy, post-orgasm coma. Two good ones in a row will do that. And I get why she had me stand where she did now because I'm holding up the wall with my head—the one on my shoulders. It's time for a nap, then another go or two.

Jamaica smacks my ass. Hard.

"Ow!" I stumble back a few steps to get out of range before she can do it again. "What was that for?"

She stands up and scowls at me. "For stopping, you idiot!"

"What?"

"You were almost there and, you *stopped!*"

How am I in trouble for trying to be nice? "I was afraid you were hurting."

Her face softens. "You'll know if I'm hurting, Austin."

The urge to kiss her grabs hold of my limbs. She's in my arms before I'm conscious of making the decision to follow through. Her soft lips mold to mine in a simple kiss—no tongue, no teeth, no heat. Still, my dick twitches to life again. *Is this woman a living little blue pill?*

Jamaica moans. One long leg wraps around my hip. "How?" she whispers.

"How what?"

"How do I still want more?"

I smile, relieved to know I'm not the only one. "I'm just that good, baby. You're welcome."

I brace for a shove, a playful slap, her to let go and withdraw behind the barricade she hides behind.

Her eyebrows arch. "*You're* welcome," she says. She grabs my face and pulls me to her for another kiss.

"Slow down, baby. We've got all night. Let's take a break, get a drink."

"Shut up and fuck me, Austin."

Well, when you put it that way. "Yes, ma'am."

Jamaica

Bzzzt . . . Bzzzt . . .

My phone rattling on my nightstand wakes me from a dead sleep. I sit bolt upright and reach for it. The arms wrapped around me adjust. Austin sighs but sleeps on.

"Hello," I answer as quietly as I can.

"You forgot to ring me," my sister pouts in my ear. "Were you *sleeping?* It's only ten o'clock!"

"Sorry. Got busy and forgot, then dozed off." All of it is true enough. I could barely keep my eyes open after Austin was finished making me come a third time.

Austin stirs. "Who's that?" he asks, though I'm not sure he's truly awake.

"Who's *that?*" Maeve asks. "Please tell me it's the bad news beefcake."

I pinch the bridge of my nose. I don't mind talking to Maeve about this, but not right *now*. "Shouldn't you *not* want it to be?" I ask her. "Hold that thought." I mute my end of the phone and try to slip away, but Austin holds me tight.

"Nuh-uh," he groans. "Stay."

It's tempting to tell Maeve to ring back tomorrow and curl up in his arms again, but I did promise to talk to her tonight. "I'll be back. I need to talk to my sister."

"Am I the bad news beefcake?" he asks. He cracks one eye open and watches me in the light streaming in from the hallway.

"Eavesdropper. Let me go talk to her."

He puts on the cutest little pout. "Only if you promise to hurry back. You're still mine for a few more hours. I operate on Pacific Time."

It takes a second to puzzle out what he means. Pacific Time means it's only eight o'clock. The day is far from over, and so is our apparent one-day lapse in judgment. "I promise."

He halfway sits up to nibble at my breast.

"Oh, my God," I hiss.

"Just making sure you have plenty of incentive." He lightly swats my ass. "I'll be waiting."

Damnit, Maeve. Her timing couldn't be worse. I should probably thank her, though. If she hadn't called, we might've slept our remaining time away.

I run out to the front room and snatch up my blanket from the couch. Without Austin beside me, I'm chilly. "Alright, I'm here," I tell Maeve once I'm wrapped up.

"So . . . Did you do the dirty with the bad news beefcake?"

I fight a smile. *Did I ever* . . . "And what if I did?" I ask, unwilling to confirm or deny anything at this juncture. She'll see right through me, but she'll answer my question.

She cackles in my ear. "Heck, yes! Get you some of that!"

"Shouldn't you want me to stay *away* from—"

"Just because Jordan was an abusive twatwaffle doesn't mean every man in the world is, Jam."

I lower my voice to a whisper in case Austin's ears are as good as his brother's. "I know that, Maeve, but I have horrible taste in men. Chances are, this one is just as bad."

"That doesn't mean you can't play hump me dump me with him."

"Excuse me?"

She clears her throat and affects a horrible London accent to sound prim and proper like she's done since we were kids. "It's only sex, Jamaica. You don't have to have a relationship with him."

And that careless attitude is how you got Shila. I love my little sister and my niece, but Maeve was not ready to be a mother. "It's hard to do the casual hookup thing when he's your best friend's brother-in-law, and you see him regularly."

"I'd think that would make it easier. He's easy to find when you want a piece."

"That's not how I define a casual hookup, Mae." By my definition, you never see them until you dial-a-dick.

"So, what are you doing with him now then?"

What am *I doing?* "I don't know," I sigh. "I think . . . Maybe . . . I was wrong about him."

"You think?"

"I don't know, Mae." I check over my shoulder to make sure Austin hasn't wandered out of my room. "At times, he reminds me so much of Jordan, but at others, he doesn't."

"Wait, so you actually *like* him? Not just his dick?"

I hesitate. There's no point in denying, though. She's our father's daughter, too. She knows the answer to that question already. "I did."

"But?"

I hold back a sigh. "It's complicated."

"So uncomplicate it."

"Come on, Maeve. You know it's not that easy after—"

"There shouldn't be an *after Jordan* version of you, Jamaica. You can't live your life comparing every man you meet to him. He's the exception, not the rule."

"Listen to you, sounding so smart." Too bad she's wrong. I *have* to live my life comparing every man to him, or I'll be stupid enough to fall for another abusive . . . twatwaffle. They seem to be my type. But Austin . . . maybe isn't that way. He was so close tonight, and he stopped because he thought I was in pain. Who *does* that?

"Jam . . . You never know unless you try. Does he know about—"

"No!" No one here knows everything about Jordan.

"Would him knowing uncomplicate things?"

I worry at my lip for a second, thinking it over. It might. But he might treat me differently in a way I don't like then. I don't want his pity; I want him to understand why the things he says hurt me. But it's not fair of me to assume how he'll react. "Maybe . . ." I admit. That's not the only reason this is complicated, but it might fix one of our problems.

The other can't be fixed, though. No matter how hard I try. Austin and I will never be together. But getting along is an improvement.

"You can't build anything with secrets, Jam," she says softly. "Not secrets like yours. They undermine everything."

"I'll try," I say softly enough she won't hear the pain in my voice.

"Good. Now, go get you some more beefcake. But I need the details tomorrow. It's been a long time . . ."

"I thought Ty was back?" He panicked when she found out she was pregnant. But he did some soul searching and begged her forgiveness.

"Oh, he is. Shila don't sleep. Hard to keep the mood when the baby is a whole mood herself."

I grin because there's a phone and a thousand miles between us. She isn't here to know that I'm holding back a laugh. "It won't last forever."

"No, neither will the beefcake waiting for you if you don't get back to him." She hangs up on me. Neither of us cares for good-byes.

I toss my phone onto the couch so it can't bother me again and go back to my bed.

I stop in the doorway to listen. The steady *whoosh* of his deep breathing fills the room, along with the occasional little purr of a snore. It's kind of cute. *Maybe I should let him sleep.*

"Austin?" I whisper so I can say I tried if he pouts later. No surprise, he doesn't answer.

Taking care not to wake him, I climb back into bed. I'd love to cuddle up next to him and absorb his warmth. Maybe he'd wrap his arms around me again. I can pretend, just for tonight, that things are different.

But I don't. It might wake him.

His breathing changes. He rolls and reaches for me. "Jam?" he asks, his voice rough with the haze of sleep.

Austin works one hand under me to pull me to his chest.

"Shh, go back to sleep." I run my fingers through his hair to lull him back to sleep.

"Sleep later. You now." He rolls onto his back, pulling me on top of him. "You're better than sleep."

"Wait." I grab his hands to stall him. "I want to talk about the party."

He blinks at me, then his eyes go wide. "Oh, God. One last time before we're fighting again, please?"

"Austin . . ."

He sits up so we're eye to eye. His fingers slip out of mine, and his hands cup my face. "Look, I'm sorry, okay? I don't know *exactly* why what I said upset you, but that was not my intention. I just wanted to see you smile and make you laugh. Can you ever forgive me?"

"Seriously?" I think back on that night. I never did explain. And he did try to apologize. All this time I've been so mad, and he had no idea why or how he kept making it worse. He was just . . . being himself, and I hated him for it. It's as much my fault as it is his. I squeeze my eyes shut so I don't tear up. *Things could've been so different.*

"Yes. It was only a joke. Clearly, we weren't close enough for such a thing. I was out of line. I never meant to hurt you. I would never intentionally hurt you, Jam."

"Accepted," I whisper so he won't hear how my voice shakes with barely restrained tears. I'm so disappointed with this whole situation—with *myself* for letting my past control me like that. Because he's right. Even though I was teased about my chest in high school, there was a time when I would've smiled and laughed at his joke because I would've recognized it for what it was instead of assuming he was another horrible person.

"And I—Wait. What?"

"Apology accepted. I'm sorry I got so defensive and wouldn't hear you out. You tried to apologize, but I was too hurt to listen."

"Accepted, but . . . Just like that?"

"Just like that. Shut up and fuck me. Unless you'd rather stay mad?"

"I dunno, the hate sex was fire . . ." He grins at me. "Water under the bridge. Now, come have a seat on my face."

Chapter 18

Austin

*G*rumbling, I paw at my watch to get it to stop its incessant buzzing before it wakes the woman in my arms. *Why the* fuck *did I set the alarm?* She sighs in her sleep and rolls over, resting her head on my chest.

Why didn't I leave? I never stay with a girl. Hair tickles my nose. I reach to move it, and my fingers encounter curls that trigger a flood of memories from last night.

Jamaica.

That's why. She fell asleep after riding me to another orgasm, and I wasn't in a hurry to get away from her. Last night was amazing.

Fuck. It's Thursday. I have to work. Mason is gone. I have to pick up the slack like I promised him I would. I can't call in today. No matter how badly I don't want to leave this bed.

Just a few more minutes. I'll do my workout after work. I can lay here a bit longer and listen to her breathe, enjoy her skin on mine. There's nothing wrong with that.

The steady rhythm of her breathing pulls me under again.

***

"Austin?" Jamaica grabs my shoulder and shakes me.

I grunt to let her know I'm listening. Sort of. It's too early for this shit. Unless she's waking me for another go. It's never too early for that.

"Your alarm . . ."

My alarm? What about it? I shut it off already. Fuck! I sit up and stop the second alarm on my watch. The one that means I have forty-five minutes to end my workout, shower, get dressed, and get my ass to work.

"Sorry," I tell her, wincing because I'm a jackass for dozing off.

"S'okay," she says, stretching and yawning.

I look over in time to enjoy a peek at her naked torso in the morning light streaming through a gap in the curtains before she pulls the blankets up to her chin. My morning wood isn't such an involuntary response anymore. It's not even a suggestion—it's a full-on demand.

I don't know about her, but an orgasm would make me a lot happier about being awake. Maybe that isn't outside the realm of possibility since we apologized. Or, perhaps we can set reality aside for another fifteen minutes of mutual gratification before we get back to the real world—the one where this never happened.

I don't like that world. And I really don't want to leave this bed or the sexy, naked woman who owns it. But first things first.

I roll out of bed and stumble to the bathroom to answer nature's call. There's time to suspend reality after.

There's a metallic clatter in the kitchen while I'm washing my hands. "Darn it!" Jamaica's sleepy voice filters through the closed door. *So much for that plan.* I can maybe coax her back to bed, though. *How do I still want more of her?* Last night should've completely satisfied this urge to be with her. But it didn't.

I go back to her bedroom and pull on my shorts so I can go investigate. "What's wrong?" I ask, rounding the corner. The problem is immediately obvious from the coffee grounds liberally coating the tile floor.

Her eyes don't leave the mess in front of her. She brings a hand up and presses it to her forehead. "I dropped the can," she whines.

I bite my lip to hold back a laugh. She looks so cute standing there in a shirt that's big enough to be mine with her curls all wild, pouting at the floor like it just told her that her birthday was canceled. *I can fix this easily enough.* "Where's your broom?"

She points over my shoulder. I turn to find a door I hadn't noticed during my previous visits. I open it and grab her broom and start sweeping. "Go get dressed," I tell her while I work even though that's the last thing I want. I'd prefer her naked, wet, and waiting again. But at least I'll still be with her. "I'll take you to get your fix."

If she's that sad about spilled coffee grounds, she must be one of those people who cannot function until they've had sufficient amounts of caffeine.

"Really?" she asks. I glance up to find her watching me with wide, hopeful eyes.

"Really. I have time." *I'll make time.* I'll work through lunch to make up for it if I'm late. It's worth it for the smile she gives me before she leaves the kitchen.

Jamaica

Austin's Corvette rolls to a smooth stop as close to the campus library as he can get me from the parking lot. Shifting into park, he smiles at me. "Have a nice day."

I smile back and hold up my steaming cup of coffee. "I will now. Thanks for this. And thanks for the ride."

His smile takes on an edge that makes my heart hammer against my ribs. "Anytime."

I fumble for the door handle and climb out of the car before I can do something stupid, like straddle him right here on campus. "Have a good day, and thanks again," I tell him while I gather my bag.

He winks at me as I shut the door between us and laughs before he drives away. *Maybe I should've taken the bus instead of asking him to drop me off*. . . I've seen that smile before. Just last night, in fact, while he—No. I can't think about that right now. I turn around and walk away, straight to the library, where I can study in peace.

I have class in an hour. If I let myself dwell on last night now, I'll never be able to focus. My education—my *future*—is too important for me to let another guy distract me. *Priorities, darn it! Degrees before dicks.*

I claim a table and unpack my backpack, but the little bag of coffee grounds he bought to last me until I get to the store again redirects my thoughts to Austin again. *So much for focusing.*

He was so sweet this morning, cleaning up the mess I made and offering to take me for coffee. He won't admit it, but I know he made himself late for work for me and—No. *Stop thinking about how great he is.* I can't have feelings for Austin. We're friends. That's it.

I'm glad we—*I*—took the time to listen last night and that he doesn't hate me for the way I've treated him since the night of Fern's bachelorette party. It's nice to know that I wasn't wrong about him when we met. That maybe I can trust myself to know a nice guy when I see one.

But that doesn't change the fact that Austin doesn't date. I don't do the friends with benefits thing—especially not after Fern educated me on the cuddle hormone and the risk it brings to such arrangements. It's not worth ruining a good friendship for sex because the stupid hormones make one of us want more. What happened last night was a one-off. Our . . . curiosity wasn't fully satisfied by our first encounter, so we had to try again. That's all it was.

I don't know that I'm ready for something serious anyway. *So, where does that leave me?* I don't want to be alone forever. Sooner or later, I'll have to face my fears. But today is not that day.

I need to accept things as they are and get over them. Over him, because, no matter how much I thought I hated him, the feelings are still there and he will never reciprocate. They never went away; I just buried them in hate and anger because I was scared of them. Scared of getting hurt.

But I've gotten over a man before. I can do it again. Since this is my decision, not his rejection, the suffering will be minimal. And I'll always have last night.

Chapter 19

Austin

"Fern, I know you're on vacation, but I need help," I say before she even has a chance to say hello. Too anxious to sit any longer, I close my laptop and hop up from the bar to pace around my kitchen. I'm an ass for calling her, but I trust her to get me through this more than some blogger who doesn't know me and her promises of easy recipes that don't sound easy at all.

"Is everything okay?" a voice that's much too deep to be hers asks.

Did I call the wrong number? I pull the phone away from my ear to check the screen, but it says Fern. "Damnit, Mase. Where's your wife?"

He snorts. "Downstairs. I'm taking her the phone, but is everything okay?"

I yank open the refrigerator and stick my head inside to survey the contents—again. "Yes. I'm trying to cook without burning down my apartment."

"I'm not sure that 'yes' is the correct answer . . ." he mutters. "I trust the plans for the picnic are coming together well?"

Picnic? Oh! The Fourth of July picnic! "Yes, as you well know because I'm sure you're monitoring everything." I don't blame him for that. It was only eight months ago that Granddad introduced Mason as the future CEO of the family business. He doesn't want the employees to think he isn't up to the task.

"Here she is," he says, ignoring my little dig at him.

"Hello?" Fern answers.

"Fern! I need to cook something. Can you please, please, please help me?"

She doesn't answer immediately. "Okay . . . What are you trying to cook? It's only been two days. You can't be that desperate already. Wait! Better question. Who are you trying to impress?"

Nice try. I am not about to tell her I slept with her best friend. That's a recipe for disaster since I don't know where this thing between Jam and me is going. "I don't know what; I'm at your mercy there. And . . . Someone special."

Saying it makes me smile. Two days ago, I never would've believed I'd say that about Jamaica. But Wednesday night was amazing. And Thursday morning. For once, I wasn't in a hurry to get away from a girl. I actually *enjoyed* the whole morning after thing with Jamaica. I didn't want to leave. Normally, it's an awkward 'bye before I run out the door. If I don't run off before she wakes.

But I forgot to get Jamaica's number. I can't text her to check on her and hopefully score an invite to visit. I need a reason to go over there. I'm not sure where she and I stand, and the uncertainty is killing me. Yeah, we apologized, but good sex makes people say crazy things. And, as much as I'd rather forget it, I need to tell her about the dare.

Checking on her like Fern requested is a good excuse to see her again, but I can't let Fern know that I'm trying to cook for Jamaica. She'll have questions, especially now.

"Someone special, as in the lady the guys dared you to commit six weeks to?"

"You got me." There's no harm in telling her that much. It's not like Jamaica and I will end up together. It's only a bit of fun. *Right?* But I still feel the need to prove myself to her—show her that I'm not the asshole she thought and we really *can* be friends. I've already bought her things—food and medicines and stuff. I need to do something big.

"Anyone I know?" she asks.

"So, what am I making?" I ask, not bothering to hide that I'm changing the subject. The only way out is lying, and that might blow up in my face more than the truth would now.

I don't regret what Jam and I did, but it changed things. I have no doubt that the truth is now a grenade. The pin has been pulled; all that's left is to hold onto it tightly until I find a way to smooth things over. I *have* to tell Jamaica. And I will. Tonight.

"Lasagna is easy," Fern says.

"I'll take your word for it." It doesn't *look* easy. It doesn't even *sound* easy. *What's with that damn 'g' anyway?*

Fern laughs. "I'll e-mail you my recipe."

"Uh-huh . . . And can you maybe walk me through it?" I wasn't lying when I told Jamaica that I burn everything.

Fern laughs again. "I'll break it down for you, but you can call if you have problems."

"Thanks, Fern. You're the best."

"You gotta let me know how it turns out! And if she likes it!"

"You got it." I can do that without telling her anything she doesn't need to know.

"Hey, Austin?" she asks, stopping me with my thumb hovering over the button to disconnect the call.

I raise it to my ear again. "Yeah?"

"Do you even have a pan to bake it in?"

"Ah . . . No. I'll buy one."

"Okay. I'll have the recipe to you before you get to a store," she promises.

***

If you can't find something, ask someone! Don't worry. You can do this. I promise it's easy. Just buy everything on the list exactly as listed. Call if you need me.

I will most definitely need her. Not yet, though. I can make it through a shopping trip alone. I bought a Crock-Pot without help. Once I knew where to find one.

Fern's ingredient list is two-fold. There's the 'if I have time' section, which involves making the sauce from scratch, and the 'when I'm in a hurry' section. I disregard the first one—time I have; confidence, however . . . I'll go for the jarred sauce. Next time, I'll get fancy. Even if I take the easy route, every woman I know will be majorly impressed. My mother will probably die of shock if she ever finds out.

Fern was careful to give me a detailed list, including brands and amounts, to increase my chances of success. *I can do this.*

Jamaica

Crap. Didn't I just read something about that? I stick my highlighter between my teeth so I don't lose it—again—and flip back a few pages in my text-book to find the right paragraph. My finger trails down the margin of the page while I skim through. *There it—*

BzzztBzzztBzzztBzzzt!

My finger slips off the page. *What the heck was that?*

Blinking, I look around, searching for the source of the noise.

BzzztBzzzt.

Oh! The door! *I did it again . . .* Book closed on my thumb, I jump up and run to the intercom. "Yeah?"

"Ready for your test?" Austin asks.

He remembers? My insides do an odd little dance before I remember that I'm supposed to be getting over him. *Easier said than done.* "I hope so," I say, praying I don't sound as excited to see him as I am. "I'm still studying."

"Got time for a break?"

"Sure," I say, working to keep my enthusiasm in check. I shouldn't be so happy about seeing him again. *Call it exposure therapy.* The more I'm around him, the easier it'll be. Theoretically. Today is session one, the first day of a new beginning. That's something to be happy about.

I buzz him in, then open the door and lean against the frame to wait for him. I hear him before I see him. He takes the stairs at a run and smiles when he sees me and my heart does a little flip. There's a stain on his dark shirt, and his hair is all over the place like he just rolled out of bed and was in such a hurry to get here he pulled on whatever he touched first and ran out the door.

"When did you eat last?" he asks, holding up a little cooler-looking thing.

Something in my chest explodes like one of the fireworks I'm excited to see next weekend. *Stop it!* "Uhh . . ."

"Wrong answer," he says. "I brought dinner, but don't tell Fern what you're having."

Why wouldn't he want me to tell Fern? She asked him to check in on me. Not that it matters. We don't normally discuss *what* I eat so much as *that* I eat. "Okay?"

He ducks his head. "I called her and had her walk me through how to make it. Told her it was for someone special."

The fireworks explode in my chest again. *Someone special?* I shouldn't read too much into that, but it's hard. A smile tries to creep up on me, so I bite my lip. "So what, I'm your first victim? If I survive, you'll treat some poor, unsuspecting girl to this lie that you can cook?"

The shy smile vanishes, and his expression quickly shifts from surprised to confused and maybe—just maybe—a little hurt.

He opens his mouth, but I don't give him a chance. We just got past one misunderstanding. It's fun to tease him, but I don't want to be in the middle of another. I like it better when he's sweet, even if nothing ever comes of it. "I'm just messing with you. Get in here."

His shoulders sag in relief. He quickly leans down and kisses me right on the mouth, only to draw back just as quickly, wearing a classic "what the heck" look. To be fair, it's probably a mirror of mine. Kissing for the sake of kissing implies a certain something we don't have—like a relationship—and that felt way too . . . right. Natural. Not something that should happen between two friends.

"Uh . . . Dinner!" he says, holding up the cooler thing again.

I get a whiff of garlic. My stomach growls. "Yes! Dinner!" *Let's not talk about what just happened.* And let's definitely not talk about how I kind of want to do it again. Throwing the door open wide, I step back and let him pass. Following him to the kitchen, I do my best to keep my eyes off his bum in those jeans. The effort doubles my appetite.

Austin sits the cooler down on the counter. "I hope you like—" he turns and catches me in a moment of weakness.

I jerk my eyes up to his, but it's too late. That crooked grin of his is already in play.

"I already know you like that," he says. "I've got the claw marks to prove it."

My cheeks flame. "You're bluffing!"

He waggles his eyebrows at me. "Wanna see?"

"Yes," I say automatically. Immediately, my hands fly to my mouth as if I can grab that word and take it back. He was only joking. Why did I say that?

Austin lunges for me. "Lasagna will keep," he mutters before his lips crush mine.

I push him away. As much as I want that kiss, it's not fair to my heart to keep doing this. And there's something important that needs to be acknowledged here. "You made me *lasagna?*"

"Yes, but . . . Dessert first?"

I freeze. "What did you come here for, Austin?" If he came here hoping to get lucky, that changes everything. He's not being sweet if he has ulterior motives. And I will not be his booty call. I can get over him, but not like that.

His brows knit together. "To bring you dinner. And because I forgot to get your number, so I couldn't text you to ask if we're really okay now. And I need to talk to you."

"So, you didn't come here hoping for . . ." I gesture between us, "this?"

"Nope. Won't complain either way, though . . ."

"Either way?" He's the one who put a time limit on last night. If he thinks he can change his mind on a whim because it worked once, we're not going to be okay now.

He lets his hands fall away. "Why do I feel like I'm being cross-examined here? I didn't come here to get laid. I never got your number, so I came here to ask how your studying is going and to make sure you eat something, but I won't lie and say I'm not game if you wanna have a little fun."

His eyes never leave mine, but the carefree sparkle that normally lights up the room is gone. I don't *think* he's lying. But I do think I hurt his feelings. "I'm sorry, I just—"

"Don't trust me? Think I only care about sex?"

"No!" *Yes. Dang it!* I shouldn't jump to conclusions like that. I should've said no and left it at that. Now, I owe him an explanation to prevent another misunderstanding. "Look, I don't like to talk about it, but I got out of a bad relationship about a year ago. Because of that, I tend to . . . overanalyze things."

Something that looks too much like pity for my liking flashes through his eyes, but it's there and gone again in a blink. "I don't understand, because I've never been through that myself, but I understand . . . If that makes any sense. Thank you for explaining."

I nod and fight the urge to jump to another conclusion. I can't assume he feels sorry for me or that it will affect our friendship. It was an apology. I explained that I have a history with bad relationships and—oh no.

What if he takes that the wrong way? Given our history, I need to fix that before it becomes a problem. "I'm not insinuating that we're—"

He purses his lips but waves away my explanation. "No, I know. I didn't think you were."

"Okay, good. Because . . . Well . . . I'm not ready to be hurt again." Speaking about it chokes me up. Jordan was the greatest guy in the world when we met, and he played that part right up until I trusted him completely. Once I was vulnerable to him, everything changed. And I won't give another guy that kind of power over me without making him earn it.

He reaches to stroke my cheek with his thumb. "The right guy won't hurt you, Jam. And none of us—by which I mean the rest of the crew and I—will let anyone hurt you. We've got your back."

Tears sting my eyes. I hate thinking about Jordan, especially when I'm so far away from my family. I always need a good hug when his name pops into my head too many times in one day.

"Hey," Austin whispers. "Don't cry. C'mere." He grabs my shoulders and pulls me into his arms. I'm not strong enough to resist the comfort. Austin has seen me naked, but he's never seen me *naked.* I hate that he's seeing it now, but it's too late.

I rest my head on his shoulder and loop my arms around his waist. He smooths my curls back and leans his cheek against the side of my head while rubbing my back. "I'm sorry I stirred up shitty memories," he whispers. "But Ronni likes to say that hugs are magic, and they make everything better."

"Ronni is a smart little girl." Hugs *are* magic. I already feel a little better. Ironic that I find comfort in the arms of a man who I thought was a Jordan-in-training just days ago. But I *wanted* to see those similarities. I fabricated reasons to hate him, and I owe him another apology for it.

"Austin, I'm very sorry about the way I behaved the past few months."

His arms tighten around me, triggering a sigh that works its way up from somewhere in my little toes. "This ex have anything to do with it?"

"Indirectly."

He snorts out a soft laugh. "I've flirted with a lot of women, Jam. You're not the only one who projects her issues onto men."

"Doesn't make it right."

"No," he agrees. "I get it, though. It's a defense mechanism. But . . . Why me?"

Do I dare? I know this will never turn into a relationship, but doesn't he deserve to know why I was so hateful? But will that break this fragile thread of friendship between us? Austin is allergic to relationships, after all. I don't want to freak him out. But it might be easier to get past if he understands.

He might stop doing things like this, things that will make moving on so difficult.

"Because I—" I pick my head up to look him in the eye to gauge his reaction and do damage control on the fly. The concern etched in his face makes the words slip my mind. Instead, I close the gap between us inch by inch. His eyes drop to my mouth, but he doesn't stop me.

My lips barely brush his, reenacting the way he kissed me before he picked me up and carried me somewhere more private. He sucks in a long, slow breath and takes his time letting it out. One of his hands comes up to cup my cheek, but he doesn't try to take over.

I do it again, giving him time to stop me because I'm not sure if I'm smart enough to.

He doesn't. His other hand comes to rest on the small of my back. He uses it to push me closer, the only sign he gives me. That and the hard length of his cock pressed against my hip.

I take one more deep breath to stall, then give in and press my lips firmly to his. He moans and hauls me closer, then must decide that isn't close enough because he picks me up and sits me on the counter, pushing my knees apart to make space for him to stand.

"I'm sorry," I whisper when we break apart.

"Don't be."

I let my arms fall away because, no matter what just happened, he's not mine to hold and I need to remember that. "I know you don't do . . . This."

His head tilts to one side. "This?"

"Relationships." I bite my lip and wait for him to understand. And, if I judged him wrong, for him to laugh.

He grins. "You said like five minutes ago that this isn't a relationship."

He doesn't get it. I sigh and force myself to look him in the eye because I am *not* ashamed of feeling what I feel. "But before, I thought I wanted it to be, and that's why I pushed you away."

Little crinkles appear at the corners of his eyes. He swallows hard. "But what if I did?"

My stomach clenches at what my heart perceives as a sliver of hope. "What do you mean?"

Austin takes a slow, shaky inhale. His arms flex around me, holding me tighter. "What if I—we—did this?"

That sliver of hope punctures my heart. "I don't do friends with benefits," I whisper. "I'm not a toy."

He shakes his head quickly. "That's not what I'm suggesting."

I bite my cheek, hoping the pain will wake me up from what has to be a dream. This isn't happening. My subconscious is playing tricks on me. "Then what?"

His shoulders shrug. "I don't know, just . . . more."

My heart quickly patches itself up and clings to hope again, using it as a dagger against my mind because I *know* this isn't a good idea. "I don't know if I'm ready for more."

Yes, I want him. Probably too much. But when he decides he's tired of being tied down, that'll leave me picking up more pieces of my heart. I'm not sure I can take that risk.

"We don't have to rush things."

I can't help my smile. "We've seen each other naked. We've passed a point of no return."

He shrugs again and slides his hands up and down my thighs. "Semantics. It can still be casual. There don't have to be any expectations. Just . . . loyalty and sex."

If that's not friends with benefits, and it's not a relationship, then what is it? That's just it, though. It *is* a relationship. To me, anyway. So what does it mean to him? "Loyalty and sex? I think the term you're looking for is mutually exclusive."

He grins, and his head bobs up and down. "Yeah . . . that."

"That's a relationship."

"Uh-huh. But . . . like . . . I can do that part. I'm already *doing* that part."

I shake my head because he's not making any sense. "What do you mean?"

His finds my hands and wraps his fingers around mine. Leaning back, he brings our hands between us and locks his gray-blue eyes on mine. "I can promise to sleep with you and only you. I haven't been with anyone else since the wedding."

"Then, what's your problem with relationships?" I ask out of curiosity. His logic doesn't make sense to me.

Austin sighs. "I don't do serious—you know this. I make jokes when we fight, which only makes things worse."

"Then what are you saying?" He opens his mouth, closes it, and swallows hard again. "What do you want, Austin?"

"I don't know! I don't want this," he lets go of one hand and swivels a finger between us, "to stop. That's all I can tell you. I don't need a label for it. I just . . . You were all I could think about since I walked out that door yesterday morning. I learned to make lasagna to have an excuse to come back here and see you, and sex wasn't the endgame. I like you, and that scares me too. That's why it was so easy to let you be mad at me. Hell, I purposely said and did things to *keep* you mad at me, but it didn't help. Here we are."

I freeze, scared to even breathe. This all sounds too good to be true. We want and fear the same things. *Can this work?* "What do you want, Austin?" I whisper, praying the answer isn't more than I can give.

"I want your phone number. I want to be able to call you or text you whenever I want. I want to sit beside you when we're out with our friends, and—" He lays his hand on my cheek. "I want to do that whenever I want, regardless of who might see. And this." He leans in and kisses me once. "But I can't do all that if I'm constantly worried that I'll say or do the wrong thing, piss you off, and you'll revoke those privileges. So can we just . . . do this, all the time? Not just when we're alone? And not think too hard about what we call it? That 'r' word gives me hives."

My heart is winning the war. He's given me enough cause to hope that my mind is seriously considering waving the white flag. What he's offering . . . It sounds nice. Scary still, but shouldn't it be? Relationships are terrifying, no matter what you call them, because you're putting your heart in someone else's hands. If the other person doesn't treasure that gift, well, I already know how that goes.

But maybe our mutual fear will inspire us both to treat that gift with more care.

"If the 'r' word gives you hives, I'm guessing the 'b' word does, too?" If we're going to do this, I need to know what he is and isn't alright with. If calling it a relationship makes him twitchy, calling him my boyfriend probably will too.

His forehead crinkles. "The 'b' word . . ." he mouths, like he's trying to figure it out.

"Boyfriend?"

His eyes widen. "Ah . . . Yeah. No one's called me that since high school." He smiles a little. "I didn't mind it so much then. It wasn't until after . . ."

"What happened?" I ask. I have no right because I won't answer the same question. At least not yet. But if he wants to tell me, I'll listen.

He shrugs, trying to play it off like it didn't matter. His eyes betray him, though. They lose that smile. "She was talking about college and our future. I made some joke about neither of us needing a degree—I don't even remember what I said anymore because I didn't expect it to blow up in my face. But it did. She told me I couldn't joke my way through life, and she couldn't be with someone who didn't take her future seriously. But the thing was, I did. I was taking our future very seriously. I had a ring. I was going to ask her to marry me after graduation." His lips twist into a bitter sneer. "And I told her that right then and there, but she thought I was making it up to change her mind."

"Austin," I whisper, my heart breaking for him. I throw my arms around his neck and lock my ankles behind him, hugging him with my whole body. The similarities give me chills. I did the same thing she did. *How does he not hate me?*

"I thought she and I would be like Gabe and Tara—minus the whole alcoholism, divorce, and second chance thing," he continues, his voice straining under the weight of the old pain.

"I'm sorry." I squeeze him again and run my fingers through his hair, offering him the only comfort I know how to give him. No wonder he's anti-relationship. He was ready to give someone everything, and she treated it like a joke while telling him he was.

"Your turn," he says.

Bands of fear tighten around my chest. I shake my head. "I can't. Not yet."

"Give me the *Cliff Notes* version," he says. "I need to know what not to do."

I sit back to look at him, taking note of the determination in his eyes instead of the sharp calculation that was always present in Jordan's. *He wants this to work too.* "Just be you," I whisper, my voice so tight from holding back tears that it breaks. There's no way he would ever treat me like Jordan did. He never intends to hurt anyone—I see that now, no matter what I wanted to believe before. This just might work.

"Someday?"

I nod. "Someday."

"Dinner?"

"Dessert?" Nothing about this discussion was sexy, but I want to be closer to him right now—want the connection. I want to lose myself in his arms and let his heartbeat chase thoughts of my past from my mind. I still have more questions than answers, but I at least know that we want the same things. We want someone, and we're both afraid of getting hurt, though he makes it out as he's scared of hurting someone.

Austin shakes his head and a pang of rejection tears through me. *Why would he decline now that we've agreed to give this a try?* "Dinner. Maybe a movie. After that, we can revisit the topic of dessert, but I don't think it's what you really want right now. And I don't want to bring *him* to bed with us."

The tears I fought back break free. He's right. It's not what I want, but it's the only way I know to get what I need right now from him. I didn't know guys could do intimacy without sex and I'm astounded that he cares enough not only to differentiate between the two but to discern what I'm after. *Further proof that he's actually a good guy.*

"That sounds perfect," I whisper. His lips stretch into that smile I always want to kiss, and I realize that I can now. I don't have to hide that I want to anymore.

I move slowly, giving him plenty of time to stop me if this is too fast for him. I cradle his face in my hands. His smile falters, but his eyes bore into mine, daring me to keep going. My lips brush his lightly, and he heaves a slow sigh that rings of contentment.

"Do that again," he whispers, as bossy in this simple intimacy as he is in the bedroom. But given what I know of his history with women, he's probably starved for this sort of affection. *And I'm not?*

I press my lips to his once more and am rewarded with another sigh.

"I can definitely get used to this. Why don't you go pick a movie? I'll bring dinner."

He turns to get plates, but something he said when he got here makes me stop him. "Wait, you said you needed to talk to me?"

He swallows hard and shakes his head. "It can wait," he whispers before pressing his lips to my forehead. "What are we watching?"

Chapter 20
Jamaica

ocus, Jamaica. I reread the passage I'm supposed to be memorizing for the fifth time, but my mind can't make sense of it. I keep thinking back on my evening with Austin.

Dinner was fantastic. I don't remember much about the movie, but I remember every beat of Austin's heart and his fingers in my hair while we watched it, and that was pretty fantastic too.

But it's what happened after the movie was over, dishes were done, and the leftovers were stashed in my fridge that won't let me focus.

One simple touch started it. He brushed a curl back, and that led to a kiss, which led us down the hall to my bedroom. There were no taunts, no words at all, actually. We smiled and laughed and kissed and touched and took our time. There was no rush for pleasure; being together *was* the pleasure. And I can't wait to do it again.

Focus, Jamaica! Degrees before dick. I repeat my new mantra a few times and reread the passage one more time.

Austin

I pause at the first flight of stairs and look back. *Keep walking, Chambers. She needs to study.* No sense of impending doom hangs over my head on my way downstairs—not like the last time I actually tried with someone. I lived on edge for weeks when I was trying to make something work with Beth, just certain I was going to fuck up. And I did eventually, in her eyes anyway.

I'm not scared this time. Jamaica doesn't want anything I can't give her yet, and she's willing to give more than I expected, based on what little I've surmised of her past. We're going to be fine because we're both willing to take this one step at a time—even if we take them out of order. *I just have to find a way to tell her about the dare without ruining everything . . .*

Leaving her bed was harder this time. There were no harsh words between us, no misunderstandings to fuel the passion. It was only that: passion. Something I'm not sure I've had in a long time, and I didn't appreciate it for what it was when I did. We weren't in it for ourselves like a random hookup; we were there because we wanted each other.

I could go back now and take her to bed. Keep her there until she can't keep her eyes open. In the morning, I could wake her up the same way I put her to sleep—with a smile on her face and my dick deep within her—but she has a test to study for. She definitely won't get any studying done while I'm around unless it's for an anatomy quiz.

Fuck, I'm turning into one of those *guys.* It's not so bad, though. Not if it means I get to call her . . . call her what? Nothing because this is not a relationship. She's Jamaica, and I'm Austin, and we are not in a relationship. We're lovers who aren't hiding that they're more than friends and that's good enough for me. *But she's mine.*

And because of that, I can wake her up with my dick another day. It's time to go home.

The humidity slaps me in the face when I step outside. *If I'm going to be sweaty and sticky, I'd rather be naked and on top of Jam.* Thoughts like that will make me turn around, so I hurry to my car before I can change my mind.

The yellow paint glows like a beacon in the cheery circle of illumination provided by the street lights that dot the parking lot. I can't help but smile every time I lay eyes on my Corvette. It's my dream car. Mom hates it. Nicole tells me to enjoy it while I can. Mason is jealous as hell of it—

though the fucker could buy his own if he really wanted to. I don't drive it to spite any of them; I drive it because I've wanted one since I had a yellow Hotwheels version as a kid. The best part of growing up is making those childhood dreams come true.

Movement outside the circle of light catches my eye. I peer into the darkness and nearly miss the silhouette of a man standing near the back of my car—a big man. He's easily as tall as Mason but broader. His eyes gleam in the light, the only indication that he's watching me. I don't know if he's the darkest man I've ever met or if he's wearing a face mask. I hope it's the former because people in face masks at night are generally up to no good and I don't want to shatter this cellular-level contentment I've got going on. *Although, I could always go back up and achieve it again . . .*

My feet slow to give me more time to assess the situation, but I don't change course. He's definitely wearing a mask. My heart beats a little harder with that revelation. I force my hands to relax when they want to curl into fists. I'm not as well-trained as Ryan, but I'm not afraid to fight. And I could be misreading the situation. He might not mean me any harm at all. He could be drunk off his ass or admiring my car from a safe distance. The mask could be his idea of fashion. Who am I to judge? As long as he's just standing there, we don't have a problem.

I nod to him as I approach the driver's door, and he nods back—only evident because a light behind him becomes visible. "Nice car," he says in rich baritone that suits a guy his size.

"Thanks." I reply as I slide behind the wheel, watching him from the corner of my eye in case he makes a move. "Have a good night."

The man turns, tossing a wave over his shoulder, and pulls his mask off, revealing close-cropped dark hair. He goes to a car two down from mine and opens the driver's door. His face remains in the shadows while he climbs in. The motor turns over before he closes the door, and he drives away.

Weird . . .

Chapter 21

Jamaica

*S*ure *is Monday* ... The gentle rain that started shortly after I boarded the bus is more of a downpour now, and I have two blocks left to walk to get out of it. *I really need to talk to the guys about finding a car.* I'll ring Fern about it tonight. She'll know who to ask. Ryan is a car guy, but his tastes skew more toward classic collectors that need a lot of work. A motor is a motor, and I'm sure he could still look under the hood of something newer and tell me if it's a sound investment, but I feel like it would be better to take someone who is well-versed in vehicles that aren't older than I am, unless I find one in that category I want to buy.

The front door of my building finally closes behind me. I stop on the rug to dry my shoes so I don't slip on the stairs and then hurry up to my floor to change out of my wet clothes. *I can't believe I didn't check the forecast today.* Serves me right. If my head hadn't been in the clouds over Austin this morning, I might've remembered. But the sweet text I woke up to wishing me luck on my test drove everything but passing that test and seeing him again from my brain. *Great, I'm dick whipped . . .* It's not so bad, though.

It's only been a few days, but things are better than I hoped they'd be. It's so easy. I live my life, he lives his, and when we both have downtime, we hang out. No pressure. Friends, but more, is indeed an excellent way to describe it, because my one experience with a relationship was nothing like this.

Something electric purple and shiny catches my eye once my head clears the top of the stairs. It's a box with a silver bow bigger than the box and it's waiting outside my door. *Awww!* I don't remember telling Austin my favorite color, but he might've asked Fern. Or it could be from my parents! Smiling so big my face might crack, I scoop it up and unlock my door. I hurry straight to the table, dropping my backpack and kicking off my wet shoes in my excitement instead of leaving them neatly by the door like I normally would.

I tear into the pretty paper with all the enthusiasm of a kid on their birthday, creating a storm of paper scraps to pick up later. The tape holding the box closed gives easily, and the first thing I find is another little box, longer than it is wide. Inside is a set of custom-made bookmarks featuring pictures of my friends and me from Fern's wedding. A reminder is emblazoned across each one, things like "time for a break," "don't forget to eat," "call a friend," "get outside."

They're gorgeous and so thoughtful I get a little misty-eyed. If this was Austin, he really went above and beyond. I can slip them into my textbooks at intervals and maybe not get lost in my work that way. *But then I won't get to see Austin as much because he won't randomly stop by to check on me anymore . . .* Nonsense. I can ring him or text him instead. He can stop by because he wants to, not because he feels like I need him to.

The next thing I pull out is a hardcovered notebook. Under that is a book about bullet journaling, a pack of fine-tipped markers, stickers, pretty tape, and stencils. In the very bottom of the box, there's a typed note that reads, 'to help you stay on track.'

A chill dances up my spine. The book is the exact one I was talking to Jordan about buying right before the dumpster that was life with him caught on fire. *It's a popular book. That's all. Nothing to get upset about.* I won't let that random memory ruin my excitement. It's not fair to whoever was thoughtful enough to buy it for me.

I check the box again for some clue about who it's from and come up empty-handed. *Odd.* Someone put a lot of effort into this and deserves to know how much I appreciate it. I set it aside, brush a few scraps of paper off the table, and arrange all of my goodies for a photograph. Once everything is just so, I snap a photo and open my texting app to send it to Austin.

Me: Thank you so much! I love it all!

The message quickly moves through sending, delivered, and read, then the ellipsis pops up to let me know he's typing.

Austin: I'd love to take credit because that's awesome, but it wasn't me. Sorry. I'm glad you like it, though!

Well, darn! I pout a little to myself. I was sure it was him. No matter. It must've been Mum. I have no idea how she would've pulled this off since there was no shipping label on the box, but Mum always surprises me. And I did send her all of these pictures, as I promised her I would. I back out of my conversation with Austin and open Mum's.

Me: Don't know how you managed it, but thank you so much! I love it!

The send button disappears with my thumb millimeters away from tapping it and is replaced by an incoming call. I recognize the area code but not the rest of the number. *Maybe it's Mum* . . .

"Hello?" I answer it after a second's hesitation. I moved here for a reason, and it's reckless to answer calls from numbers I don't recognize, but it's too much of a coincidence. Mum *knows* I'm back from class by this time.

"Jam?" a woman asks. Her voice jars more buried memories loose, and I lower my phone to end the call. "Oh, God, don't hang up! Please!"

The desperation in her plea stalls me. I shouldn't—this could be a trap—but I bring the phone back to my ear. "Why shouldn't I, Leesa? And how did you get this number?"

Jordan introduced me to Leesa, and she proved to be one of my worst tormentors, using our supposed friendship against me. I thought she was jealous at the time, but I've learned it was probably self-preservation. Jordan didn't have friends; he had people who were too scared of him to upset him.

"He's out, Jam! I don't know how long ago it happened, but I just found out today. I called in a favor with a guy I know and had him find your number. I wanted to warn you."

Another chill traverses my spine. A moment of blind panic urges me to flee before it's too late. Then reality sets in. I'm safe here. This is the last place Jordan would think to look for me. I hate the heat. I hate the grass.

I'd hate everything about this place if it weren't for my new friends. "Thank you for the warning, Lees, but I'm safe. He'll never find me."

"That's why I'm calling you, girl! I moved and changed my number too, but Charles was too damned stubborn to do the smart thing," she says, naming her twin brother who was equally deep in Jordan's circle. "Charles says Jordan's figured out where you went. I don't know if I believe him, but I thought you needed to know."

The rest of what she has to say is lost in the roar of blood pounding in my ears. The room spins. My knees go weak, and I fall backward onto my butt. *This can't be happening.*

It has to be one of his tricks, him trying to get someone to tell him what they know. He did that all the time. None of them know anything, though. I'm still safe here. I just have to be smart. Buy some mace. Don't go anywhere by myself, just in case. There's no reason to be afraid. I just have to be smart.

Besides, even if he is out, he's surely on parole. He can't leave the state without permission from his parole officer, and there's no way they'll let him. He's dangerous. *Then why did they let him out?*

"Jam? Jamaica? Hello?" Leesa's tinny voice pierces my daze, calling my attention to the white knuckle grip I have on my phone.

"Yeah, I'm here, Lees. Sorry, just kinda freaked out for a minute," I tell her, willing my hand to relax.

"Girl, so did I," she says. "Listen, no one wanted to tell you before because . . . you know, but his last ex turned up dead." A knot forms in my stomach. He never mentioned an ex, but I know what she's going to say before the words leave her lips. I know Jordan. "It was ruled suicide, but none of us believe that. We were too scared to snitch, though. You know what he'd do if he found out? Damn, I get chills just thinking about it. I'll call you if I hear anything else, but don't call me. It's not safe for either of us. I moved, but I didn't *move*. Not like you did. He could still find me."

Not like I'd ring her anyway. I might know why she was the way she was, but I still hold it against her. "Yeah, I hear you. Thanks for the warning. Take care, Lees."

I hang up without waiting for her to say goodbye and ring Fern. I have to tell my family too, but I need to talk to someone who isn't scared of him first. And I can't tell Austin. Our . . . thing isn't ready for this. I need an ear, not a solution, and he's a problem solver. He'll also freak out, and that's *not* what I need right now. I'm still not scared. Jordan will never find me here.

"Hey, Jam!" Fern answers, her usual, cheery self. Distantly, I hear Ronni squealing and the rush of the surf on her end of the call. "What's up?"

A rush of guilt has me second-guessing my decision. Maybe I should tell her I'm calling to check in and then talk to Mum. "I'm sorry, I know you're on vacation."

"I don't stop being your friend because I'm on vacation," she says, cutting me off. "What's going on?"

I swallow hard, take a deep breath, and let it out slowly. I hate the idea of casting a shadow over her beach getaway, raining on her metaphorical parade. "I need to talk about Jordan."

The silence is pierced by another little girl squeal and her father's deep laugh. I'd give anything to be there right now, outside under the bright sunshine despite the heat and the grass, instead of sitting alone in my little apartment. ". . . Okay. I'm here."

"C-can you tell me about where you're at first?" I ask. I push myself up to my feet and stumble to the door to check the locks, then to my couch to wrap up in a blanket to pretend I'm basking in the sun, willing the coldness in my belly to melt away, while she paints me a picture of the beach right outside their back door, right down to the rocks and the gulls trying to raid their picnic basket.

"Alright, I'm ready," I tell her when she pauses for a breath. Imagining myself beside her makes it so much easier for the words to flow. I start at the beginning, with the first time I ever laid eyes on Jordan Graham, and end with the fire that displaced my family and led me to flee Chicago for somewhere far out of his reach.

Chapter 22

Austin

I check my watch again for the tenth time in ten minutes. I'm supposed to be enjoying this time with Jamaica, but I'm too anxious to get into the movie—even though she let me pick. She's been different lately.

Quieter.

More alert.

Almost jumpy.

But when I mention it, she smiles and says it's nothing and she's only being silly. And I let her because this is obviously one of those things she's not ready to talk to me about yet. It sucks, but I'm sure she has her reasons. And I'm not sure I have any right to press her since this is *not* a relationship. Pressing would change that.

That's not what has me wound tight today, though. Mason and Fern should be home any minute now. I've already scheduled the pizza delivery because I know what's going to happen. Mason is going to call and growl at me to get my ass over there and help him undo the mess I made. I promised Fern I'd clean Ronni's room and put away the dishes—and I did. I made no promises about what else I'd get up to while they were gone.

My phone blares the chorus from The Pretty Reckless's "Follow Me Down." Beside me, Jamaica jumps. I hide my frown at the reaction. Maybe it's not related to whatever is going on with her right now, or maybe it is.

"Huh . . ." I say, looking at the name on the caller ID. Things are about to get interesting. Jamaica still doesn't know what I've been up to while she's studying and I'm not busy with arranging the company Fourth of July picnic this weekend, but she's about to find out. I couldn't tell her and risk her warning Fern. It would ruin the fun!

"What?"

"I was expecting Mason, not Fern." I swipe to answer. "Hello, sister dearest."

I don't care that she's only my sister on paper. Mason chose her. She's my sister as much as Nicole is, just like John is my brother.

"Get. Your ass. Over. Here," my brother growls in my ear. I check the ID once more, but it says Fern, and that was her ringtone.

"Fern! Have you taken up smoking? Your voice has changed!"

"Cut the shit, Austin!" Mason snaps. "My phone is dead. I forgot to plug it in on the way home and I *can't fucking charge it here!*"

If I try to speak, I'm going to laugh. I sit quietly, shaking with the effort it takes to stay quiet, waiting for it to subside enough to taunt my brother some more. "Why ever not?" I finally ask, infusing my voice with innocence he'll see right through.

"Austin . . ."

I give it up and laugh. "Alright, alright. I'm on my way. I promised Jamaica I'd pick her up, though." That's stretching the truth a bit. Jamaica has no idea what I've done to my brother. I did promise she could ride with me when I went to visit later, though.

"Whatever. Just get here and help me fix this." He ends the call.

Jamaica is watching me when I look up, her chin tucked and her eyes slightly narrowed. *She must've heard Mason.* "What did you do?"

I grin at her. "What *didn't* I do?"

"Better question, what are you dragging me into?" she asks, her brows arching toward her hairline.

"Dinner," I tell her. "And, if you're okay with it, I thought we could . . ."

I don't know what I want to say and the silence stretches on until she asks, "Could what?"

"Maybe not *tell* them, because there's nothing to tell, but just . . . not hide what's going on here?" We've seen each other almost daily since our talk twelve days ago. I'm not sure why I'm counting, but I am. It's a big deal for me. We're coming up on the longest relationship I've had since high school. I don't want her to think I'm hiding anything and hurt her feelings.

It's a risk, but Mason and Fern won't rat me out before I have a chance to tell her about the dare. Telling them has nothing to do with it, either. My six weeks aren't even up yet. I've went above and beyond what I intended to do, though. This is so much more than a friendship. *So much* better.

"How do you mean?" she asks.

Grinning, I grab her chin and give her a quick peck on the lips. "Like that." I find her hand and lace our fingers together. "Or that." I slip my free arm around her shoulders and haul her a little closer to me. "Or that."

"Or this?" she asks, laying her head on my shoulder.

"Mmhmm," I agree, nearly purring with contentment.

"I think I can live with that. You know they'll have questions, right?"

I shrug, moving her head along with my shoulder. "We're not obligated to make sense to them."

Really, I doubt they'll care. Too much. Until this comes to an end. *But what if it doesn't?* Oddly, that thought doesn't make me panic. This thing we're doing right now is something I could get used to. Exclusive, but free. She has her place and her thing; I have mine. We come and go as we please, and we *come* a lot.

I've liked the few times I woke up next to her, but I also like knowing that I can flat out tell her I need some space and she doesn't overthink it when I only mean I want to go home for the night.

"So, should we go then?"

I'm not ready. I give her a little squeeze. "Not yet. I like it right here."

"Okay." She throws her legs over mine and snuggles in closer. "Hard to believe we're here."

"Mmm." *Hard to believe I actually enjoy this.*

Hard to believe we wasted time being mad over nothing. Maybe it happened for a reason, though. Maybe we wouldn't be here if we hadn't. There wouldn't have been anything to apologize for after the wedding. I wouldn't have chased her into the timber or made her feel good behind that tree. I wouldn't have wanted her so much I couldn't take it anymore two weeks ago.

She never would've owned up to her crush. I wouldn't have given her a chance had she tried.

"Shall we?" she asks after a few minutes.

"Yeah, let's go." I've indulged myself long enough, and even my brother's patience has its limits.

Jamaica

Mason yanks his front door open before I'm out of the car. The blinding smile I'm used to seeing on him has checked out. "Seriously, Austin?"

"What?" Austin asks, trying—and failing—to sound innocent. He walks around the car and holds out a hand to help me out, though he knows it annoys me. I don't need help getting out. *"I never said you* need *help. I do it for every woman who gets in my car. You're no exception. Don't like it? Get out faster. It's how I was raised."*

Mason crosses his arms over his chest. "We got home, and the lights wouldn't come on. Anywhere. So I went downstairs to check the breaker box . . ."

Austin slaps a hand over his mouth as if he can physically restrain his laughter.

"Where are the breakers?" Mason asks, nostrils flaring.

Coming between them doesn't seem like a smart thing to do. Ordinarily, I'd laugh at the idea of Mason stooping to violence, though I know he's capable. I've never seen him so angry. I fall back a few steps in case things get physical. Fern could stop them, but I'd end up an accidental casualty. Absentmindedly, I reach for the thin white line on my cheek where Jordan's ring cut me when I tried to break up a fistfight between him and JT.

"I left you clues!"

"Austin!"

"Alright, alright," Austin sighs. "You're no fun."

"Pranks aren't supposed to involve my family, too!"

"Hey!" Austin snaps. "I didn't do anything that isn't a minor inconvenience. If you'd played along instead of throwing a hissy fit, you'd probably have power back by now."

"Is this like . . . a thing you two do?" I hear myself ask. Mason's eyes land on my face while Austin turns around. I take another step back to be safe. They're both angry now.

Austin's eyes flare wide when he sees me. All traces of anger disappear, and a smile softens his handsome face. "Yeah, but it's all in good fun. Most of the time. Usually, to break the tension after an argument or something, but it's been a while, and I thought it would be funny."

Men are so weird. My sister and I just stay mad until we find a way to get even if we fight. We don't put effort into planning it. The opportunity will eventually present itself.

"But it's not supposed to involve other people," Mason says, pointedly looking at his brother.

Austin coughs into his fist, but it sounds suspiciously like, "Pepper spray!"

Mason's jaw clenches. "But people have occasionally been indirectly affected . . ."

"You *maced* your brother?" I ask. That seems a little extreme.

Mason winces. "It, uh . . . It seemed like a good idea at the time. The prank to end all pranks . . ."

"Nicole and Mom happened to be downwind at the time," Austin adds.

"What did you do to deserve it?" This is Austin we're talking about. I'm sure he wasn't *completely* innocent.

"He shaved my eyebrow off while I was asleep," Mason says, absently touching the feature as if to make sure it's still there.

"That's horrible!" Maybe not mace worthy, but still . . . I bet he looked funny for weeks.

Austin curls his upper lip. "Yeah, well, he ate the last of the ice cream . . ."

I cross my arms, feeling like my mother when she would scold my sister or me as children. "So you shaved his eyebrow off?"

"It seemed reasonable at the time! I was eighteen! And drunk!"

"For the love of dirt," I mutter, borrowing one of Fern's funny sayings.

As if summoned by the thought, Fern comes bouncing out of the house, bumping Mason out of the way with her hip. "Power's back!" she says lightly. "That was fun, Austin."

The tension between Austin and Mason vanishes, washed away in a wave of Fern's enthusiasm. *Thank goodness!* Someone needed to defuse that situation, and I wasn't doing a very good job.

"Yes!" Austin cheers. He holds his hand up, and she high-fives him on her way to me.

"What are you doing here?" she asks through a smile. Her eyes betray her worry, though. It's better than pity, which is what I expected now that she knows. She grabs me and hugs me tight.

Did Mason not tell her I was coming? Should I have stayed home? I wasn't really invited, after all. Not by Fern or Mason at any rate, and I've already intruded on their time once. And Austin is only here right now because he stirred up trouble. Maybe they want to settle in before people beat down their door to see them. Fern isn't the kind to tell anyone they're not welcome. Ever. Even if company is the last thing she wants.

"Austin said he would be summoned when you got home and asked if I wanted to ride along," I tell her, squeezing her back as hard as I can without hurting her. "I can go if—"

"Nonsense."

"But you just—"

"But nothing. Come on in. You can help us figure out what else Austin did to the house while we were away. I'm sure he didn't tell you anything."

"Correct!" Austin tells her. And I did ask on the drive over. A lot.

That actually sounds fun. "Okay."

She grabs my hand and leads the way. As we pass Austin, he checks his watch. "Pizza should be here in a half-hour."

Fern drops my hand to grab Mason's face and pull him down for a kiss. "Smile! It's a joke," she tells him. "There's no reason to be a grump-opotamus. Austin didn't get mad when you Saran wrapped his car doors closed three months ago. And you knew this was coming when he didn't go overboard on the car after the wedding."

Grump-opotomus? I'm going to have to remember that one.

The corners of Mason's eyes crinkle like they do when he smiles. His shoulders sag, and he presses his forehead to hers. "Thank you."

"But of course, my love." She kisses him once more, then bounces back into the house to tackle whatever mess Austin made like a kid diving into a ball pit.

Sighing, Mason scrubs his face with both hands. "Sorry," he says, extending his hand to his brother.

Austin knocks his hand aside and hugs him, displaying the same level of enthusiasm as Fern now that Mason isn't a grump-opotomus anymore. *He thrives on chaos.* There's never a dull moment with him around, though.

***

The furniture is all right-side-up again. All of the lightbulbs are back where they belong. The electronics in the house have their power cords back. The Saran Wrap has been removed from all of the toilet bowls. Everything in the kitchen is back where it belongs, but there's nothing to be done for the labels on the canned goods. Luckily, Austin wrote on the bottom of each can with a permanent marker. But he is still smiling like he knows something we don't, so I'm sure there's more to discover in days to come. *Maybe I can get him to tell me on the way home.*

Ronni is upstairs, having already inhaled two slices of pizza so she could go play *Minecraft* with her friends. The rest of us are taking our time, enjoying good food and better company.

"So, Austin," Fern begins. She laces her fingers together and rests her chin on them. "How's the dare going?"

He stills beside me, his whiskey halfway to his mouth. "Good."

"What dare?" I ask. *This oughta be good.*

"Oh, you didn't hear?" Fern asks. "The guys dared him to commit to one woman for six weeks."

"I haven't been with anyone else since the wedding." Austin told me that the night we agreed to be more. That six weeks must be up by now. No . . . She asked him how it's going.

"Jam," Austin whispers. Under the table, he grabs my knee and squeezes. I ignore him, too afraid to see my suspicions confirmed in his eyes. Mason's eyes dart back and forth between us. Fern doesn't seem to notice that anything is wrong, though.

"When did that happen?" I ask, forcing myself to act casual. Maybe it just happened or something. That's it. It was after that day in my kitchen and Austin didn't say anything to them because . . . We wanted Mason and Fern to hear about our pseudo-relationship from us.

"At Gabe and Tara's a few weeks ago."

The cold, hard truth hits me upside the head. I've been played. Austin had ulterior motives the entire time. He might not be like Jordan, but he's a different sort of monster.

"Jam," Austin whispers again.

My heart pounds in my ears. *This isn't happening.* It's a joke! That's it. Austin told them already to prank me.

Then why aren't they laughing?

"Jam? What's wrong?" Fern asks.

Slowly, I turn to look at Austin. *Please, let him be smiling.* I grew up Catholic, but I've never prayed so hard in my life.

The beautiful smile I adore so much is absent. His mouth is set in a grim line. There's no laughter in his eyes, only panic. *I'm such a fool.* I was right all along.

"Excuse me," I mumble. I push my chair away from the table and hurry from the room. Behind me, Fern cusses and Austin calls my name. Heavy footfalls follow me, so I run. I don't want to do this here. I don't want to do this anywhere, really. I don't need another fake apology from him.

I burst through the front door and run around to the house where Fern showed me Len, Mason's scary driver and security chief, lives. He answers after two knocks.

"Miss Gunn?"

"I'm so sorry to bother you. Would you mind taking me home? I'll pay you, just—"

He steps back and opens the door wider. "Come in while I get my shoes."

"Thank you." I step inside and out of the way so he can close the door behind me. Surely, Austin won't think to look for me here.

"So you found out?" Len asks from another room in the cute little house. I try not to look around—I don't want to invade his privacy more than I already am—but I can't help it. There's a lot of military memorabilia on the walls.

"Found out what?" I ask, hoping his question isn't related to the reason I'm here. *Did everyone else know?*

"About the dare."

"How did you know?" He wasn't at Gabe's, so he wasn't there when it happened. That means . . . I'm a fool. That's what it means. Austin told everyone else so they could laugh along with him.

"I notice things," he says, walking back into the room he left me in. "Fern and Mason were talking about the dare in the car one day. Austin doesn't know how to walk away from things like that, so I knew he'd do it. But I didn't *know* it was you until you knocked on my door."

Oh. So maybe he didn't tell everyone. But he's still a jerk for using me. My vision blurs with tears. "I'm sorry," I tell Len again. "I didn't know what else to do."

"Miss Gunn, Mason might sign my paycheck, but his family and friends are all good to me. I don't draw the line at Mason, Ronni, and Fern. You coming to my door when you didn't know where else to go to feel safe means I'm doing something right." He pushes a button on a monitor I hadn't noticed, and it powers on to display a divided screen. "Austin is in the backyard. I'm ready if you are."

"Yes, thank you."

"Come with me then. We'll go out the side. It's closer to the garage."

Chapter 23

Austin

I round the corner into the front yard just as Mason's Tesla pulls into the street. *No!* I run after it, after *her*, but a strong hand grabs my arms and stops me.

"Austin, let her go," Mason says. "You know you'll never catch up. Come inside, tell us what's going on, and figure out how you're going to fix it."

"I *can't* fix it!" I shout. I wrench my arm out of his grasp, but he catches me again in two steps. *I need to do more cardio.*

"Everything can be fixed, Austin."

"Not this time," I say, shaking my head. She'll never listen to me now. I've already blown my second chance, and I know she won't give me a third. I know down to my soul that she's already lumped me in with *him*. And I don't even know what kind of company I'm in.

"I didn't know you had it in you to give up," Mason says.

"I'm not giving up!" I shout, disgusted with him for even suggesting it. "You're making me! I'd still be chasing the car if it weren't for you!" *Why the* hell *did I decide to drink tonight?*

"That's not going to solve anything, Austin. Come inside, let us help you."

It *might* solve something, but only if she looks back and sees and decides that my willingness to chase a car means something. *Not likely.* Maybe it's better to let her go. It was so easy for her to believe I'd do something so horrible. That's got to be some sort of sign that we were never destined to work out.

Dejected, I let him drag me back to the house and push me down on the couch because jumping in my car and chasing Jam across town isn't an option right now. I can't do that to Fern. I only had a drink with dinner because Jam was going to drive home.

Fern is already waiting for me. Without a word, she hands me a lowball.

"Keys," she insists, holding out her empty hand.

I know better than to argue. A drunk driver turned her life upside down before we met her. She doesn't get too demanding as long as it's only *a* drink, maybe two, if I'm going to be here a while, but dinner wasn't that long ago, and we both know I'm not stopping at two right now. If I don't hand them over, she'll slash my tires so I can't leave here. She probably won't pay to replace them, either. She'll shrug and say 'play stupid games, win stupid prizes' with a smile on her face because I'm still alive to bitch about it.

Once she has what she wants from me, she sits on the loveseat and tucks her legs underneath her. "Alright, what happened?"

I look around for Mason. This isn't something I want to explain twice. Once is bad enough.

"He's getting himself a drink," she says.

"I can hear you," he calls from his office.

I eye my glass and toss back half in one swallow. The burn makes my eyes water, but it feels better than the numbness that set in when I saw that fucking car pull out of the drive.

"Bring the bottle, Mase," Fern calls to him.

"Planned on it, sweetheart."

"I'm sorry," I whisper to her. Sorry I'm here, ruining their day. Sorry I hurt her friend. Sorry I'm putting all of them through this. I remember how I felt when Fern thought leaving Mason was the best course of action. It was almost as hard as watching him struggling for breath in the grass that day. I have a fairly good guess at how they both feel now.

She shakes her head and leans forward to pat my arm. "Just tell us what the hell is going on, Austin."

Mason takes the seat next to her and leans forward to refill my glass. After another gulp, I'm out of excuses to put off explaining. So I do. I start with the bachelor party and the words just keep coming—things I didn't even know I thought or felt—until I get to today.

"I meant to tell her. I was waiting for the right time," I whisper into my glass before I swallow the last of my third refill. I've put away too much too fast. Either I'm listing left, or everyone else is leaning right. I don't particularly care, though. Jamaica isn't here. That's the part that matters. I had my chance to tell her—to make things right—and I blew it. Again.

"I love her."

Fern leans forward. "What did you say?"

"I don't know. It doesn't make sense. We've only been doing this . . . whatever you want to call it, since you left." *Twelve days. That's all it took for me to fuck up.*

"Nothing about love makes sense, Austin," Mason says. "It didn't take a month for Fern and me."

"No, but you two knew each other for years! I met Jam . . ." I stop to count the months on my fingers. "Six months ago!"

"And?"

Is he serious right now? I *just* told him how we spent *months* at odds. "And we *hated* each other."

Fern smiles. "No, you didn't. You didn't understand each other. And, maybe, you were both trying to push the other away to avoid *this*."

"What? Heartbreak?" I ask. Yep, I avoid that. I thought once was enough to learn that lesson, but apparently, I needed a refresher course. I was right before. Relationships aren't worth it. *If it isn't worth it, why does it hurt so much?*

I wish we'd never left her couch today. None of this would be happening. Everything would be perfect.

Fern leans forward to backhand me on the arm. "Feelings. A relationship. I know Jam's last boyfriend was an asshole of the lowest order. Has she talked to you about him?"

I shake my head. "Just that it was a bad relationship and she wasn't sure if she was ready for another one yet."

What happened to her? I can't shake the feeling that knowing the answer would help me a lot right now. I couldn't push Jamaica for answers, though. I wanted to wait and let her tell me in her own time. I wanted to earn her trust and the right to know.

"What do I do?" I ask without any real hope of an answer. The biggest fight these two have ever had was a minor disagreement over what the caterer would serve at their wedding reception. I have to try, though. No matter what I want to tell myself, she is abso-fucking-lutely worth all of it.

Even when we're not getting along, she makes me happier than I ever remember being. I can't lose that.

"First, you're going to call her," Mason says.

"She won't answer." Even if she does, she's more likely to misunderstand what I'm saying. Her shields are higher, and her tongue is sharper when she's upset. There's only one way to get through to her right now, and I'm not going to shove my way into her apartment. Things between us are bad enough. They'd be worse if I did that. She'd never trust me again.

"I didn't say she would. You're going to call her and leave a message. Apologize. Tell her it's another misunderstanding, and you want to talk it out in person to avoid more misunderstandings."

Sounds reasonable. If she'll listen. "And then?"

"Then, you're going to leave her alone for a few days, except for the *occasional* text message. And by occasional, I mean no more than three a day. Ideally, right after you wake up and right before you go to sleep. Hopefully, she'll reply, and you'll go from there."

Fern arches her eyebrows at him.

"What? I spent a lot of time groveling for Felicity's forgiveness," he says. I roll my eyes at the mention of his leech of an ex.

She shakes her head. "Just impressed."

"And after a few days when she still won't speak to me?" I'm no fool. Jamaica won't be that easy to sway.

"Then, you're going to go to her apartment."

"And?"

"And that's all I've got. I only made it that far once, and she—" he cuts off abruptly and looks at Fern. "Never mind."

Fern rolls her eyes. "I heard the story, down to the last detail, the next day when she called her besties to brag."

"I love you." He says it like an apology, though. That had to have happened more than a year before he started dating Fern, so I'm not sure why he feels bad. *I* haven't heard this story, though. But I'm not going to pester him for details when his wife is right here, and I have problems of my own. That's a story for a happier night.

"I love you too."

Ignoring the way the world around me sways, I push myself up off the couch. It's time to step up and do the thing that scares me. I can't hide behind my sense of humor this time. It doesn't matter that she knows it's my thing; she's too hurt to see through it right now. I have to face this head-on. The alternative is losing her, and I'm not okay with that. "Okay. I'm gonna go call her."

"You can use the office," Mason says.

"Thank you," I say, grateful for the privacy. I stumble my way there and close the door behind me. Phone in hand, I fall into the desk chair and tap the picture of Jamaica on my home screen to call her.

"This is Jam! I'm probably studying. Leave a message, and I'll call you back when I take a break!"

I take a deep breath and remind myself of what Mason told me to say, only to forget it all when I open my mouth. "Jam, please. I know what you're thinking . . . Actually, I don't, but I can guess how that sounded to you. I swear, the dare had nothing to do with it. Please, call me back. Give me a chance to explain." Three little words burn my tongue, or maybe it's the alcohol. I want to say them. I want her to know. But this isn't the right time. She'll know I'm drunk and think it's only another lie to salvage what we have.

Jamaica

"Thanks again, Len," I tell him as I reach for the door handle. "I really appreciate it."

"My pleasure, Jam," he says, a smile cracking the veneer of seriousness he usually maintains.

I climb out and walk behind the car so he doesn't have to wait, but he stays until the door closes behind me. The only sound of his passage is that of stray rocks on the asphalt crunching under the tires of the electric car. My phone vibrates in my pocket as I mount the stairs. *Probably Austin.* I ignore it and begin the trudge up the three flights of stairs to my landing. The buzzing stops somewhere on the second flight, only for my phone to emit two short, polite buzzes to alert me to a voicemail as I reach my door.

I ignore that too, but get my phone out to text Fern to let her know I'm home. On my way to my room, I kick off my shoes and leave them where they land. I'll pick them up later. Probably when I trip over them.

I stop at the foot of my bed and fall face-first onto the mattress. My phone rings again. Since it's still in my hand, I lift my head and peek at the screen. *Fern.* I should've expected her call. I wouldn't put it past Austin to try to use her phone to call me, but I know in my bones she wouldn't let him do that. It would be easy to blame her for this mess as well, but it was apparent she had no idea what was going on until I ran away from the table. And no one *forced* Austin to do what he did.

"Hello?" I answer.

"Jam." The tears in her voice come through loud and clear. "I'm sorry."

"For what?" I ask her. I'm still too numb to cry, but it's coming. None of this is her fault.

"For not putting a stop to the dare before it started. No one thought it through, but none of us intended for anyone to get hurt. We thought he was already seeing someone casually and this would just . . . encourage him to make it something real."

"It's not your fault, Fern. He made the decision. He's the one who lied to me about everything," my voice breaks over the last few words, and a tear rolls down my cheek.

"Did he really?" she asks.

"Lies of omission are still lies."

"I get why you're upset that he didn't tell you, but are you sure he lied about *all* of it?"

Suspicion makes me wary. *Why would she ask that.* "What do you know?"

"He told us everything, Jam. I know you didn't answer his call, but . . . I think you should talk to him. I think this is another misunderstanding."

I really hope everything *doesn't include what happened at their reception.* I don't regret *what* we did, but the timing and location are unfortunate, and I do feel bad about that. "I'll take it under advisement."

"Are you alright?"

No. "Define 'alright.'"

"I'm sorry. I feel awful."

"I'll *be* alright." And I will. Eventually. I've survived worse than some jerk pretending to like me for a dare. I know Fern means well, but the probability of her having a blind spot for her brother-in-law is high. And Austin might've lied to her, too.

"If you decide you want to talk to him tonight, he's here. I'm making him stay."

"Alright, thank you."

***

The backlight on my phone is the only light in the room. I like it that way, though. I can ignore the fact that the other half of my bed is empty. Pretend today didn't happen, and he's there, sleeping or texting or something. I tap the play button next to his voicemail again, then turn on the speaker and let his voice fill the room.

"Jam, please. I know what you're thinking . . . Actually, I don't, but I can guess how that sounded to you. I swear, the dare had nothing to do with it. Please, call me back. Give me a chance to explain."

I can tell he was drunk when he called me. I kind of want to hug Fern and Mason for keeping him there tonight because I know Austin would be beating on my door and playing *Pony* right now to embarrass me into opening it. I wouldn't put it past him to bring in a Bluetooth speaker powerful enough for the entire building to hear it.

I hit play once more and close my eyes. How could I be so stupid? How could *he?* It's hard to misunderstand any of this. He accepted that dare, then wormed his way into my life and my bed, and somehow convinced me that he actually liked it here when I was ready to kick him out. And I fell for it.

He might not be as bad as Jordan, but he still lied. I trusted him, and look how that turned out. *Men aren't worth it. The good ones are all taken or off-limits.*

I play the message again.

My brain knows it's all a lie, but my heart wants to believe him after talking with Fern. She knows him better than I do, but she's also biased. I want to phone him back and tell him to come over and make me understand why I should forgive him. Again. I wanted him to apologize and make it all better once before, and all he did was make it worse. I can't expect this time to be any different.

But I was wrong then. Or was I? Was it really a misunderstanding, or did he back off and play a different angle when I stood up to him?

Bah! I play the message again and lose myself in the sound of his voice, memorizing the words, along with every pause and drunken slur.

Why did he have to make me love him?

***

My phone rings, pulling me from the depths of my study daze. Studying is the only refuge I have from thoughts of Austin, and now he's ruining that. I nearly failed a semester once because of a guy; I'm not going to let it happen again. I even put my bookmarks away so I won't see the pictures and think of him. *I need to remember to thank Mum for those.* I never did send that text. I don't want breaks right now, though. And I don't want to talk to Mum until things are better. I don't want her to worry about me.

Sighing, I swipe the screen and raise the phone to my ear. *Better to get this over with now.* Fern asked me to think about it, and I have. How am I ever supposed to trust him? There's no reason to prolong the torment.

"Hello?" My voice, rusty from lack of use and from crying, cracks over the word and I wince. I don't want him to hear how he's affecting me.

"Jam!" he says much too loudly. I jerk the phone away from my ear. "Sorry," comes his tinny voice at a much more reasonable volume. "I didn't think you'd answer. Look, I'm sorry I didn't tell you. I tried, I swear, but there was never a good time! It has nothing to do with—"

"Austin," I say, cutting him off. "Please, stop."

Sleeping on it didn't help. Sleep brought dreams of the days before I learned the truth. The sun rose, and everything was still the same. The sting of betrayal lingers. The uncertainty of being lied to. They're familiar feelings.

"I'd say that I've never felt so betrayed—so *used*—in my life, but that isn't true. You lied to me for a *dare*, Austin. Everything we had was *fake!*"

"No! Please—"

"I forgive you, but only because I refuse to live with the burden of this hurt. Please, leave me alone, Austin. Maybe someday I can move past this, but today isn't that day." It's childish of me, but I disconnect before he has a chance to defend himself. Even as hurt as I am, he got his hooks in deep enough I might fall for whatever lies he's selling this time. I let the phone slip from my fingers and fall to the floor as tears overwhelm me again.

Chapter 24

Austin

*O*ut of desperation, I push the buzzer for the apartment next door to Jamaica's—the one where the old lady lives who was very curious about the strip-o-gram. I haven't seen Jamaica for nearly forty-eight hours, and I'm coming apart at the seams. It's a Thursday night. I know Jamaica is home. I miss her. Our one phone call didn't go well. I'm tired of being ignored. And I'm willing to play dirty. Mason said to give her space and text for three days, but I can't do that. Even one day without at least talking to Jam is too long.

"Yes?" a fragile voice answers.

"Hello, ma'am. I'm very sorry to bother you, but my girl—" I nearly choke on the word. I haven't had a girlfriend in years, but that's what she is. She's mad at me right now, but I know I can get through to her if she'll just *listen*. "My girlfriend lives next to you. She and I had a misunderstanding, and now she won't let me in so I can apologize."

"Who's your girlfriend?"

"Jamaica Gunn."

She harumphs loudly. "Are you aware that someone sent your girlfriend a *stripper* a few weeks ago?"

"Ma'am, I was the stripper." I'm not above twisting the truth a little bit right now. No one took their clothes off, but it was me at the door that day. Maybe the old lady is a romantic and will believe it was love at first sight. And I'll get a real kick out of hearing all about her asking Jamaica about her stripper boyfriend when this is all over.

"My word!" She presses the button to let me inside.

"Thank you so much!" I shove the door open and sprint up the stairs. I have no idea what I'm going to say to get Jamaica to open the door, but at least I'm in the building.

I knock on her door, knowing she won't answer. The carefully scripted words, repeated until I could speak them in my sleep, echo in the hallway. "Jamaica, please. You don't have to open the door. Just listen. I'm sorry. I feel horrible. I swear, the dare had nothing to do with anything I said or did! There was a loophole. I only ever intended to repair our friendship— which was something I wanted anyway! But things didn't stop there. I didn't do this to hurt you. I got to know you better and—"

The door flies open. My heart does a flip. *It worked!* Then, I get a good look at the angry snarl contorting Jamaica's face into something right out of my nightmares.

"Go away, Austin. I already told you I forgive you because I refuse to carry this . . . this *pain* around longer than necessary. But I can't forgive myself for being so stupid as to give another man the power to hurt me like that."

"Jam—"

"No! I don't believe any of it, Austin. Not telling me was bad enough, but then you stood in my kitchen and listened to me tell you I just got out of a horrible relationship and kept right on doing what you were doing. You even told me some sob story about your high school sweetheart to get me to let my guard down. Was that even true?"

Hope surges through my chest. *Here's my chance!* "Ye—"

Something that looks a lot like regret softens her face a little, but it doesn't slow her down. "Never mind! I don't care!"

No! Damnit, not again! I have to get her to listen! "Jam!"

"No! Go away. I don't want to hear it. I don't want to hear any of it!"

I cross my arms. "I'm not leaving until you tell me about your ex."

"Hope you brought a pillow." The door slams in my face before I can stick a foot out to stop it. *Well, shit.*

Now, I have to sleep out here to prove a point.

The door to the apartment next door opens and her neighbor pokes her curler-covered head out. "Oh my," she says. I recognize the voice from the intercom.

"Thank you for letting me try, ma'am," I tell her, rubbing the back of my neck and casting about for the best place to get comfortable and wait.

She shuffles out into the hall and right up to me, pulling her housecoat close. "You're not giving up, are you?" she whispers.

"No, ma'am. I'll sleep here for a week if that's what it takes," I whisper back. The truth of that statement takes my breath away. I said it as a joke, but I do mean it. I'll set up camp out here if that's what it takes for her to realize I'm serious. Hell, I'll have someone drop my laptop off and work from this hallway if I need to.

Her smile takes me by surprise. I expected her to be angry with me for not listening to what Jamaica wants. "Good. I don't think she meant anything she just said. I've heard her crying a lot. If you need to leave to get anything, you can buzz me to let you back in."

"I appreciate that, ma'am." I pull out my wallet and grab one of my business cards to give her. "If you ever need anything, I owe you."

She winks at me. "I didn't know strippers had business cards." She takes the little white rectangle and looks it over. "Chambers Freight International . . . What a coincidence! My grandson, Darren, works there!"

What are the chances her grandson is Mason's assistant? I'm sure we employ more than one Darren, so I don't ask. "Did he invite you to the picnic this Saturday?"

She beams. "Of course!"

"I'll be sure to watch for you." Her door isn't even ten feet away, but I offer her my arm and help her back because I'd want someone to do the same for my grandmother. "Have a good night, ma'am. I'm sorry we bothered you. I promise there won't be any more yelling."

She waves away my apology. "It happens, dear. Sometimes, it's a good thing. Sometimes, it's not. In this case, I think it means you both care. Wait right there."

I do as she orders. She comes back to the door with a pillow and a couple blankets that bring with them the faint scent of mothballs and roses. "Here. If you're serious, you'll need these."

"I am very serious," I assure her. I will do whatever it takes to get Jamaica to hear me out. *Anything.*

"Good night, Mr. Chambers."

"Good night . . ." I realize I never got her name.

"Rose," she says. "Rose Craig."

I give her my best smile. "Good night, Mrs. Craig."

Once she's safely shut away in her apartment and I'm sure the door is locked behind her, I make myself a pallet on the floor, pondering her words while I do. Sometimes, what someone isn't saying is more important than what they are yelling.

Jamaica

I can't sleep. I've cried bucketfuls, waiting to sink into the unconscious oblivion of slumber so I can dream of Austin. It hurts when I wake up, but my dreams are better than reality. But sleep doesn't come for me, and I toss and turn in the dark.

The hallway is quiet now. It has been since I opened the door to yell things I didn't mean, trying to drive him away without hurting him the way he hurt me. I don't know why he insists on trying. This was never real, not to him, anyway. I was a means to an end no matter what he intended.

"I'm not leaving here until you tell me about your ex." Why does he even care, though? He made it clear he wasn't looking for a relationship. Neither of us was, really. We only wanted the comfort of one. The ease. The familiarity. None of the risk.

Surely, he isn't still out there.

Austin is stubborn, though. There's no telling what he'll do. I tiptoe through my apartment and crack the door open. Something heavy pushes it out of my hand. It flies open, and something falls at my feet with a loud *thud.*

"Jamaica?" a groggy, masculine voice asks.

Shrieking, I run back to my room, slam that door and lock it for good measure. *Oh, my God. He stayed.*

"Jam?" Austin asks right outside my bedroom. "I'm sorry I scared you."

"Go away!" I hiss.

"Tell me about him."

"I don't want to see you. Go away!" If I see him, he'll smile at me. And if he smiles at me, all is lost. I'm powerless against that stupid crooked smile of his. I only hope he doesn't know it. I need more time before I can face him.

"You don't have to see me. I'll stay on this side of the door. Just talk to me. Please."

Telling him will get him to leave. It might even get him to give up his crusade to get back in my good graces. He'll understand why I can't trust him anymore. And the sooner he leaves me alone, the sooner I can get back to life and pretend he never happened. Our mutual friends will be tactful enough not to tease me about him. I think. And someday, seeing him won't hurt anymore. I just have to take it one day at a time.

I rest my back against the door and slide down until I land on my butt on the cheap carpet. Through the door, I tell him, "Jordan was . . . the Earth to my moon."

That's the best way I've found to describe the nearly magnetic pull I felt the instant I laid eyes on him. From that day, I was drawn into his orbit. "It was love at first sight for me. We met in class one day. He was older, a TA, and he wouldn't give me the time of day. By the time semester was over, I was mostly over him because he wasn't very nice about letting me know he wasn't interested in me. He was graduating anyway, so I wouldn't see him anymore. That's when he decided that maybe I was worth his time after all."

I swallow down the tears that always come with remembering him. In hindsight, the way he treated me before we were anything to each other should've been my warning. But I didn't want to see it.

There's a soft thud against the door, then the sound of Austin sliding down it as I did. I imagine him sitting much as I am, back to the door, head tipped back as well, maybe with his knees bent, arms draped over them while he listens.

I don't like the catch in my voice when I tell him, "Things were great at first. We didn't spend much time alone together. It was always double dates and hanging out with his friends. He was the perfect gentleman, opening doors, paying for everything while we were out, buying me presents . . . His friends were great, too. They were always happy to see me. Invited me to hang out all the time.

"Then we started hanging out alone at his place. It was simple little things at first. He'd invite me over for a movie but never watched the one I wanted to see. It was like he waited until I chose one to make up his mind."

It was so *frustrating*. I wondered why he bothered to ask if he wasn't going to take my choice into account. But I was young and dumb, and it didn't seem important.

"It escalated from there. On our first real date, he took me out to his favorite Italian restaurant. He asked me what I wanted, and when I told him, he said no. He said that he was paying, so I'd get what he wanted me to have.

"Little by little, he took all of my decisions away from me and convinced me that I hated things I loved and loved things I hated. He even picked out my clothes every night. When we were intimate . . ." I suppress a shudder at the memory of his hands on my body. "He told me that I was lucky he decided to take a chance on me because no other man would want a scrawny little black girl with no bum, no hips, and no tits." Admitting that is still hard, but I promised Austin the whole story. And now he should understand why his joke bothered me so much.

"Shit," Austin mutters. Something *thunks* against the door, causing me to jump. "I'm sorry, Jam."

I don't think he's apologizing for scaring me, so I don't acknowledge his apology. None of what Jordan did is his fault, and I'm tired of people apologizing for something they had no control over.

"He slowly turned me into a mindless puppet. Everything was about him. Every word that came out of my mouth was one he put there. That's when he started driving a wedge between my family and me. He spouted nonsense about them, telling me they didn't want me to be happy because they didn't want me to be with him."

Out of everything he put me through, that part hurt the worst. Choosing between him and my family was easy at the time because he was so convincing. I was sure that they hated me then and never wanted to see me again anyway, but I didn't understand why they hated me and didn't want me to be happy. I couldn't see what I'd done wrong for them to turn their backs on me.

I suck in a deep, shuddering breath that nearly turns into a sob before I continue, glossing over the way he sabotaged my schooling and how his friends' behavior toward me changed, culminating in his fight with JT that landed us all in jail.

"My parents bailed me out and basically kidnapped me to get me away from him. That night really opened my eyes, though, and I didn't want to go back to him." My hand raises automatically to touch the scar on my cheek from that fight, a permanent reminder to never let a man manipulate me again.

"After that, the threats started coming in. I blocked his number. He borrowed a friend's phone. Then he got all of his friends to phone and text me, telling me he would kill my whole family and me if I didn't go back to him. I ignored it for weeks. I mean, who would do that? He had to be bluffing. Then, someone set our house on fire in the middle of the night. We were lucky to get out."

My voice breaks. I take a deep breath to try to keep it together. After everything I put my family through while I was with Jordan, they had to endure the loss of everything they had. The home my parents were so proud of was gone. Everything they had worked for . . . And it's my fault.

They tell me that things don't matter. We still have each other. That's the important part. But I'll always carry that guilt.

"I went to the police after that," I tell Austin when I can talk without fear of breaking down again. "He went away for a while. That's why I transferred down here and why I don't have social media. I don't want him to find me. But he's out now . . . and I recently learned that his previous ex-girlfriend died under suspicious circumstances. It was ruled suicide, but . . ."

The past few days, I've been so upset over Austin I didn't have the capacity to worry about Jordan too. And now, I'm too numb to care. Not that it matters. He won't find me here if he's even looking. I still don't believe it, and I refuse to let fear rule my life.

The silence stretches on so long, I begin to wonder if Austin fell asleep. Or left.

"Jam, can I come in to the out now?" he finally asks.

The request doesn't make sense at first, then a scene from a kids' movie we watched last week pops into my head, and I laugh. I laugh so hard, I cry. As jokes go, it's kind of weak. But I needed it.

I stand up and open the door. His arms engulf me immediately. "I'm so sorry, baby," he whispers.

I didn't even know I needed a hug until it happened, but I can't let it happen. I brace my hands against his chest to avoid the temptation to lean on him. I'd love nothing more than to let him make me forget the last three days ever happened, to lay my head on his shoulder and pretend we're fine. But we're not, and it wouldn't be fair. "I forgive you, Austin. I wanted to blame you—to doubt your intentions—but I know you wouldn't do anything to purposely hurt me. You can go home, and you don't have to bother Mrs. Craig to get in. I'm not mad at you. We can be friends again."

"What if friends isn't good enough?" he asks, his voice a little deeper, a little rougher than it usually is.

My heart takes off like a surprised alley cat. "That's all I've got, Austin. This just proved that I'm too damaged to do this again, especially with you. You wanted someone who expected nothing more than loyalty from you. When I heard about the dare, I acted like you owed me something more. It's not fair to either of us. I am sorry that I didn't trust you. You are a great guy, and you deserve so much better. I know she's out there."

He shakes his head. "Jam, don't."

"Go home, Austin. I'll see you this weekend at the picnic."

"You don't mean it," he says, scowling down at me.

"I do. It's better this way. Neither of us will get hurt," I lie. I'm already hurting, even if I hide it well. I don't know why I dared to love again. I knew it would never work. Jordan saw to it that I could never be with anyone else because I can't trust myself. How am I supposed to trust a man when I can't trust myself?

He pushes a curl out of my eyes and cups my face in his hands. Slowly, he leans in, angling for a kiss.

It would be so easy to let it happen, but I shake my head, and he stops. I know what he's doing. If I fall for it, I'll never end this. I don't want to push him away, but I do. I have to. We had an agreement, and I can't keep my end of it. "I'll walk you out."

He goes without protest, confirming my theory. This was nothing more than a bit of fun to him. He was so desperate to apologize—to make amends—because he's a good guy and he genuinely feels bad for hurting me. He never meant for me to fall for him.

At the door, he stops to gather the blankets and pillow he was sleeping on. "Would you give these to Mrs. Craig for me, please? And tell her I didn't give up?"

"Um, sure," I say, chuckling at his odd message. "I'll do that in the morning."

"Thanks. I'll see you tomorrow."

"Tomorrow?"

"Yep. This isn't over yet." He uses my surprise against me and steals a kiss. "I said I wasn't leaving until you told me. You told me. I'm going home since you don't want me to stay. Good night, I'll see you tomorrow."

"Austin—"

"Good night, Jam."

Chapter 25

Austin

I hate leaving her like this, but it's what I said I'd do, and she didn't ask me to stay. Since I tend to do or say something to make things worse, this is for the best. I can still fix this, though. I will find a way, but it starts with keeping my word.

This gives me time to think about what I need to do to get through to her too.

I had theories about her ex, but none of them were close to reality. He wasn't just a bad boyfriend who didn't value a good woman; he was a bad person who tried to break her. It's amazing she can even contemplate letting someone close again. A weaker person would've avoided any semblance of a relationship after what she's been through, but she didn't. And I was lucky enough to be the man she tried to trust.

Now I'm going to show her that I deserve that trust. Somehow.

I shut the door quietly behind me and check to make sure it locked before I make my way down the hall to the stairs. I don't blame her for having trust issues. If I'd known sooner, I would've proceeded with more caution. I would've made sure to tell her about the dare day one. We would've been on the same page from the start instead of me thinking we were. I'd be with her right now, helping her forget that fuckwad was ever born. I'd be telling her I love her without fear of her thinking I'm using it to fix things.

The door to the building slams behind me, echoing slightly in the quiet of the early morning hours. Goosebumps pebble my arms. *What the hell?* It's not cold enough out here for that. Now I'm jumping at shadows like she has lately. She didn't say *when* she learned he got out of prison, but I have a pretty good guess. *I wish she would've told me that too, so I could comfort her.*

I stroll through the parking lot, forcing myself not to walk faster or tense up. A dark figure near my car slows my steps further. He's dressed head to toe in black, a face mask, long sleeves, and pants in the middle of summer. The light reflects off the blade of the knife he's using to clean under his fingernails. I shudder.

Is he fucking crazy? He'd scare the shit out of a kid. How has no one reported him yet? What if it were Jamaica out here right now? It would freak her out, especially since her ex is out of prison. And sweet Mrs. Craig . . . She can't even run from him!

I don't care if he does live here or has family in the building; I'm reporting him. If nothing else, the local PD will increase patrols. That might ease Jamaica's mind.

He doesn't move as I approach, and he's not just near my car. He's fucking leaning on it! Anger shoves my caution to the side, and I march right up to him to find out what the fuck his problem is.

He looks up when I stop in front of him but continues to groom his nails. Something about his face is familiar. Under different circumstances, I'd tell him he has beautiful eyes just to see his reaction. And I wouldn't be lying. He has the kind of eyelashes that women think are wasted on men framing hazel eyes that are sharper than the point of his knife. Prudence stops me, though. *No one will believe that.* Ryan puts off a fuck you vibe; this dude's is more of an "I'll kill you and go home and sleep like a baby." Not someone I want to fuck around with and piss off tonight.

"Hey man, do you mind?" I ask, gesturing toward my car. "You shouldn't touch someone else's car without permission."

He smiles and the light glinting off his teeth triggers a memory. *That's it.* We've done this before, sort of. He was the guy checking out my car the last time I left here in the night. Fear batters at my chest, but I fight it down, refusing to show him weakness. I thought he was drunk that night. I was obviously wrong. He's clearly crazy. Who *leans* on someone else's vehicle?

His eyes travel to my feet and back up as if taking my measure but he doesn't say a word. He only sneers.

The back of my neck prickles as if I needed a warning that something isn't right here.

He points the knife at me and shoves away from my car with his hip. He looks me up and down again and strolls off into the darkness that swallows him up as if he never existed.

Is he here for me? Have I done something to piss him off?

I hurry into my car and lock the door. I start it up so I can leave if he comes back, but I get my phone and look up the non-emergency number for the police department.

I'll have to ask Jam if she's seen him around tomorrow. I can't exactly make her move, but if he's dangerous . . . I don't know what I'll do, but I'll figure something out. He obviously hasn't posed a problem for her before, or everyone in our circle would know it, so asking her can wait until the sun is up. But I'm not leaving here until an officer knows that there's some creepy motherfucker lurking around the parking lot.

An operator answers my call, takes the essential details, and promises an officer will be right over to take a report.

***

Sunrise finds me still awake, tangled in my sheets from tossing and turning. Every time I get close to dozing off, some part of Jam's story would pop into my mind. The sadness in her voice while she talked about how Jordan tried to destroy her relationship with her family hits me particularly hard. *She misses them so much.*

Maybe there's something I can do to bring a little piece of her home to her here.

Me: I need your help.

I have no fear of waking Fern at this hour. She's one of those dreaded morning people. Sure enough, the ellipsis pops up almost instantly.

Fern: Shoot.

Me: Do you still have Jam's mother's number? Or her sister's?

Seconds later, my phone buzzes again with contact info for both.

Me: You are amazing. Do you know if it's too early to call?

Fern: You'll be alright with Gloria. Maeve will murder you if you contact her before noon. It's been nice knowing ya! ;)

I thank her one more time, take a deep breath, and dial Gloria Gunn's number.

Chapter 26
Jamaica

lmost there. Standing at the bottom of the first flight of stairs clutching my meager haul, I'm not convinced I have the energy to make it to my third floor apartment. I couldn't sleep after Austin left last night. I'm running on coffee and a prayer, and the caffeine is but fumes now. *Looking won't get me there.* I step onto the first riser, and they suddenly seem to stretch on forever like that hallway in *The Shining*.

Pretending to be okay for Tara's benefit long enough to get through an impromptu errand run with her was exhausting. Taking Target by storm didn't seem so bad when I was still too emotional to be tired. That emotional fuel was no match for the subsequent stops on her hunt for beads in just the right shade of pink. Apparently, her normal supplier messed up the order and can't make it right in time.

My phone rings, startling me out of my groggy daze. My zombie-like climb stops in the middle of the second flight of stairs. One corner of my phone catches on my pocket, holding it hostage. Groaning, I try to wiggle it free only to lose my grip on the bags clutched in that hand. They hit the ground, and their contents spew forth, rolling and bouncing down the stairs to the landing.

"No!" The tears that I so carefully kept at bay in Tara's presence spring to my eyes. I give up and let them fall. I'm too frustrated—and tired—to hold them back any longer.

I check the ID and swipe at the screen, and the stairwell falls silent except for my ragged breaths. "Hello?"

Ignoring the urge to sit on the steps and cry like a little girl, I tap the icon for speakerphone and put the darn thing down on a step while I collect my spilled belongings. If I sit now, I'll never make it inside. I'm too tired. This day has been too long.

"What's wrong?" Maeve asks.

"Oh, nothing," I tell her, downplaying to the nth degree. I don't want to tell her and relive everything yet. I need to wait until I'm emotionally derailed as opposed to an emotional trainwreck. Otherwise, the trainwreck will get worse. Talking to Austin last night didn't help anything, not that I really believed it would. "I just dropped some stuff."

"And that made you cry? What broke?"

My heart. "Nothing. I'm just . . . It's just . . ." I don't know what to say to get her off my case. But I had to answer. She worries too much if I don't answer her calls.

"Hold the fibs and serve the tea."

I pause and glare at my phone, wishing we were on a video chat for her to see. "Darn it, Maeve." She isn't going to let me take the easy way out, whatever it might be.

"Yeah, I know. You hate it when I catch you trying to downplay things. Deal with it. I hate it when you feel like you can't talk to me."

Sighing, I give in to the inevitable. "Let me get this mess picked up and get inside. How's Shila doing?"

Maeve tries not to be one of those mothers who talks incessantly about her child but asking opens the floodgates, and she happily fills me in on everything I've missed since we last spoke while I trudge down the steps shoving things back into bags as I go. It won't let me off the hook, but it's a nice distraction for both of us, even if I'm only half-listening.

"—It was *hilarious*, Jam! Ty just *had* to be the one to feed her green beans for the first time, and she spat them all over him!"

Hilarious. Yeah. *Have kids, they say* . . . Somehow, no one remembers such things when encouraging unwitting young couples to have children. It's all rainbows and unicorns to them then. I suppose, in the long run, it's worth it. Even if things like that do happen. It didn't seem to dampen Maeve's enthusiasm for motherhood.

"Alright, I know I just heard your door shut," she says. The baby anecdotes have bought me as much time as they could. "Tell me all of it."

Just thinking about telling her everything makes me tired but I know I'll feel better once I have. She'll help me figure everything out.

I work while I talk, putting away my new acquisitions to keep my hands busy and my thoughts divided to keep myself from crying again. She's a noisy listener, interjecting growls and groans at appropriate intervals. When I've laid it all out for her, she falls silent. That silence stretches on long enough I begin to fidget.

Unable to take one second more, I finally ask, "Are you there?"

"Yes," she says, followed by a heavy sigh. "Processing. Let me see if I've got this straight. You two first hooked up at his brother's wedding?"

"Right." Maeve won't tease me about it. She's done worse.

"And again what . . . six weeks later?"

"Approximately. I didn't count," I lie. I did count—every last day. I'm not sure why. Knowing didn't solve anything. I sink onto the couch and let my head fall back to stare at the ceiling. I have too many memories of Austin here I'd rather not relive right now.

"And he says there was no one else during that time?"

"He says." As much as I don't want to, I believe him. Something stops me from telling Maeve that, though. Defending him isn't my job. I need to take care of myself.

"And the dare happened when?"

"Like . . ." I open my calendar app and count back to the day of the party at Tara's, "ten days before the second time? Does it matter?"

"Yes."

I scowl at the wall. The only reason it matters is that he used me to win it. If he'd just waited a few more weeks . . . I give her a beat, but she doesn't elaborate. "How?"

"Well," she says, stretching the word out, "it does to me anyway. If he's such a player that his friends are daring him to commit such a short amount of time to one woman, I'm sure he had other options. So why you?"

That's a good question . . . One I've avoided thinking about because the answer might change things. If he has a good reason, I don't have a reason to keep him at arm's length anymore. *That's not fair of me.*

"Do you think I'm being ridiculous?" I ask anxiously. I need her to tell me no, that I'm doing the right thing, because the more time that passes, the more I wonder if I am. I miss him so much, but I'm scared.

"I think you're protecting yourself and I admire you for it . . ."

That's not what I asked, but her redirection is an answer itself. She's not going to tell me what I want to hear. I'm not sure why I expected her to. She isn't afraid of hard truths. "But?"

Maeve sighs again. Shila cries in the background, and she asks someone—presumably Ty—to get her. "But I'm not convinced that you need to protect yourself in this case."

How can I not need to protect myself? He was using me so he could win that dare. That's the part I have to remember. I was a means to an end. Plain and simple.

"But he doesn't *want* a relationship! He said it himself. If it weren't for the dare—"

"You're making excuses," she says flatly. "Each time I shoot one down, you'll have another. There's more to it, and you know it, or you wouldn't be fighting so hard to convince yourself that you're doing the right thing."

Her logic leaves me speechless. *Darn it.* I guess I am. But why shouldn't I examine every angle? It's what lawyers do. Tears well in my eyes and I have to swallow several times before I can speak. "I don't like it when you're right."

"Hear him out, Jam," she says firmly. "You can't live your whole life alone because your first real relationship was a disaster. I know you're afraid, but Jordan was the exception, remember?"

"I remember." I actually believe that now, too. But only because of Mason, Gabe, Chris, and Ryan. *And Austin . . .* "But I'm not ready for a relationship! That's not why I'm here! I came to finish school, and that's what I need to focus on!"

Austin didn't keep me from studying. My degree was important to him, too, unlike Jordan. But that's not a good enough reason to give him another chance to hurt me.

"That's another excuse, Jamacia Marie Gunn!" Maeve snaps at me. "Relationships don't care if you're ready for them. They happen. They're not always perfect. You have to decide if it means enough to you for you to fight for it. I wasn't looking for Ty. He wasn't looking for me. You know it wasn't always great, but we didn't give up. We made it work."

A tear glides down my cheek to drop off my chin. I know she's right, but it's so hard. *Maybe I'm just not cut out to make them work.* Especially not now.

"I know you're scared," she says when I don't respond. "That's why I know you want this. If you really thought it was nothing to him, you wouldn't be afraid."

"Maeve . . ." I don't even know what to say. I was counting on her to support my decisions, not poke holes in them with such astounding accuracy.

"Jamaica, if he's still trying, you're more to him than a means to an end. You speak so highly of his brother and sister-in-law. Would they let him hurt you for the sake of a dare?"

Her words sink in slowly, working their way in deep and leaving me cold. Fern and I haven't talked about it since the night it happened, but she knows Austin is still trying to wiggle his way back into my good graces. She actively encouraged me to hear him out . . . "Fuck."

"Jamaica Gunn!" Maeve gasps. "Mum would wash your mouth out with soap! Good for you!"

She says something else, but I don't hear it. I'm stuck on the fact that Mason would eviscerate his brother for hurting me over a dare, and that's *after* Fern was through with him. Whatever he's said to them, they believe it. And they haven't stopped him from contacting me.

Someone rings the buzzer. "I've gotta go, Maeve. Love you. Thank you."

"Mmmmhmm. Love you, too. Let me know!"

Chapter 27
Austin

*J*amaica readily—if a little tersely—answered all of my texts to-day, but I still hold my breath while I wait for her to let me into the building. Just because she told me I don't need to bother her neighbor anymore to get in doesn't mean she'll actually let me in today. Last night was . . . fucking intense. *Like sex while camping. Ba-dum Tsss.*

Today wasn't much better, though. I've jumped through hoops, pulled strings, and cashed in favors to organize a surprise for Jamaica. And it's all for nothing if I can't convince her to come with me.

"Yeah?" her voice rings clearly through the intercom.

"It's—" I begin, but it comes out garbled, so I stop and clear the rust from my throat. "It's me."

That oh-so-suave proclamation is followed by a heartstopping moment of silence. Then the buzzer sounds. In a rush, I throw the door open and run to the stairs, which I also take at a run. Outside her door, I stop dou-bled over with my hands on my knees to catch my breath. *Need. More. Car-dio.*

The door opens. She catches me huffing and puffing, too breathless to speak when there's so much I need to say. *Probably for the best.* I'll either say the wrong thing or blurt out everything I want to say before she's ready to hear it.

Her lips twitch but don't make it to a full-blown smile before she gets them under control again. "Hey."

I suck in a lungful of air and will my body to stop acting as if it's going to die. *It was three flights of stairs, not a 5K. Get it together.* "Hey," I reply. "This place needs an elevator." Her smile breaks free, brightening the dim hallway.

I'm too anxious for jokes—a first for me—because too much rides on getting her to hear me out. Clearly stating my intentions up front is probably the best course of action. It can't hurt to try anyway. "Jam, I know you don't have a lot of faith in me right now, and I know that asking you to trust me is asking a lot, but if you don't have plans, could I persuade you to join me for dinner?"

Her eyebrows shoot toward her hairline. She closes her teeth on her bottom lip but nods. "Alright. Let me change."

Seriously? That was . . . suspiciously easy. What's going on here? Before she can rethink my invite and change her mind, I glance down at the cami and cut-off shorts she's wearing. "Nah, you're perfect."

She cracks a smile. "Let me get some shoes, then."

My eyes drop to where she's wiggling her bare, purple-painted toes in the carpet and shrug. "Okay. I don't care if you go barefoot, though."

"The restaurant might."

"Ah . . . This one won't. It's a 'come as you are' kind of place."

She opens the door wider and disappears to get her shoes. I step inside and close the door behind me, then wait patiently next to it. Despite our history, I'm treating this like a first date—sort of. A lot rides on my proving to her that I'm serious. Hopefully, actions speak louder than words for her because I'm sure I'll say things I shouldn't, which is why I didn't call her to ask her out. It seems like the sort of thing I should ask in person.

The shrill siren of a car alarm sounds in the distance and shuts off almost immediately. *The owner probably pushed the wrong button.* I hate it when that happens.

There's a series of loud crashes from the construction site on the next lot. It's odd that they're working after hours coming up on a holiday weekend, but maybe they're behind schedule on the new apartment complex they're building.

Fifteen minutes later, Jamaica emerges wearing a cute little sundress. The scent of her favorite perfume, something that makes me think of the ocean, wafts across the room, and her eyes stand out more than normal.

The effort she put into getting ready sends my heart floating away, clinging to a balloon of hope. Maybe she'll be ready to listen tonight.

Her eyes land on me, still waiting at the door, and she frowns a little. "You could've sat down. Not like you've never been here before."

Yes, I have, and I have memories everywhere. I shrug and smile. Her tendency to read more into my words than I mean has me scared to speak—just like last night. There was so much I wanted to say to her, but I held back for fear of making things worse. "I knew it wouldn't take you long. Ready?"

She slings her little purse across her body and opens it to check for something. Satisfied, she snaps it shut and nods. "Yeah. Where are we going?" she asks while she closes the door behind her and checks the lock.

"You'll see." My hand reaches for her before I remember I can't do that anymore. *This will be harder than I thought.* I alter my trajectory and run my hand through my hair instead to cover the flub.

"Would you like to drive?" I ask to fill the awkward silence as we make our way downstairs. I did promise her she could drive my car someday. Today is as good as any, even if we aren't going out of town like I said we would. We can do that later.

"Yes!" Her hand shoots out, palm up, for the key.

Chuckling, I shake my head and explain, "You don't need it as long as it's in the car. Oh shit! You probably can't drive standard, can you? I didn't think of that before." She would've said something by now if she can't, but I can't resist the opportunity to tease her a bit.

She shoves me playfully, and I let her push me into the wall. "Yes, I can!"

I hold my hands up in surrender. "Just checking. Don't want you grinding gears."

She rolls her eyes and bounces down the last few stairs. "Why did I agree to this again?"

"Because you like me and you like to eat?" I ask, hoping like hell I'm not pushing my luck too far.

"Most of the time," she mutters.

A swooping sensation, like going down a big hill on a rollercoaster, moves through my chest. *She's joking with me!* That has to be a good sign. I catch up with her and casually snag her hand, lacing our fingers together before we step out into the warmth of the evening. That sensation makes another pass when she doesn't pull her hand away.

I don't know what's happening here. It's a far cry from last night's insistence that we're just friends. But I'll take it.

"Oh, my gosh! Austin!" She points with the hand I'm holding, directing my attention to a pile of shattered glass and dented yellow metal that vaguely resembles my car.

The bottom falls out of my stomach, which is interesting because the urge to puke is overwhelming. The blood drains from my face fast enough to make the world spin. I stumble forward, trying to reconcile the battered heap in front of me with the pristine Corvette I walked away from not thirty minutes ago.

That was my car alarm.

The construction site is dead.

"Be careful!" Jamaica cries, grabbing my hands when I reach to touch the ruin. "There's glass everywhere."

She steps in front of me, putting herself between me and my car, and throws her arms around my waist. "I'm so sorry, Austin," she says softly.

Questions rocket around my brain, ricocheting off each other until they're one big snarl and I don't even know where to start.

"Austin, love, you need to ring the cops to file a report."

"Okay." That's a good place to start. I should do that. But I stand there staring, unable to make myself move.

"Just don't touch anything, love. I'll do it."

I'm vaguely aware of her talking to someone on her phone, but the details don't pierce the rage that's slowly burning its way through my body. A quick glance tells me what I need to know. Someone was targeting me specifically. No other car in the lot is damaged. This was personal.

They were determined too. They didn't have much time to pull this off. And in broad daylight . . . They're sending me a message, saying they can get to me whenever and wherever they want.

Someone just started a war they will *not* win.

"An officer will be here soon," Jamaica says, taking me in her arms again. "Do you want to wait upstairs?"

"No." I wrap an arm around her and pull her away from the puddles of glass at her feet. She's in sandals. One misstep and she'll get a shard in her foot. "You don't have to stay here, though. I'm sorry, dinner is—"

"I'm not worried about dinner, and I'm not leaving you to deal with this alone!"

"I'll call Ryan," I reply automatically. He seems like the logical choice.

"Ryan? Why not Mason?"

"Mason is busy." I love my brother. Truthfully, he's the first person I want to call whenever something doesn't go right in my life, but I've bothered him enough this week. "Ryan will be the guy I call to fix her anyway. He might as well come see what he's dealing with now."

"Alright," she says reluctantly. "Want me to ring him?"

"If you would, please." I'm not in the right frame of mind to deal with anyone else right now. Keeping my shit together for Jamaica is hard enough and only accomplished because I can't afford to alienate her further. I need a little more time to get my anger on a leash before I'm suitable company for anyone else.

***

Mason's Tesla stops beside us a short while later. *What the hell are they doing here?* I glance at Jam, who grimaces and ducks her head. *That answers that question.* Doors open and awed swear words flow freely along with a handful of the more colorful phrases creeping back into Fern's vocabulary now that she's happy.

"I did say I wished I would've got the convertible," I tell them, reverting to jokes because the alternative is yelling and no one here is to blame for this. It would make me feel better, but it's not worth having to make it up to them later.

Fern inserts herself into my arms, taking the spot Jamaica ceded for her. I tried several times to convince Jamaica to go back to her apartment. There's no need for her to stand around in the heat—which she hates— waiting on something that could take hours. She ignored me every time, and I'm selfish enough to admit I am grateful for her company. Especially when she wrapped an arm around me and laid her head on my shoulder.

I lean forward to rest my chin on top of Fern's head—a running short joke between us—and sigh, but my eyes never leave the wreckage of my car. "Helluva way to go about it," she says, playing along with me.

"Where's the midget?" Ronni would be a great distraction right now. I would have to keep my shit on an extra short leash for her.

"Sleepover with Nicole's crew."

Damn.

"You weren't *in* it, right?" Mason asks.

I pull my eyes away from my car to look at him. He and Len are standing on the far side—the driver's side—staring at the door. I didn't notice before, but it's slightly ajar. Whoever did this must've hit it hard enough to damage the locking mechanism, or they jimmied the locks before batting practice. "No. We found it this way just before Jam called."

Jamaica edges around the car, taking care not to get glass in her sandals, and stops next to Mason to take in the damage from a different angle. Mason drops an arm around her shoulders and hugs her, propping her up the way Fern is for me.

Len grunts and kicks a tire. "This wasn't gang related. They would've tagged their work. It's personal."

"I figured that, but I don't know why," I mutter. My money is on the creepy asshole who likes to prowl around the parking lot at night, but I still haven't mentioned him to Jamaica, and I don't want to upset her more right now. I'll discuss it with the cops when they arrive and with her at a later date.

"Pissed anyone off lately?" Fern asks.

"N—" I almost change my answer, but a glance at Jam makes me decide to ride it out. "No." I can't imagine what I would've done to deserve this.

Mason frowns at me. "Cops on their way?"

"Yeah, Jam called them."

He nods. "Alright. Ladies, why don't the two of you go pick something up for dinner? Len and I will keep Austin company while he waits, but it might be a while."

"Preference?" Fern asks no one in particular.

"Finger food," Len says, watching me closely. "You're not going to get him to a table anytime soon."

"Good point," she says.

I lift my chin and let her go, but she doesn't move. "That thing you asked us to do?" she asks, her voice pitched low enough it won't carry.

I cringe. This whole evening is seven different kinds of fucked now. "Yeah?"

"It's handled. They should land in thirty minutes. Transportation is handled. Once we're gone, you might call and update them."

"On it. And thank you. You're an angel." I have no idea how she convinced my brother to go along with this harebrained scheme of mine, and I may not want to know. But she did it. That's another reason I don't think twice when she asks me to do something. She will move heaven and earth to make things happen when I ask. I can do the same for her.

She beams at me. "You're very welcome. Don't stress. It'll all work out in the end." She grabs my hand and squeezes, then goes to Mason and pushes up on her tiptoes to kiss him before they fall into a discussion about what to order for dinner.

Jam steps away and comes to stand beside me; close enough I can feel her warmth but not so close that we're touching. I shift a little, edging a bit closer to her under the guise of transferring my weight to the other side to give my leg a break. When I take a breath, my arm brushes hers. It's not much, but it does the trick.

"I hate leaving you right now," she says.

I paste on a smile because I can feel her eyes on me. As touching as her concern is, it's misplaced. I'm going to be fine. It's just a car. Yeah, it sucks. I love my car. But things could be so much worse. "It's okay. Thank you for letting me blank out there for a bit."

"You're welcome. I'm so sorry," she says again.

"Hey, not your fault." I wish I hadn't lost the privilege of hugging her because I'd really like to do that again. I hate that she feels like she needs to apologize for this. It's not her fault at all. How could it be? "I'll get her fixed up good as new. It was just . . . the shock of it."

The sadness in her eyes is killing me. She was supposed to be happy this evening. *I'll find a way to get her where she needs to be.* "I know how much you love your car, though," she whispers.

"At least it was the car and not either of us." That's what is really important here. What if we *were* in it when the asshat came out to play?

She gasps. "I didn't really think of that."

I shake my head and fight the need to kiss that worry away. "Don't. Don't worry about what might've been. You're fine. I'm fine," my stomach growls, interrupting me, and she giggles.

"You must be fine; your appetite is intact."

Grinning for real, I clutch my stomach and exaggerate a groan. "I might not be fine if I don't get food soon!"

Jam rolls her eyes at me. "We're going, we're going."

Len tosses the key to Fern, who catches it one-handed. "Ready when you are," she tells Jam.

Mason and I watch while the girls climb into the front seats. We watch them drive away, then Mason rounds on me. "Now, you wanna tell us what's going on?"

Disgusted, I turn my back on my car and scrub my face with my hands. "Not really, no."

"But you're going to."

I feel like a dick for not explicitly telling Jamaica not to call them. They're busy setting up for the firework show tomorrow, and I've already been a pain in their asses by asking them to help me surprise Jam. "I'm sorry. I know you're busy today. I didn't know she was going to call or I would've told her not to."

He crosses his arms over his chest and turns to me. "Austin, I'm your brother. If you can't call me, who can you call?"

I don't answer because I don't have an answer he'll like. I knew if I called he'd feel obligated to come, just as he has since Dad died. I don't want to be his obligation anymore. I'm supposed to be returning the favor at this point in my life. *Never mind that I'd be pissed if our roles were reversed and he didn't call me.*

"Besides," he continues, "Darren and Grandma have everything well in hand. At this point, it's standing around, barking orders. Darren likes that part."

"Good point," I concede on a sigh. "I guess we should pull up a bit of curb while we wait."

Mason and I sit, but Len stalks around the parking lot like he's searching for something. "I've had a couple run-ins with a guy when I'm leaving here at night," I begin, and I explain both in as much detail as I can remember, right down to the guy's hazel eyes.

Jamaica

"Thanks for this," I tell Fern. I've only said it about twenty times now but I can't seem to stop myself. I know they're busy today, but I knew Austin would feel better having Mason there. Thanking her repeatedly is better than reliving the moment we rounded that last corner, and I saw the destruction. *I was going to drive it today.*

The look on Austin's face . . . Despite his nonchalance about letting me drive it, Austin loves that car. Destroying it is only a step or two below hurting his family.

"Jam," she says patiently, never taking her eyes off the road or her hands off the wheel, "if you thank me one more time, I'm going to assume you're in shock and I'm pulling this car into the next convenience store and buying you something loaded with sugar."

"I'm sorry! I just don't know what to do with myself right now!"

Fern blows out a breath, puffing out her cheeks as she does so. "Talk to me."

"About?"

"What are the chances this is related to what you called to talk to me about?" she asks.

The world around me spins at the vague mention of my ex. I bend over and shove my head between my knees, which is neither easy nor safe in a car, but it's better than puking all over Mason's new ride. "I never considered that," I said, my voice muffled by the odd position.

"Have you told Austin about him yet?"

"I told him about our history. And that he's out. Jordan won't come here. His parole officer wouldn't allow it. I didn't want Austin to worry over nothing." *Jordan's not going to waste that much effort on me.* I can't count the times he told me I'm worthless. He got his revenge when he burnt the house down. He was bluffing when he told Charles he found me. That's all it was. He did things like that all the time, trying to catch people withholding information.

"Then why do you need to stick your head between your knees when I mention him?" she asks.

"I hate that idea that my troubles could've cost Austin something he loves so much," I answer easily. I've hurt Austin enough. I'd never forgive myself if my past came back to bite him in the bum like that.

"Well, hopefully, there are cameras in the parking lot. We'll find out who did this soon enough."

"Yeah." Somehow, that isn't as comforting as it should be. What if it *was* Jordan?

I shudder. If it was him, I'm in trouble. He burnt down my house and maybe—probably—killed his ex. I can only imagine what he'll do if we come face to face. *I need to tell Austin.* But not yet. He's got too much on his plate already. Waiting another day won't change anything.

"When we get back, you should pack a bag and crash at my place tonight. I'll sleep better if I'm not worrying about you there with whoever did this still running loose."

That's another thought that hadn't crossed my mind yet. I swallow hard and try to convince myself that I won't spend the whole night jumping at every little sound now. And I fail. "Yeah . . . I'll do that. Thanks."

"Anytime. So . . . You and Austin are . . . ?"

I sit up slowly and look out the windows to get my bearing and to cover my silence. I don't know what to tell her. I was so excited when Austin showed up and invited me out. But then . . .

"I don't know," I confess, hanging my head. "Last night was a mess. I told him we weren't working out and we could still be friends. Then my sister called today. Some of the things she said made sense. She got me thinking about what happened differently. I was so excited to see him. I thought we were going to get a chance to talk things out, and I could apologize, but we found his car and . . ."

I stop talking in favor of fighting tears. *Everything is such a mess!* And it keeps getting worse! I don't want to have a breakdown right now. Austin will notice when we get back and—

Fern takes a hand off the wheel to grab my arm. "Slow down, Jam. Everything is going to work out. The car is . . . just a speed bump."

"I know, but I feel like I need to fix this soon or I'm going to lose him! I've given him no reason to keep trying! I don't even know why he came over today!"

"Jam, if he were that easy to get rid of, our conversation would be very different right now. Take a deep breath. You'll have time to talk after he's handled the car. In the meantime, just be there for him."

"I can do that," I whisper.

Chapter 28

Austin

*T*he girls return with dinner before the cops arrive. Pizza in a parking lot isn't what I had in mind for tonight. It's a big letdown after spending hours studying a recipe and prepping to cook Jamaica's favorite for her.

Jamaica offers to go upstairs for plates, but Fern stops her. Pizza comes with its own plate—the box. I'll use them to be polite when necessary, but they're mostly a waste.

Fern opens a box, glances inside, and hands it to me. "All meat," she says with a smirk.

"What else is there?" I ask, remembering that night in Mason's kitchen—*their* kitchen now—as I'm sure she is.

Next to me, Mason sighs and shakes his head as he accepts his pizza, which is probably all meat too.

"Don't say it," I warn him, knowing he's about to dust off his *Jeopardy* joke. As much as I love it when we dig at each other for funsies, I'm not in the mood for it right now. "I will glitter bomb your fucking office."

He narrows his eyes at me. "You wouldn't dare."

"Try me, motherfucker."

Mason shudders because he knows I'll do it. There's still glitter floating around from the time I got Darren, and that was nearly two years ago. "Someone is in a mood."

I wave a slice of pizza toward the remains of my car. "Some dickweasel used my car to practice his fucking golf swing! I think I'm entitled."

"Here," Jam says, holding out a styrofoam cup. "This will help."

I take it from her gladly. "Please tell me that's spiked."

"Um . . . I don't think 'spiked' really covers it." I shift a little to give her room to sit, but she walks over to Fern and sits down, opening the box between them to grab a slice.

Fern leans around Mason and grins at me. "I spiked your whiskey with soda. Does that count?" she asks before taking a big bite of the supreme pizza she's sharing with Jam. There's a fourth box, which is probably for Len, but he's still patrolling the lot like someone is paying him to. And since that's exactly what my brother pays him to do, I suppose it makes sense.

I take a tentative pull, bracing for the obnoxious burn of cheap whiskey grabbed in a hurry from whatever liquor store they found first. I should've known better, though. Even in a hurry, Fern would never be so thought-less. She went for the good shit. The first sip goes down smooth.

I pop the plastic lid off my cup and get a good drink. "So, who is car-rying my ass home?"

"Me," Ryan says from somewhere to my right. I jump, slopping a good bit of the precious liquid in my cup onto my lap. *Fucking great.* Now it looks like I pissed myself. That is just what this day needed.

It could be worse.

I locate him stalking our way and wait until he's close enough to see me to waggle my eyebrows at him suggestively. "Is that a threat or a promise?"

He grins and winks. "Whatever you want it to be."

I hold up my cup. "I can no longer consent to anything. Alcohol is in play."

Ryan's shoulders slump. "Damn the luck. There's always next time."

"I'll hold you to it."

"You guys are so weird," Fern grumbles.

"You love it," I tell her.

"Yeah . . . But it needed to be said."

"You want the good news, or the bad?" Ryan asks.

"*Is* there good news?"

"I *can* fix this, but it will take for fucking ever," he says, holding up a finger to forestall my complaint. "*And* I can't accept insurance. But I know a guy."

"Fuck. I didn't think about the insurance thing." I pay for it, might as well use it.

"Already got Darren on it," Mason tells me. "He says you owe him a beer for his services and they'll be here soon."

I salute him with my pizza. "Done."

"Doc will take good care of her," Ryan says.

"Tell me he doesn't have an assistant named Dopey," I mutter under my breath.

Mason snorts and chokes on his pizza.

I drop the slice I'm holding onto my box and pound on his back. "Oh no, you don't, you fucking asshole!"

"Don't make me laugh!" he sputters when he stops coughing long enough to take a breath.

"If you're going out early, I'm taking you there."

"Hey!" Fern calls. "Get in line!"

"I knew him first!"

"I live with him."

"Gee, I can really feel the love here, you two."

"You are all crazy," Jam says, but she sounds happy about it. That makes me happy because she belongs here with us. With me.

I lean forward to smile at her. "It keeps life interesting."

"You get used to it," Ryan tells her.

A police cruiser rolls by and stops behind my car. The big motor falls silent, and both front doors open.

"Hey, you guys? In case I forget later . . . Thanks for being here." It means a lot to me, especially the lengths they're going to in order to cheer me up, but I can't do the emotional stuff right now.

"Well, this looks like the right place," the older of the two officers says before anyone can try to turn my gratitude into a sappy moment. *Perfect timing.* "Is one of you Austin Chambers?"

I jump to my feet and wipe the pizza grease on my jeans before extending my hand. "That's me," I say, squinting at his name tag in gloom of the evening. It's still too early for the streetlights to be on, but dark enough it's difficult to make out the writing.

Officer Dorn is clearly a grizzled veteran of the force. His dark skin is deeply lined, especially around his eyes, and his tightly curled hair and neatly groomed mustache are shot through with gray.

His partner, Underwood, is a big man. I guess him to be about fifteen years younger, but he's not exactly a spring chicken, either. Still, he moves with a grace that belies his size and age. His close-cropped hair is still dark as night.

"Do you know the woman who called this in?" Officer Underwood asks, glancing behind me at Fern and Jamaica.

"Yes, my—" I stop myself before I screw up. "My friend, Jamaica. She was with me when we found it. I wasn't up for making phone calls at the time."

"I understand," the older officer says, offering me a smile. "I'd be upset if it were me, too. We'll need statements from both of you. Then we'll need to get some pictures. You can go ahead and call a tow company if you'd like."

"Not necessary," Ryan calls over. "I brought a trailer."

The officers and I look around. It's a big parking lot, but it's packed, and there's no trailer in sight.

Ryan laughs. "I had to park down the street. I'll move it closer when we're ready. She should drive long enough to load."

"I'll take his word for it," Officer Dorn says.

"Me too."

Officer Underwood calls Jamaica over. "We'll need to talk to you too, Miss. If you'll come with me, we'll step over here, and I'll take your statement."

Chapter 29

Austin

*I*t's fully dark by the time we pull into the drive at Mason and Fern's. My head is still spinning from all the questions the officers asked. I'm sweaty, tired, and Ryan ate my pizza. Fern saved my drink, though, but only because he had to drive. I just want to get home, find something to eat, and stand in the shower until the world makes sense again.

"Hmm," Mason hums from the front seat. "Wonder when they got here?"

I lean to look through the windshield and see Tara's SUV parked in front of the door. That must be what Fern was talking about when she said transportation was handled.

"I dunno," Fern says brightly. Guilt is eating me alive. I hate that things didn't work out as I planned them. But she's here now. That's the important part. I just hope they don't hold it against me.

It takes way too much effort to open the car door and traipse up the stairs behind Jamaica, who somehow ended up coming along to stay the night—probably Fern's handiwork. I'll have to thank her for looking out for me later.

Someone turns the kitchen light on, and four of the seven people gathered around the kitchen table yell, "Surprise!"

The noise wakes Jamaica's niece, who starts to cry. *I hear you, Shila.* I just want a nap too.

The bag Jamaica is carrying hits the ground with a muffled *thump.* Her hands fly to her mouth, and she takes a step back, bumping into me. "Oh, my gosh!" she cries.

"When did you get here? How?" she asks while her family mobs her for hugs. I give her a slight push forward and attempt to edge out of their way, but someone grabs me by the wrist.

"Where do you think you're going?" Mrs. Gunn asks. We spoke on the phone this morning, but her strong accent still catches me by surprise. *Was it really only this morning?* She pulls me to the table and pushes me down in the chair Gabe abandoned at some point after we walked in.

More chairs scuff the floor, and the rest of Jam's family joins me at the table.

A hand lands on my shoulder. I look up into two nearly identical faces, one on either side of me. Now that I'm looking for it, it's easy to see that Jamaica got most of her features from her mother, but, as she said, she clearly owes her tall, slender figure to her father. "*You* did this?" Jamaica asks.

"Yes," I tell her, swallowing a tired sigh. "I'm sorry. We were supposed to be here before they were."

She squeezes my shoulder. "I don't understand."

I try to smile, but I probably just look tired. "I called your mom this morning to ask her what your favorite food is and how to make it," I explain. "I wanted to do something to make up for . . ." I glance around at our audience and decide that if they don't already know why she's upset with me, I'm not going to tell them and have them upset with me right now. I can deal with that tomorrow. "You know . . . And I knew you missed your family. I thought one of your mom's recipes might cheer you up."

"And I told him it was a pity we didn't live closer because I'd just teach him how to cook it!" Mrs. Gunn chips in, excitement glowing in her dark eyes. *Jamaica's eyes . . .*

Smiling at Mrs. Gunn's enthusiasm, I pick up where she left off. "And that got me thinking. A few phone calls and gross misuse of the company's private jet later, here we are. We were coming here for dinner—neutral territory. Your mom was going to teach me how to cook jerk chicken."

And instead, you got mediocre pizza in a dirty parking lot.

I meet Mrs. Gunn's steady gaze. The last thing I need is for two out of three Gunn women angry with me. Apologizing now might save my skin. "I'm sorry it didn't work out that way. I tried to figure out a way to get her here sooner, but she had to give a statement too." I still could've got her here sooner. I could've asked Fern to bring her while Ryan and I were loading my car.

Mrs. Gunn starts to speak, but Jamaica cuts her off. "That isn't your fault! I didn't want to leave you alone!"

"I wasn't alone," I remind her. "You made sure I had my brother and Fern. Thank you, by the way. But now, if you don't mind, I'm going to butt out and let you enjoy some time with your family."

"But—"

I cut her off so we don't spend the next hour arguing about something asinine. "I'll see you tomorrow at the party, right?" I planned to go to bed tonight secure in the knowledge that I'd see her tomorrow. I was already making plans to officially introduce her to my mom and grandparents— assuming everything went well tonight.

But everything didn't, so I still don't know where we stand. She never said the words "we're over," but the words she *did* say weren't terribly encouraging.

Her eyes fill with tears. "Can I talk to you? Please?" she asks, her voice thick with emotion.

I stifle a yawn and stand, stretching out the need to sleep. "Sure."

Mrs. Gunn clears her throat. I freeze instinctively, battling the urge to ask to be excused. It's not me she's glaring at, though.

Jamaica cringes. "Oh, sorry," she murmurs. "Dad, Maeve, Ty, this is Austin."

It's not hard to figure out who's who. Her father is tall, lean, and pale, with bright green eyes and dishwater blond hair. Maeve got his thin lips and upturned nose, but she has her mother's eyes and her curly hair. And, of course, Jam and Maeve both have a blend of their parents' skin tones.

Her dad stands up and reaches across the table. "Call me David."

"Nice to meet you, sir," I say, grasping his hand. "Sorry to run off so soon, but it's been a long day."

"I heard that," Maeve mutters. She stands up with Shila on her hip and walks around the table. "I'm a hugger," she says unnecessarily as she throws her free arm around me.

"Hugs!" Shila twists and wraps both of her chubby arms around my neck.

"I think she likes you," Maeve cackles.

Kids are the best. "Oh, thank you for the hug, precious. That was the best hug I've had all day."

"Don't let Ronni hear you say that," Jam says, poking me in the side. She has a point, but there's no danger of that right now.

Shila lets me go, and I shake Ty's hand. Jamaica told me once that he ran off when he learned Maeve was pregnant. I expected a scrawny kid barely out of high school, not a giant with shrewd eyes that give nothing away. He has two inches on Mason and could probably bench press him too.

I make some general inquiries about their flight—smooth, except for the crying toddler—before Jam drags me from the room.

My apprehension grows with each step. We were supposed to have time to talk things out before her family arrived, but that didn't happen. For all I know, she's going to tell me she never wants to see me again.

She stops in the family room, but turns around to frown over my shoulder at the kitchen, then grabs my hand and tows me toward the door to the basement, closing the door behind me. I hit the light switch so we don't miss a step and break our necks and follow her down the stairs and through the first door she comes to. She shuts that door as well and fumbles for the light switch. I beat her to it on muscle memory alone.

The lemony-scented cleaner Fern uses is no match for the old sweat, metal, and rubber permeating the air here. It smells like every gym everywhere—maybe better because she doesn't try as hard to cover it up as some places I've been. It's comforting to me, in a way. My brain associates it with effort and the satisfying ache of a good workout. I suck in a deep breath and let it out slowly, like a smoker enjoying his first drag after a long day. It's not that it's a pleasant smell, but it clears away some of the grogginess.

Jam whirls around, keeping herself between the door and me, and plants her hands on her hips. "You're not really leaving, are you?"

She wouldn't ask that if she wanted me to leave, would she? I blink, ignoring the way the sandpaper standing in for my eyelids scratches my eyes. "Yeah. I didn't get back to sleep last night, and it's been one helluva day."

"You could stay . . ."

The knot of tension in my chest eases. "Nah. I know they have the room, but there are enough extras here right now."

Jam nibbles at one corner of her bottom lip, something she does when she's thinking hard and doesn't have a pen to chew on. "I'm sorry," she whispers.

I breathe freely for the first time since she ran out of this house. If she's apologizing, we can fix this. "For what?"

"For being so suspicious all of the time. I ruin everything."

"What are you talking about?" I ask, struggling to connect her apology with anything that happened today. It's not her fault everything went sideways. *I hate that she blames herself for everything.*

"The dare," she whispers.

Oh. That . . . This was definitely on the agenda for this evening, but that was before. I'm too tired to do this right now. Too tired to carefully plan my words to avoid another misunderstanding. But I have to say something. "You didn't ruin anything, Jam. *You're* the one who decided you didn't want *me* anymore. I never said I didn't want you. I never said I was done. I believe I said a lot of things to indicate the opposite."

"Austin, I—"

I let her stop me before because I didn't know what to say to make it better, but it's not happening this time. "Yeah, it sucked that you didn't have more faith in me, but fuck, Jam . . . I set myself up for that. We both did. We didn't want promises from each other because we didn't want to be hurt and that backfired spectacularly!"

A tear rolls down her cheek. I reach to wipe it away with my thumb. "Austin—" she begins, her voice strained with the effort of holding back more tears.

I cut her off again because there's still more that I need to get off my chest—things she needs to know before she makes any decisions about us. "But tonight was supposed to be me trying to show you that things changed. I started off wanting to make amends for that stupid joke, but it became so much more. It's scary, and I don't understand it, but I'm ready to make promises. I don't care if that means I get hurt from time to time because you're still struggling to put your past behind you. I'm here for it— for *you*. I'm not giving up on you, but you can't give up on me, either."

"I know."

"And I—wait. What?"

"I'm not giving up on you. I didn't mean what I said. I was scared and lashing out to try to protect myself."

"I'm not giving up on you." A huge weight lifts from my chest, leaving me sagging in relief. I don't even know what to say anymore. "Oh . . ."

Jam steps forward and throws her arms around me, holding on as tightly as she did that day in her kitchen when I told her about my botched proposal to my high school sweetheart. On reflex, I heave a contented sigh. I know we're not fixed yet, but this proves there's something here still. Something worth fighting for.

"Maeve called me today," she murmurs. "Did you have something to do with that?"

"No," I answer honestly.

"She told me that I needed to hear you out."

"Oh?" I don't know much about her sister, other than that she calls me the bad news beefcake, which I still don't understand. "Is that why it was so easy to get you to agree to dinner?"

"Yes," Jamaica answers through a laugh.

Apparently, being the bad news beefcake isn't a bad thing, and I need to thank Maeve for her behind-the-scenes help.

"She helped me see that I was a little . . . extreme and not thinking things through clearly."

"I see . . ." While I agree with her sister, it's probably best to keep that to myself. I don't want to do anything to jeopardize this fragile forgiveness.

There's a smile in her voice when she speaks again. "She reminded me that not every man is like Jordan and that Fern and Mason would have you drawn and quartered if they thought you were intentionally trying to hurt me."

"She's not wrong there," I mutter to myself. If they suspected I was playing this woman, they wouldn't even need a Q-Tip to clean up my remains when they were done with me. There would be nothing for a crime scene analyst to find. I'd just cease to exist entirely.

Jam's laughter tickles my neck, raising goosebumps that spread from head to toe. "Yeah. I felt ridiculous when she pointed that out because Fern encouraged me to hear you out too. I didn't want to listen. I was making excuses to drive you away, but I did it to protect us both because neither of us was ready for a relationship, and I was starting to care too much."

I hold my breath. *Is she saying what I think she's saying?*

"And Maeve pointed out that relationships don't care if you're ready or not."

"I hear that."

"And that you wouldn't be trying so hard to make things right if you didn't care too. That if you were the asshole I wanted to believe you to be, you'd just walk away."

It took Maeve one phone call to accomplish what I've spent days trying to do . . . My sister only ever makes my life more difficult. *I need to trade her in for a newer model or check her for updates.* I wish Jam would've come to *me* to talk about this, but I guess it's not so different from me talking to Mason. *We'll work on it.* "I really like your sister."

"I think she'll like you too once she gets to know you."

"Why does she call me the bad news beefcake?" I ask.

"Ah, you remember that?"

"Uh-huh."

"The picture before the escape room," she explains. "She asked about the beefcake next to me. I started to tell her that you were a Jordan clone, but I was beginning to realize that wasn't true, so I called you bad news instead."

"I see . . ." I have been called worse. And it's sort of fitting. I *am* a beefcake, or so I've been told.

"Sorry . . ."

"Jam," I say on a sigh. "Stop apologizing."

"No! It was wrong of me."

"Alright, let's make a deal. Right now, we're both going to issue a blanket apology that covers anything that happened until this moment, known or unknown, and that's the end of that. Because we're never going to move forward if we both keep tripping over things that already happened."

Eyes squinted, she watches me, and I can practically see her scrutinizing each word in her mind, looking for loopholes. "Deal," she finally says. "I'll go first."

"Aright."

"I'm sorry for anything I may have said or done to upset or hurt you up until this moment."

Relived, I parrot her words back to her, confident that we can get somewhere now—until she frowns again. "What?"

"Should we shake on it?"

"I'd rather kiss on it, but if shaking makes you happy," I hold out my hand and watch her eyes bounce between it and my mouth.

"Just like that?" she asks. I arch an eyebrow in a silent request for clarification. "We're just going to pretend that the last few days didn't happen?"

I shake my head. "Oh. No, not at all." Ignoring it won't make it go away. I'd prefer that method, but it won't keep something like this from happening again. And I never want a repeat of this hell.

She breaths out a laugh. "That's not the answer I expected from you."

I shrug and let my hand drop because we're apparently hashing this out before sealing our agreement. I know the answer she expected of me. Once upon a time, just a few days ago, in fact, I would've been perfectly content to sweep that whole thing under the rug and get back to our regularly scheduled life. But she ran away from me, and that changed things.

I back up until I run into a wall and lean against it, shoving my hands in my pockets to keep from fidgeting. It's got to happen—I know this—but talking about feelings makes me antsy. "Every time I've closed my eyes since Tuesday night, I see the look on your face when you put two and two together and thought I was just some assclown using you for a win. I see you running away from me and Mason's car leaving with you in it, and there was nothing I could say or do to stop you. So no, we're not going to pretend it didn't happen. We're absolutely going to talk about it, but we're not going to do it from defensive positions on opposite sides of an uneven playing field. We're going to sit down and figure this shit out together, even if that means I have to deal with the hard shit because I fucking love you and I never want—"

Jamaica throws herself across the few feet separating us into my arms, cutting me off with a short, sweet kiss that leaves me breathless. "You love me?" she whispers against my lips.

"I'll tattoo your name on my ass to prove it to you if that's what it takes." I wince as soon as the words are out. *So much for being serious.* Though, I'm not opposed to following through if it'll make her happy . . .

She laughs until her head falls back and her whole body shakes with it. It's the happiest—most genuine—laugh I've ever gotten out of her, and I love it. I'll do anything and everything to hear it again. When she rights herself to look at me again, there's a glow in her eyes I've never seen on her before, and I love that too. Making people laugh has always made me happy, but making Jamaica laugh like this . . . It's next-level happy. Nothing else in the world matches this feeling.

Jamaica smiles happily and wipes at the tears caught in her lower lashes. "I love you too."

My stomach does a flip. *So, I was wrong.* There's no way anything could come close to topping the sheer ecstasy that comes from hearing her direct those words to me. I've heard them fall from her lips many times when she's on the phone with her family, but said to me . . . *Breathe, Austin.*

Her eyes fill up with tears that quickly stream down her cheeks and drop off her chin, knocking me off the cloud I was floating on. "I never thought I'd tell you that," she says in a high, tight voice that flays me open and exposes all those sensitive bits I hide behind a shield of humor. "I never thought you'd want to hear it. I realized it somewhere in the middle of crying myself to sleep listening to your drunk voicemail. It wasn't supposed to happen. We had an agreement. I thought there was no way you'd ever feel the same, which is why I fought so hard to drive you away."

I squeeze my eyes shut to hold back tears and hug her tight, leaning to bury my face against the soft skin of her neck. "I wanted to tell you when I left that message, but I was terrified you'd think I was using it as a Band-Aid to salvage our arrangement."

She gasps and leans away to look at me, an unspoken apology in her dark eyes. She whispers my name and pulls me down for another kiss.

Chapter 30

Jamaica

*H*e says I didn't ruin anything, but he's wrong. I ruined two whole days, robbed us of this happiness because I was scared. I was scared of his rejection—of loving someone incapable of reciprocating—but mostly, I was scared of myself. Of getting hurt again. I didn't want to believe that little voice in the back of my head telling me that Austin is a better man than I was giving him credit for being, all because of Jordan.

But standing here in Austin's arms, I know this is right. This is where I'm supposed to be. It's where I want to be. I don't know how it happened or when, but it doesn't matter. I love him, and somehow, he loves me too. *I never want to let go.*

What matters is that, despite how hard I tried to push him away, Austin came back. What he couldn't say with words he said with actions. And while I was fighting to save both of us from hurt, he put aside his fears and fought to keep us together.

"How can you still love me after the way I've treated you?" He probably thinks that's a ridiculous question, and he's right, but I have to ask. The last man I left set my house on fire. I know that's not normal, but part of me is still waiting for the other shoe to drop. It's what *he* conditioned me to do. Nothing was ever this easy when I messed up.

Austin sighs and rucks the back of my shirt up to rub my back. My body melts into his, finding comfort in his touch. "Because I knew it was a misunderstanding—again. And . . . Mrs. Craig said something to me last night that made a lot of sense."

"What's that?" I ask, wondering how big of a "thank you" I owe that sweet old lady.

"Well, in a nutshell, she said that you wouldn't be yelling if you didn't care. I thought about that last night before I fell asleep and I realized that there were things you weren't saying, but the yelling made it hard to hear that."

"And what wasn't I saying?" I said a lot of things, some I meant and some I didn't, and all of them were calculated, to drive him away. I can't see how he found any sort of hope for us from any of it.

"That you hated me and never wanted to see me again. That it was over." He leans back to look down at me. Whatever he sees makes him laugh. "Oh, you came close, but you never actually said it was over and it got me thinking that maybe you didn't really mean it."

"But how? And *why?* Walking away would've been easier!" And that's Austin's M.O. He takes the easy road. Or . . . he did until recently. That changed that day in my kitchen when he said he wanted us to be something. But he wanted something uncomplicated, and I complicated it to the extreme.

I can't see it from where my head rests on his shoulder, but I feel him nod. "Yeah, it would've. But I'm not the kind of man to walk away from a challenge, which is sort of how we ended up in this situation to begin with. Besides, you're talking to the king of deflection, Jam. I joke my way through uncomfortable situations. You . . . take a different approach."

I duck my head, hiding it against his chest, embarrassed by his assessment. It's spot-on, though. I get loud and refuse to listen to anyone else.

He hugs me extra tight. "I suspect it's a recent development for you . . . Learned behavior after what Jordan put you through?"

"Yeah," I whisper, amazed that he puzzled out. *He notices more than anyone gives him credit for.* That's by design, though. He likes to be underestimated, written off as the joker. But how are we going to work if one of us yells and the other jokes their way through confrontations?

"We'll figure it out," he murmurs, addressing the question I didn't give voice to. "We'll learn, just as long as we don't give up on each other. And I don't give up easily."

I squeeze him as hard as I can. My breath shudders with the sobs I'm holding back. *How did I end up here with him?* A better question would be, what did I do to deserve him? "Why are you fighting so hard to hold onto me when all I've done is complicate your life?"

His hands slide around to cradle my face. He leans back until I'm looking him in the eye and smiles at me. "Because you're worth it. Life might've been easy, but at what cost? I'm happier with you than I've ever been, even when we're fighting, because life has meaning with you in it. I think of you first thing each morning and last thing each night and every other minute in between. When we're not together, I can't wait to see you again. I can't wait to tell you jokes and hear you laugh and do little things just to make you happy. That is my purpose in life, Jam: to make you happy. And I like to think I'm good at it."

"You are," I whisper through the lump clogging my throat. All those things he said, they're true for me too. It's more than enough for me but can he say the same? If so, will it still be true when the new wears off? "But what do you get out of this? Because it sounds very one-sided."

"I get you," he says with a smile. "I get to tell you I love you and know that you don't doubt it. I get someone who doesn't hesitate to challenge my bullshit when I go too far. I get to watch you heal and know that I helped you do that." His eyes light up with excitement, and he asks, "Did you notice how nervous Fern was walking down the aisle?"

The question is completely off-topic, but I humor him. "Yes."

"And did you see how she relaxed the second Mason took her hand?"

I think back and smile reflexively at the memory. "Yes."

"That's their love," Austin says, surprising me with his perceptiveness again. "That's what it does. Mason anchors Fern, and she helps him let go of everything weighing him down. Together they fly. Everyone has something different. This is ours. It'll change over time, I think, but for now, you get to heal, and I get to love you without fear of rejection. I am enough for you as I am. You don't demand that I change, but you make me want to be better. And apparently, you'll love me either way."

"Yes." My whisper turns into a sob and tears break free. How could I do anything else? This man has seen the shattered facets of who I am and saw something worth salvaging and treasuring when others would've thrown me away.

"That's our love. We don't have to understand it. We just have to accept it. I stood beside my brother at his wedding, thinking to myself that I'd never have something like that. But here I am, and here you are, and we do. We only have to accept it."

Austin's confidence wears through my fear. The scars on his heart are different from mine, but if he can do this, I can too. I just have to have faith. In him. In myself. In *us*. It won't be easy, but as long as we love each other, we'll get through it.

"Alright," I whisper, then pause for another kiss. He groans and teases the seam between my lips with his tongue, fanning the ever-present spark between us into a flame. He might not want me to apologize, but I can make it up to him in other ways. I can show him that I know he's not Jordan. "But you still owe me a pair of boxers, and I intend to collect."

His lips stretch into a smile. "I can arrange that. You can raid my underwear drawer tomorrow night."

I shiver, thrilled with the promise of tomorrow. But . . . "I'm partial to the ones you're wearing."

Austin slips his hands to my bum and pulls me close enough to feel him hardening for me. "Mmm. I like the way you think. But I'm exhausted, and your family is here. Raincheck?"

"Raincheck," I agree, albeit reluctantly. We probably have another fifteen minutes before anyone comes looking for us. But he's right. My family is here. He made that happen for me, and I'm not properly appreciating that gift. "Could you stay for just a little longer, though?"

He cradles my face in both hands and lets his thumbs skim across my cheekbones. "Anything to see you smile."

"A kiss would make me smile," I whisper, inching closer.

"I love you," he murmurs, then closes the scant distance between us.

His lips are hot against mine, hot enough to light a fire in me that begs to burn unchecked. Balancing on one leg, I wrap the other around his hip. He slides his hands down my body to grasp my bum.

"Don't tease me like this, baby," he groans.

"But I'm not teasing."

He chuckles. "Don't test me, then. I won't be able to look your mama in the eye when we go upstairs if we keep this up."

I *do* want Mum and Dad to like him. "Fine. But later . . ."

"Tomorrow," he promises.

***

Austin shuffles along behind me. I almost feel bad about asking him to stay longer, but I've missed him so much. And I really want my family to meet him.

Conversations stop when we walk into the kitchen. Mason, Fern, Gabe, and Tara are huddled around the table along with my family—a sight that nearly brings me to tears. Both of my worlds are colliding before my eyes, and it's wonderful.

Mum turns in her chair to face us. Her narrow-eyed glare stops me in my tracks. I ease to the side a bit, putting myself between her and Austin. We *just* figured things out. I don't want her scaring him off already. Austin squeezes my hand and moves to stand next to me, though.

"And where will you be staying?" Mum asks him.

Gabe and Mason exchange grins. Mason mimes eating popcorn, and they both lean back in their chairs to watch Mum put Austin through the wringer. As much as I don't want this to happen right now, it's probably best to get it out of the way. The longer Mum waits, the more ammunition she'll have.

Austin squeezes my hand again, shifting his weight from foot to foot under the weight of that glare. "Uh . . . I'm going home."

"You're not going to wait until we turn in and sneak into Jam's room?"

Maeve and I lock eyes, and I have to bite my tongue to keep from laughing. Her lip disappears between her teeth like she's struggling to do the same. We both know her stance on such things; we're grown and not doing anything she didn't do.

I know exactly how it feels to be the object of that glare, but I also know that Mum is only testing him. I'm not worried about him failing as long as he doesn't do a runner. She's already decided she likes him, or she wouldn't bother.

"Oh, no! I would nev—"

"Don't insult my intelligence, boy," Mum snaps. "I was young once."

Maeve and I give up the fight. Our laughter draws Mum's ire for a moment, but she dismisses us with a roll of her eyes. Maybe I should've warned him, but it's best to let the two of them feel each other out.

Austin shoves his hands in his pockets. "I'm just going to shut up now."

Mum's head bobs. "Good choice. I may not like the truth, but I'd prefer it to a lie."

He frowns at that. "I wasn't lying—at first," he adds quickly when she raises a questioning brow. "I didn't plan to stay here tonight. I asked you to come so that Jamaica could have time with her family."

"But you don't want to spend time with us?" Mum asks. Dad might be the lawyer, but Mum could hold her own in a courtroom any day of the week. If he'd said he was staying so he could get to know them better, she would've asked why he invited them if he wasn't going to give them time with me.

Austin opens his mouth and abruptly snaps it shut again. He exhales sharply, then tries again. "With any luck, there will be plenty of opportunities for me to spend time with you all in the future. Time with you now was my gift to Jam, and I want her to have that without feeling obligated to pay attention to me."

Mum turns her head my way and raises her eyebrows. "I like him. He doesn't try to butter me up. You should convince him to stay."

I breathe a small sigh of relief even though I knew he would pass her tests. She doesn't care so much about the answers as she does the intent behind them—will they say what they think she wants to hear to win her over, or will they tell the truth at the risk of displeasing her?

Fighting back a proud smile, I look at my boyfriend. "You know Fern will cook breakfast."

"Cinnamon rolls," Fern adds. She looks at my dad and smiles. "And Irish coffee."

Austin squints at me, then at her. "Why does this feel like a trap? The cinnamon rolls are bait, aren't they?"

"*That's* your plan to convince him?" Mum asks on the heels of his questions.

I roll my eyes at both of them. "Just wait until you try the cinnamon rolls," I tell Mum. "And Austin can't resist food. He's . . . snacktivated."

"Snacktivated?" Maeve asks, beating Mum to it.

I nod. "It sounds better than calling him treat trained! The man loves food!"

Austin's stomach growls as if following the conversational cues. "She's not wrong . . . Snacktivated," he murmurs. "I like it."

The legs of Mum's chair scrape across the tile floor, and she crosses the room at the same unhurried pace at which she does everything. She isn't tall, but she isn't short either. Maeve and I can look each other in the eye over her head when she keeps her hair short. But she has to pull Austin's face down to her level to kiss him on the cheek.

"You've been good for my daughter," she tells him. "Do you know how long it's been since I've heard my Jamaica make a joke?"

His eyes find mine, but their customary sparkle is gone, replaced by a grimness that makes me squirm. "No, but I'm going guess the answer is too long."

Mum tips her head to the side but then nods. "Yes. Too. Far too long."

"I can't take all the credit here," Austin tells her. "Fern started it."

"Yes," she tells me, patting his cheek. "I like this one. You can keep him."

***

The sunny yellow walls of the room Fern assigned me give the room a cheery glow. Next door, in the blue room, Ty and Maeve are arguing about something. *When* aren't *they arguing?*

I unzip my backpack to change into my pajamas while Austin showers and my plans get sidetracked by the little book I shoved in as an afterthought. I never did remember to thank my mother for her thoughtful gift that day. *I better do that now.*

Mum and Dad's door is open, so I tap on the frame as I walk in.

"Aren't you supposed to be sleeping?" Dad asks from the desk where he's probably reviewing a case file because he doesn't know when to quit working, either.

"I'm getting there." I hold up my journal so Mum can see from the bed. She closes her book on her thumb, giving me her undivided attention. "I found this in my bag while I was getting my pajamas and remembered that I never called to thank you the day I got it. So, thank you! I love it!"

Mum scowls at the book, and my heart sinks. "I don't know what you're talking about, Jam. I didn't buy you that."

"Y-you didn't?" I don't know why I'm asking. Mum wouldn't tease me like that. Especially not after Jordan. Who else could have given it to me, though? Fern wouldn't leave it outside my door like that. And we talk to each other almost daily. She would've mentioned it by now.

"No," she says, shaking her head.

My eyes slide to Dad, but he shakes his head too. "Maybe it was Austin or one of your friends?"

"It was probably Fern," I say. Maybe she got busy and forgot to mention it? *Or maybe it was Jordan . . .* I paste on a smile to hide my fear. I'm safe here behind Mason's gate, his security system, and Len's watchful eye. I don't want to ruin my parents' holiday with my worries that are probably nothing. "I already asked Austin."

"Fern is a good girl," Mum says approvingly. "I like all of your new friends so far."

"Jam?" Austin calls softly from the hallway.

"And him," Mum says. Almost as an afterthought, she adds, "And he's cute, too. Well done."

"Oy!" Dad cries. "I resent that."

"Oh, hush. You resemble that." Having mollified Dad, she looks at me and winks. "Good night, Jam m'love. I'll see you in the morning."

"Good night," I whisper on my way out the door. *I'll tell everyone Sunday. I don't want to ruin their celebration.*

Chapter 31
Jamaica

"Morning, sunshine," Fern greets me when I stumble into the kitchen, rubbing my eyes and fighting back a growl at her effervescent cheerfulness. *How can anyone be that happy before noon?*

"Morning," I grumble. "Where's Austin?" I woke up disoriented and alone; neither did anything to improve my mood.

"Outside with your mom," she says as she sends a plate loaded with a cinnamon roll the size of my face sliding across the counter toward me.

"Your dad is an accomplice in Austin's torture," Mason says from the table, causing me to jump. I missed him there when I walked in.

Torture probably doesn't begin to cover it. He accused me of cross-examining him once. That was nothing compared to what my parents will do to him. They'll have him so turned around he'll admit to things he's never thought about doing. "Crud. I guess I'm going to go rescue your brother."

"Oh, I dunno," he says. "Maybe we should give them a few more minutes. It's good for him. I enjoyed watching him squirm last night."

Fern heaves a falsely exasperated sigh. "You're terrible."

I slip out the back door to rescue my boyfriend from the torture chamber. Instead of cries of pain or pleas for mercy, I'm greeted with laughter and Shila's happy shrieks. No matter what I tell myself, some small part of me is relieved.

Mum and Dad are seated on one side of the massive picnic table, and Austin and Shila are on the other. Shila is sitting on the table in front of him, happily engaged in a game of peekaboo.

"Peekaboo!" Austin coos, sending Shila into another fit of squeals. *The phrase "made my ovaries explode" makes perfect sense now.* This isn't the first time I've ever seen a man playing games with a kid. Apparently, it takes just the right man. And I'd very much like to drag this one back upstairs for a different sort of game.

Shila holds her chubby little hands up over her eyes. "Boo!" she shouts, thrusting her arms up into the air.

Austin grabs her ankle and holds it up, ducking down to pretend to hide behind her foot. He sits up and cries, "Peekaboo!"

Mum spots me watching and greets me with a smile and a wave. "They've been at it for ten minutes," she chuckles.

The seat next to Mum has a better view of their antics, so I take it. "Well, I think he's a toddler trapped in a man's body, so . . ."

I cut a bite of my cinnamon roll and sigh happily when the sweetness hits my tongue. *Worth getting out of bed for.* Okay, Austin and Shila were totally worth getting out of bed for. The food is just a bonus.

"How long have you been up?" I ask Austin.

"Long enough I've got a workout and a shower in," he says, switching to tickling Shila's sides so he can talk without punctuating with random "peekaboo's."

I shudder. "Yuck."

Mum and Dad laugh at my reaction, though there's nothing funny about it.

Dad grins at me. "What's the plan for today?" he asks.

"Mason and Fern will leave soon to finish setting up for the picnic, which officially starts at noon," Austin says.

"Wow, why so early?" Mum asks.

"So the employees can come early if they have other plans for the evening," he explains. "They're leaving the keys to the Tesla for you."

"But—" Mum begins, but Dad cuts her off.

"Really? I was rather keen to drive it!"

"Yep," Austin tells him. "Fern mentioned a rental car. Mason said there was no need. You'll all fit in it. You're welcome to go wherever you'd like. Don't worry, he has good insurance."

Lord help us all. Dad will be like a kid with a new toy.

"And where will you be?" Mum asks him.

"Following orders."

I choke on my cinnamon roll. Austin? Follow orders? "Is there food in it for you?" I ask to tease him.

His eyes get the same dreamy, unfocused look to them Shila used to get when she was milk drunk as a baby. "So much food," he murmurs.

Mum turns to stand up from the bench. "Are Fern and Mason still in the kitchen?"

"They were when I came out," I tell her.

"If you're looking to argue with them about the car, you might as well save your time," Austin says, addressing Mum. "Those two redefine stubborn."

"Look who's talking," I mutter.

His smile becomes a deep scowl that doesn't suit him at all. "That's enough wisecracks from the peanut gallery."

"No," Mum says before Austin and I can start bickering.

Oh, my gosh. That's how we *flirt!* We're those people. Fighting is . . . foreplay. Almost every conversation I've ever had with Austin replays in my head in the span of a heartbeat. This revelation makes me view them all in a new light.

"I want to volunteer to help today," Mum says, distracting me from rehashing the day I met Austin.

"What?" Dad asks. "We're on *holiday,* Gloria!"

"And?" she asks, almost making two syllables out of it.

It's all the warning Dad needs. Her mind is set. This is happening.

Dad sighs. "And . . . that sounds like a lovely way to spend the day," he says sadly.

"It'll be fun, Dad. I said I'd help ages ago." I figured I might as well. Fern will be busy anyway. I don't know if the others will be there or not since they're not CFI employees. And if they are, they'll probably help too.

"You can still take the car," Mason says. Mum, Dad, and I all turn quickly, like children caught misbehaving, to find him just outside the door, a smiling Fern tucked into his side. "There's not much left to do at this point, but someone has to be there to handle any crises that pop up."

"And our grandparents are much too old to deal with all that," Austin says. I don't need to see his smile. It is plenty evident in the tone of his voice.

Mason grins. "Let them hear you say that. I *dare* you."

"You know," Austin says, "I think I've had enough dares for a while."

I turn around to smile sweetly at him. "Fine. *I* dare you. But I want to be there to see the look on Miss Lola's face when you call her old." That old woman can work circles around just about anyone I know, in heels, and look poised and polished while she does it.

"Challenge accepted."

Mum looks at me. "You'd best get dressed. I'll go wake your sister."

"Good luck with *that*." Maeve hates mornings more than I do. She'll be an absolute bear, especially when Mum tells her she's getting up to go work.

Mum smiles like she has a secret to tell. "It's not so hard anymore. I'll just tell her Shila got her favorite lipstick and drew on the walls. She'll bounce right out of bed."

I scramble off the bench and follow her because this is something I didn't know I needed in my life. "This I've gotta see."

***

The sun just barely kisses the horizon, painting the sky with brilliant, bold strokes of oranges, blues, purples, and pinks. Sunset doesn't bring the promise of cooler temperatures, though. Darn it. I swipe at a bead of sweat about to roll down my face and grab the steering wheel of the nearest pedal tractor to pull it back to the starting line. Mason said there wasn't much to do today except stand around and handle crises, but he seriously underestimated the number of crises that would occur. They call it a picnic, but it's a whole *event*—games for kids and adults, food trucks, a BBQ contest, craft vendors, the works. It's a street fair shoved into a car park.

It was all hands on deck from the moment we arrived, and I was tasked with helping an elderly couple, the Hopewells, run their kiddie tractor pull. Mrs. Hopewell fell and broke her arm last night, so she can't do most of the things she normally would. It's not what I planned to do with my day, but it *is* fun. The kids are so cute, from the big 'uns determined to win the gold plastic championship cup to the ones who can barely climb on the tractors by themselves.

"What the hillbilly hell is this?"

I stop. My stomach churns, threatening to reject its contents. That voice . . . It sounded like Jordan . . . I quickly scan the crowd, ready to run for Austin or Fern or someone, but he's nowhere in sight. *The heat must be causing me to hallucinate.* Or maybe one of the men in the crowd has a similar voice. That's all.

Still, I can't shake the sensation of eyes tracking my every move. *I need to tell Austin.* It won't stop my foolishness, but at least he can help reassure me. *Tomorrow.*

I finish lining up the pedal tractors and step aside while the next wave of kids swarms to the starting line. There aren't as many this time—more tractors than kids—so I clear away the vacant ones while Mrs. Hopewell goes over the rules. *I can recite them in my sleep at this point.* The air horn blasts, and off the kids go, pedaling with all their little might.

One little girl can barely reach the pedals. She's probably too young for this, but the couple doesn't turn any child away as long as they can get in the seat by themselves and don't try to cheat.

Once the bigger kids are far enough ahead that no one will cry foul, I sneak over and give her a push in the right direction. Getting the tractors moving is most of the battle. As long as she pedals, she'll make it to the finish line.

She tips her head back to smile at me and nearly topples backward off the tractor.

I lunge to stop her from hitting her head, but she catches herself. "Pedal, sweetie!" I cry over the commotion of cheering parents. I give her another little nudge in the right direction and step back. She's not the first kid I've given a boost to today, but I draw the line at doing all the work for them.

This time, she doesn't look back. "You can do it!" I cheer, clapping for her.

An arm wraps around my waist from behind. Still jumpy from hallucinating Jordan's voice, panic grabs my heart and squeezes until I notice the ring Austin never takes off. It was his father's.

"Sorry, didn't mean to scare you," he says, his lips brushing my ear.

"It's alright," I tell him, feeling foolish all over again for my jumpiness. There really is nothing to worry about. There's a perfectly logical explanation for everything that doesn't involve Jordan. I don't know why any part of my brain is wasting time on him. "I missed you." This is the first time we've had a chance to talk since about ten minutes after we arrived.

"I missed you too. You were adorable with that little girl. Had to give you a hug."

"I'll take it. Aren't you supposed to be sweating your butt off somewhere else?"

"My booth closed down."

"What, did you scare everyone away?"

"Nope, ran out of paint."

"Paint?"

"Yep. Pretty sure I left my mark on every kid here."

"Uh . . ."

He snorts out a laugh. "Yeah, that didn't sound good. I was at the face painting booth. One of the helpers had to go home—heat exhaustion."

"I hope they're okay."

He kisses the side of my head. "They will be."

The little girl finally makes it across the finish line, and I clap and cheer along with her family.

"Gotta go," I tell Austin, wiggling out of his arms. The jog to the finish line is short, but it's a lot easier than dragging the tractors back. They're *heavy* for something so small.

"You can go after this one," Mr. Hopewell says once we've got them all lined up again. He takes off his hat to mop his bald head with a handkerchief, which he then shoves in his back pocket. "We're about done here. The kids are getting tired, and so are the parents."

"Are you sure?" Yes, I want to go with Austin, but I was given a job to do, and I don't like to leave anything unfinished.

"Yeah, I can handle it. Thank you for your help."

"You're welcome, Mr. Hopewell."

Mrs. Hopewell calls for the kids to pick a tractor. There are even fewer this time, proving Mr. Hopewell's theory. We remove the extra tractors, and Mrs. Hopewell blasts the air horn again.

Mr. Hopewell offers me his hand. "Go on and enjoy the rest of your evening, Miss Gunn. And thanks again."

"No problem!" I grasp his hand, then jog around the edge of the makeshift race track—white lines spray-painted on the asphalt—to tell his wife goodbye.

"Jam!" Austin calls. When I look, he holds up his phone and jerks his thumb over his shoulder toward the lot next to the car park. I give him a thumbs up to let him know I understand—he's got a call he's going to take out there so he can hear better.

"Hello, dear," Mrs. Hopewell greets me. "Calling it a day?"

"Yes, ma'am. Mr. Hopewell told me to take off."

Her broken arm doesn't stop her from bestowing a hug upon me. I hug her back, taking great care not to jostle her. "Thank you for your help today. Was that your husband?" she asks, nodding in the direction Austin went.

"My boyfriend," I correct her.

"Good. You're too young to be married," she says, throwing in a wink. Then she smiles and adds, "We were married right out of high school. I don't regret it, but sometimes I think we rushed."

"But you made it work," I say, thinking of my parent's whirlwind romance. They met while Dad was on holiday in Jamaica. Four days later, he proposed.

"Oh yes. Work. And speaking of, I'd best get back to it." She pats me on the shoulder, and I'm dismissed. I weave my way through the scant crowd, following the glow of Austin's phone in the rapidly growing darkness.

Chapter 32

Austin

"Mr. Chambers, thank you for returning my call." The tightness in Officer Dorn's voice is telling. Something is wrong. "Of course, officer. Did you find them?" I ask, cutting to the chase. It doesn't take me long to put enough distance between myself and the parking lot. The hum of the festivities fades away with every step until I don't have to strain my ears to hear his delayed answer.

"Not exactly." Something is definitely wrong, and I get the feeling he doesn't want to tell me. "It's about Miss Gunn. She isn't answering her phone. We're concerned enough we reached out to you hoping you might be together."

I take a deep breath and exhale, releasing the urge to yell for him to quit stalling and tell me. "I just saw her. She's helping at my family's company picnic."

"Good, can you have her call me as soon as possible?"

Another deep breath in and out. Jamaica will just tell me anyway, so we might as well save us all some time. "I'm sorry, Officer Dorn, but if you're concerned enough to reach out to me, can't you tell me what's going on?"

A long pause follows my question. "What is your relationship to Miss Gunn?"

"I'm her boyfriend," I say, my chest swelling with pride despite the apprehension his dodginess triggers.

"That's what I thought, but you two were fighting or something yesterday?"

"Not exactly . . ." If he's perceptive enough to pick up on that without us telling him my answer will not fool him. I may as well explain. "We had a misunderstanding and were in the middle of working things out. We're good now."

Another long pause. "It's about her ex," he finally says.

I seethe at the mention of him. "Jordan? What of him?"

"So you know about him?"

"I know he wasn't good to her and that he was in prison, but he's out now."

"Okay, good. I don't feel bad for telling you then."

Something about the way he says it has warning bells going off in my head. "What do you mean?"

"Maybe I'm old fashioned, but it's one of those things you should hear from her. But . . . under the circumstances . . . Jordan Graham has disappeared. We have reason to believe he might be here. He stopped showing up for meetings with his parole officer. He's not answering calls. His family hasn't seen him, and they won't cooperate. There's a warrant out for his arrest. Due to his history, he is considered armed and dangerous. Miss Gunn needs to know he could be looking for her."

Several things click into place all at once. Her sudden jumpiness. The man in the parking lot. The gift outside her door. My car. It could all be related. "When did he get out?"

"A few months back. I don't have the exact date in front of me right now."

"That's okay. When did he disappear?" I ask, my feet already carrying me back the way I came. I've got to get back to Jamaica.

"His P.O. hasn't heard from him since mid-May. Why?"

I stop while I count the weeks. "I'm just . . . Trying to figure some things out. The first time I saw the man I told you about in the parking lot was a little over two weeks ago. That's around the time someone left a present outside her door. She assumed it was from her parents and that's the last I heard of it. But now . . ."

"Now, you're wondering if they're all related or if you're paranoid?"

"Yes."

"I wouldn't say you're paranoid."

"Austin?" Jam asks, startling me.

There's no reason for me to feel guilty, but I still look over like Jam caught me doing something I shouldn't. Backed by the glow of the parking lot, it's hard to see her face, but her smile still knocks me out. "Jam."

Her beautiful smile fades away. "What's wrong?"

In my ear, Officer Dorn asks, "Are you with her now? Is something wrong?"

"Yeah, she's here," I tell him. To her, I say, "Officer Dorn was trying to reach you. He called me when he couldn't."

She reaches for me, so I open my arms and hold her close.

"Baby, no one has seen Jordan in weeks."

Her arms tighten around me, and she hunches over to hide her face against my chest. "No," she whispers. Her voice is thick with tears when she continues. "This can't be happening!"

I take a deep breath and exhale slowly to dispel the urge to grab Jam and shake her until her teeth rattle. I'd never hurt her, but *fuck*, she doesn't sound surprised by the news. "You knew he was looking for you?"

"I . . . Had a call from an old acquaintance warning me that he might've figured out where I went."

"Are you getting this?" I ask Officer Dorn, wanting to keep him apprised. On his affirmative, I return my attention to Jamaica. "Why didn't you tell me, babe?"

"I thought it was one of his tricks!" she says in a voice so small it brings tears to my eyes. "I figured you'd get all overprotective because it's what Mason would do to Fern and I don't need another man trying to dictate my every move."

"Babe . . . Yeah, I get where you're coming from. I probably would've gone a little overboard, but I wouldn't stop you from living your life! I'd just . . . help you live it safely."

Len has some friends in the security business. Big goons who scare the bejeezus out of hardcore gang members, according to Fern. For the right price, I'm sure one of them would guard Jam indefinitely. And I'm willing to pay whatever they want.

Something hard presses against my spine, just above Jam's arms where they're looped around my waist. "Hang up the phone."

Jamaica gasps. Her arms constrict around me like a vise grip. Something about the voice is familiar. If it weren't for our current conversation, it might've taken me weeks to place it. As it is, images of a man dressed all in black in the darkness of the parking lot materialize in my head.

"I said—"

"I heard you!" I snap at him. He doesn't have a knife or I'd be bleeding already. I haven't heard a gun cock, but he could've done that before he got here. Either way, it's not worth the risk. Yet.

Instead of dropping my phone, I slowly crouch down to lay it in the grass. Jam moves with me, and so does the gun jammed against my back. "There's no need for the gun," I say loudly.

Jordan ignores me. "Good. Now, no one needs to get hurt as long as you're not stupid," he hisses.

"Jordan, just stop this!" Jam cries.

"No!" he shouts into the night. "You're mine, not his. I'm here to bring you home! He can't stop me! I'll fucking kill him!"

My heart leaps into my throat. *You'll take her over my dead body.*

Jam shakes in my arms. Her eyes, barely visible to me in the moonlight, go wide. It takes everything I have not to turn around and knock his delusional head off his shoulders. But I can't provoke him. Not yet. Not until she's safely away.

"Okay!" she says quickly. She lets me go, and I miss her arms around me as soon as he does. I have less faith in him than she does, and if I'm going to die, I'd rather have her holding me. *It's better this way, though.* "Let him go, Jordan. I'll do whatever you want. Just let him go."

"I know you will. Come here, baby. I'll keep you safe."

The thought of her getting closer to him has bile climbing my throat. Can he not see that he's the only danger here? She was safe until he came back into her life. I open my mouth to ask but stop myself. *Not yet.*

"How did you find me?" she asks, clearly stalling him.

He snorts. "I applied for a job at the Chicago branch of Chambers Freight and guess who's pretty face I saw plastered all over their website?"

Jam gasps. "The form I signed," she whispers.

"It wasn't hard after that. I just followed that Chambers asshole around until you turned up where he was."

I squeeze my eyes closed. Grandma put the wedding pictures on the company website. He must've followed Mason.

"Now, get. Over. Here."

"Promise me you won't hurt him!" Jam cries.

"He stole you from me!" Jordan snarls, prodding me with the gun again. "Why do you care?"

"You know I don't like to see people get hurt!" Jam says quickly. "Th-that's why I ran away. People got hurt and—"

"I know, baby," he coos. "As long as he's not stupid, no one needs to get hurt."

That's not a promise . . . Regardless, I want her well away from me. At this range, if he shoots, the bullet will go right through me and into her. I can't count on him being lucid enough to realize that. If he thinks *I'm* the man here who hurt her, he's got issues.

"Okay," she says. She sidesteps to my right, holding her hands above her head so he can see them.

"Jam, run," I whisper to her. I don't care what happens to me. I'd rather die to give her a headstart than live knowing she suffered another second at his hands. "Just go."

"Shut up!" Jordan snarls. "Don't listen to him, baby! He can't hurt you anymore!" He prods me in the back in warning. "I swear to God, I will shoot."

"No! Don't!" she screams.

I look over her head at the parking lot packed with people, hoping that someone didn't hear her scream and decide to come to investigate. Unless it's the right people, they'll only make things worse. Jordan is unstable. That kind of pressure will send him over the edge. *But if the right people hear* . . .I know I saw Len and his buddies earlier, watching the kids doing rubber duck races, of all things.

I just have to stall him. There has to be something I can do to get Len's attention, or to distract this madman long enough for me to come up with a way out.

"Come here!" Jordan shouts at Jam. "The fuck away from him!"

I fight the overwhelming need to hold her back. I need her to move, but I don't want her closer to him. She moves slowly, whether playing for time or hoping not to startle him into doing something stupid. I turn my head to watch her as long as I can and breathe a sigh of relief when she's behind me and the gun.

I get another prod in the back. "Stop looking at her! She's mine, and you can't have her. She wants *me*, not *you*, you arrogant asshole with your nice car, thinking you can have whatever you want because you have money! Well, she's mine! You can't have her!"

Funny, I got that the first time you said it. "Whatever you say, man," I tell him, hoping to pacify him. Play his game like she is. He can believe whatever he wants. I know the truth. Jamaica belongs to no one, but for all intents and purposes, she's *mine*. I'm hers. That's just the way it is. But I'm not going to bait the guy with the gun to my back, and I'm not going to let him get under my skin. He's already lost this game; he just doesn't know it yet.

The *thwack* of flesh striking flesh rings clearly through the darkness. Jam cries out in pain. *Game over.*

I pivot to my left and grab his wrist with one hand and shove his arm down and away with the other. He screams, and a shot rings out.

"Austin!" Jamaica's scream is distant even though she's not two feet away. *At least I can still hear.*

Hugging his wrist close, I grab the gun with my empty hand and crank it back towards his body, forcing him to choose between releasing it or letting me break his wrist. I'm good with either option because they both end with the gun in my hand.

"Get my phone!" I shout over Jordan's screams. Jam frowns and pulls her own phone from her pocket. I shake my head. "Officer Dorn is still on the line."

I feel something crack in Jordan's wrist. His screaming intensifies, but the gun is mine. Relief makes me a little dizzy, but I've come too far to fuck this up now. "You move, and I shoot," I tell him.

He ignores me, or maybe he didn't hear me over his screams, and falls over, curling around his injured wrist. *Guess I can allow that.* He could try to come up off the ground and tackle me, but that wrist is going to slow him down.

"Got it!" Jam calls, though her voice is muffled to me still.

"You're going to have to talk to him. That shot wasn't good to my ears."

Flashlight beams knife through the darkness, swinging wildly as if the people holding them are running. I suppose an entire parking lot full of people heard that shot and freaked the fuck out, so it makes sense.

"Austin!" Mason's voice is identifiable even with broken ears. "Jamaica!"

"We're fine!" Jam shouts back.

Len and his goon squad materialize seemingly out of nowhere. One of them grabs Jordan by the good arm and hauls him to his feet.

"I'll take that," Len says, relieving me of the gun.

The weight of that responsibility falls off my shoulders like a fucking avalanche. I take a step back, then another, calling for Jamaica. He hit her hard, and if he broke any part of her, I'll break more of him. Turnabout is fair play, after all.

I turn around to look for her, and an octopus attacks me. Four different pairs of arms engulf me from all sides. They're all talking, but I can't understand a word any of them are saying. I doubt I could even if my ears weren't still ringing like a sonofabitch.

"Jam!" I shout again, hoping to get my point across. I'm sure I love everyone who is fussing over me right now, but none of them were just attacked by a psychopath from their past. I *need* to see her.

"Give him some space," Mason yells to the others, leading by example and stepping back.

I take them all in with a quick glance, then get back to my search for Jam. There will be time for hugs after I find Jam. Mom, Tara, and Nicole will just have to understand. Jam needs me.

"She's fine," Mason says, but it's not assurance enough.

"Where?"

"Grandma and Fern took her to the first aid tent, but Fern said something about the hospital."

"*What?*" I shout. I shove my way through the growing crowd and sprint for the tent. Jam isn't going anywhere without me.

Chapter 33

Jamaica

One whole half of my face is a throbbing mass of pain. I have a headache that is threatening to split my skull open any second since Jordan failed to do it. My jaw aches. And it's all getting worse by the second as I come down off the adrenaline high.

It all happened so fast. One second, it was Austin and me discussing the odds of Jordan wasting his time to find me. Then he was there, as loud and angry as ever, and he had a gun.

"Jam!" Austin's shout rachets the pain in my head up a notch, which makes me wince. He throws himself through the opening of the tent and then to his knees in front of my chair hard enough to make me cringe in sympathy for his knees.

"Out," my mum orders, grabbing Maeve and Ty by the arm and bodily dragging them from the tent. Fern, Miss Lola, and the nice EMT tending to my face follow before she can come back and drag them too.

Austin carefully brushes a curl away from my good eye. "Oh, babe. I'm so sorry. I should've—"

"Stop." I don't want to hear an apology from him. If anyone here needs to apologize, it's me. I told myself I needed to be smart. Smart would've been telling him that Jordan might've found me. *I should've told all of them* . . . It's too late for that now, though. It's time for me to face this head-on like I should've done from the start. *Hopefully, it's not too late.*

The irony isn't lost on me. We *just* fought about him withholding information from me, although I didn't see that I was doing the same thing until it was too late. I intended to tell him. *Just like he intended to tell me.*

I lower the ice pack covering the entire left side of my face and lay it aside so I can grab Austin's hands. His eyes dart back and forth, taking in the swelling, and widen in horror. I knew it was bad. People took one look at me and got the heck out of our way.

I raise his hands to my lips and carefully kiss them both. "If not for you, things could've been so much worse. No, not could've, *would've.* You saved us both, Austin."

"He never should've had a chance to lay a hand on you," Austin growls. "I should've—"

"No," I cut in, squeezing his hands to stop him. "Don't do that. You should've done exactly what you did."

I point to my face. "This is not your fault. The blame lays squarely on his shoulders and mine, and I refuse to let you carry any of it. I let him make me a victim last time. I worked hard to overcome that, and I'm not going to let him do it again—to either of us. I'm a survivor. So are you. End of story. Blanket apology."

I worry my bottom lip while I wait for him to answer. Like last night, we won't get anywhere if we don't acknowledge our intent to forgive each other upfront. We need to put the blame game aside and get to the heart of the problem, whatever it may be. That's easier to do, for me at least, when we both know we haven't done irreparable harm to our relationship.

Austin takes several deep breaths and nods, and my anxiety melts away. *We'll get through this.* "Blanket apology. Why didn't you tell me you knew he was here?"

I knew that would be the sticking point for him, not the withholding of information. He'll view it as a trust issue when it was anything but. "I . . . was warned that he might know. And I chose to believe he was bluffing, trying to trick my old acquaintances into telling him—not that any of them knew. So I didn't tell anyone except Fern because I didn't want you to worry about something that probably wasn't an issue."

"Why didn't you trust me to share that burden, though, Jam?" *Called it.*

"Trust had nothing to do with it. I watched my family live looking over their shoulders just like I did before he went to prison. I didn't want to see you lot doing the same. I was trying to protect you from the Bogeyman, but, in this case, he was real."

He sighs. "Babe . . . I don't know what to say. Like, I'm pissed that you didn't tell me, but . . ."

I try to smile, but the pain stops me. "But you've already forgiven me, so being angry is pointless?"

Austin winces sympathetically. "That, and it's impossible to be mad at you with half your face swollen like that."

"I love you."

"I love you too. Let's get you to the hospital. You need to get that checked out."

Epilogue
Austin

I stand in the middle of Mason's backyard and turn in a slow circle, taking everything in.

It's hard to believe how far we've come—all of us. Two years ago, we gathered here to celebrate my brother's upcoming wedding. Now he's married and has another rug rat running around. Gabe is happier than I've ever known him to be, and an excellent father. Ryan's relationship is everything he never wanted. And Chris finally learned to trust someone again.

I have so many great memories with the people gathered here, and tonight promises to be another. I spent a lot of time planning the when and where of this. Her graduation day was a top contender, but I want that day to be special for nothing other than her hard work.

Near as I can tell, everything is perfect. Things might not be exactly where they were that night, but they're close enough.

My survey of the yard ends with Jam. As fate would have it, she's sitting in nearly the same spot she was the night it all started. She's not hunched over, trying to be invisible this time, though. She's laughing with Fern and Tris, bouncing Fern's little one on her knee.

She catches me watching her and smiles. *I love making her smile.* And I'm here to do it again.

I walk the few feet separating us and literally fall to one knee in front of her because my joints go weak with nerves. Fern quietly takes her baby under the guise of a diaper check, freeing Jam's hands.

Even though most of the others are busy with beer pong, cornhole, or one of the other games strewn about my brother's backyard, they know why I organized this shindig. Desi pauses the music, and everyone falls silent.

Jam is so beautiful I forget everything but staring into her eyes, marveling that I get to call her mine.

"Austin?" she asks, snapping me out of my daze.

I clear my throat and reach for her hand. I'm not given to fancy speeches, but many things have changed since the night Jam, and I walked away from here hating each other. "Jamaica Gunn, two years ago today I sat down next to you at this very table, and we had our very first fight. I walked away from here thinking you were the most impossible female in the entire world. Little did I know, that fight would be the first of many misunderstandings.

"I don't know if it was by accident or by design, but we couldn't stay away from each other. Slowly, those misunderstandings became an understanding. That animosity became love. And I'm here, where it all started, to ask you to be my wife, so I can be the man who gets to annoy you for the rest of our lives."

Jam's chest heaves with a cross between a sob and a laugh. "Yes!" she says, breaking into hysterical laughter. "Yes!"

A note from Cara

Thank you for reading Dare To Love! If you enjoyed reading it as much as I enjoyed writing it, I hope you'll consider taking a moment to leave a review and share your thoughts. Reviews are magic fairy dust readers use to help good books fly. Your review could help other readers decide to read this and the other stories in the Tarnished Hearts series.

My newsletter is a great way to stay up-to-date with the newest releases. If you haven't already signed up, you can do so on my website, carad-smith.com. You'll get a free short story about the day Ronni, Fern, and Mason from I Kinda Do met when you sign up, and there are sure to be more short stories made available to subscribers along the way!

CARA D. SMITH

Acknowledgments

Thank you to my Mister and my Little Mister for your patience and understanding. And to Mom and Dad for your support. I can't say this one wasn't crazy too, but we're getting this writing and editing thing figured out. I'm sorry I get a little grumpy when that deadline is approaching and things just aren't working the way I want them to.

Once again, thanks to my awesome team of friends, Kelsey, Katie, and Shannon, my alpha readers, the ones who put up with the crazy questions, the angst, and all of the re-writes. I couldn't do it without you.

Thanks to Nancy, Dawn, and May for your efforts to make each story the best it can be.

And, last but not least, thanks to the readers for every page you turn. A lot of work goes into every book, and you make it all worth it.

Follow Cara

My website:
www.caradsmith.com

Facebook:
www.facebook.com/CaraSmithAuthor

Instagram:
www.instagram.com/caradsmith

Also by Cara D. Smith

Tarnished Hearts:
*Hired—Newsletter bonus short story
I Kinda Do—Mason and Fern
*Surprise!—Deleted Epilogue
Right By You—Gabe and Tara
Dare To Love—Austin and Jamaica
(TBD)Tarnished Hearts 3.5—Noel and Colton
It's Not You—Ryan and Trista
A Second Glance—Chris and Heidi
(TBD)—Logan and Madi

Each book in the Tarnished Hearts series is a stand-alone, meaning each story is self-contained and they can be read in any order. Some jokes, conversations, and references might make a little more sense if you read them in the order in which they were written, but it is not necessary. Each story has a guaranteed HEA.

*Find these on my website, caradsmith.com

Right By You is available now! Why *does* Ryan enjoy teasing Trista so much?